TIME TO EXPIRE

Chris Ramos

www.ten16press.com - Waukesha, WI

This book is dedicated to my Dad, Tony.
Taken before your time, you taught me the meaning of family.

And to my Mom, Donna.
You showed me how to make every moment count.

PROLOGUE

The red-orange rays of the setting sun climbed over the steep plasteel roof and were diffused through the auto-tinting plastique window. Walsh walked past the window, his movement causing a breeze that fluttered the curtains. The rays had a fleeting moment of freedom, dancing around the room briefly, until the silk settled back against the window. Walsh stopped his pacing as his attention was drawn to a glint of metal showing from under the couch. He leaned down and retrieved a long-lost lapel pin, one of his favorites. He stood up, laughed at the poor timing of his discovery and tossed the pin back under the couch. It was too late for that now, too late for such trivial material discoveries. He reached in his pocket and retrieved his pocket watch, depressed the side button, popped the cover and checked the inside timing. He smirked to himself for checking the watch so often; it really hadn't changed much in the last minute. Or the minute before that. It was still counting down. Walsh closed the lid. Instead of dropping it back into his pocket, he set it down on the low table and walked away to resume his pacing. The glowing LifeSpan logo on the watch cover slowly dimmed.

Walsh was waiting. His expiration was eminent, and he paced his small home with a deep sense of apprehension. Of course, he had known about this date, this hour, even the second he would expire the very day he was born. Everyone knew when their own expirations were. That was one of the many luxuries living under the splendor of the global corporation, LifeSpan.

Walsh smiled and reminisced. He was rather impressed with the efficient LifeSpan administration, especially after his most popular publication: *LifeSpan by the Numbers: From Neanderthals to Nimbus*. It was a history of humanity, detailing the long road to their current prosperous status. LifeSpan effectively conquered illnesses of every kind, improved industrial production and forged a global economy. These accomplishments alone had easily catapulted LifeSpan into the most powerful and influential company the world had ever seen. Of course, you couldn't admire LifeSpan without paying homage to the single most influential LifeSpan innovation: lifting the veil on the unpredictable time of death. Consequently, everyone was assigned an individual expiration date, calculated at birth and accurate to the millisecond.

Walsh paused and admired his many awards hanging in the front entry. His most prized digital plaque was from the LifeSpan Digipost World Library. This was in recognition for his recently completed *Your Expiration Date: A Lifetime Management Manual*. Also hanging next to this reminder of his accomplishment was a digiframe cycling through numerous digital reviews, boasting the manual as the top digiloaded publication three months in a row. Ever since LifeSpan abolished paper resources, everything from the daily news to publications of any kind were digiloaded. With thousands of publications loaded hourly, it was truly an accomplishment to be the most read in any category.

Reminiscing during his great success with *Expiration Date* reminded Walsh of his timepiece still sitting on the front coffee table. His moment was almost here. Finally, it was his time to expire. His life's work was complete, for that was a benefit of knowing your expiration date: everything was carefully plotted and planned for. There was no project left unfinished. Humanity across the globe had become incredibly efficient.

He continued to the table and scooped up the silver timepiece. The LifeSpan logo emblazoned on the cover glowed a pale blue again when it was in his hand, recognizing him as its one true owner. This was another innovation of LifeSpan, for coursing through each person's bloodstream at that very moment were millions of tiny nanobots, giving each individual a unique nano signature. His assigned pocket watch was only attuned to his identity, keeping the watch locked at all times, unlocking only when it recognized his touch.

Walsh pressed the small, recessed button on the side of the watch, releasing the cover latch. The lid rose to reveal a series of dials and clock faces inside.

There were five clock faces in total: the largest was used for counting down the years, the next smallest counted down by days in the months, and three small dials counting down hours, minutes and seconds. Each dial moved counterclockwise, a flurry of larger pointers and smaller, lapping dials, spinning in harmony for one purpose: a constant reminder of the countdown to your expiration. Usually the dials were all moving in concert. Only two of the five dials were moving now: the minutes and seconds. The year, day, and hour dials were already at their zero mark. He was close to his expiration now, but he was not afraid. With LifeSpan, there was no fear of death; it was as expected as the sun rising.

The minute hand was finishing its final lap, and rested precisely at zero, never to start another lap. This left only the second hand to finish a sixty-tick countdown. Walsh stood with the watch open in his palm, less than sixty seconds of life remaining. He adjusted his tie with his free hand and glanced around the empty room, waiting.

"So long, and thanks for the memories," Walsh whispered to nobody.

The second hand closed the gap. 3 . . . 2 . . . 1 . . . 0.
Walsh collapsed. His timepiece fell from his limp hand.
The Collectors arrived.

PART ONE: THE MOTHER

*Today began as many have before, planned and perfect. I awoke, looked outside and watched our solar panels slowly change direction and catch the sun's light. Ate a quick breakfast with momma and ran off, down the block to school. Everyone lined up outside the walls, waiting for the doors to open. As we passed into the halls, we were handed our daily program. Same familiar schedule — school lunch menu, assembly after school, daily student expirations. A boy named Johnnie was expiring today; he is in my science class. I should say, Johnnie **was** in my science class. He was pretty neat, but I'll find another. I always find another friend. We stood in class reciting our daily LifeSpan oath. It changes every day, with Tuesday being 'The future was dark. LifeSpan is the light.' When we were done, everyone sat back down and pulled in their chairs. Today, I remained standing. "Why do we repeat that? Who says we have to keep doing that?" I don't think teacher liked my question. So, here I am, typing and being watched by an unhappy LifeSpan counselor. Another day in detention. Like I said, today began as many have before.*

NIMBUS

Moving swiftly over the open countryside, the dark clouds rolled above the mountains, churning and building into a blue and gray mass, ready to explode. Finally, they began to empty their soaking payload onto the sprawling town below. Nimbus watched this powerful show from atop his high tower located inside the LifeSpan grounds. As the highest populated structure in the country, he always thought about the rain touching him first, and then moving on to the ground below. He imagined each raindrop asking him for permission to continue. Nature itself was seeking his consent to carry on. As it should be.

Nimbus was tall and very lean, with well-defined muscles showing through his formfitting silk robes. His hair was jet black with speckles of gray on the sides. His face was chiseled with a pointed chin and a sharp nose to match; his silhouette was more like a rough-cut piece of wood than of flesh and blood. These were not his most distinguishing characteristics; those that had come face to face with him were immediately struck by his eyes, the hue of which seemed to change with the lighting of the room. His pupils were surrounded by a haze of colors, constantly shifting like mother of pearl. Not many had the opportunity to be caught in his gaze, for he was above them, above everyone. Nimbus answered to nobody because he *was* LifeSpan.

His attention once again was pulled to the roiling clouds above. *Right on schedule*, he mused. The cloud formations were actually responding to the large atmosphere collection towers strategically placed across the mountainous geography. These tall, thin spires reached to the skies above and pulsed with atmospheric pressure, encouraging a storm. His gaze traveled slowly from one collection tower to the next, as far as the eye could see. These were the property of LifeSpan. As chief commander of the globally spanning company, he had unrivaled power in his hands. These towers had helped propel LifeSpan's climb to power.

Many years ago, early in the company's timeline, the sky was clogged with pollution. The oceans were losing valuable organisms, crops were failing, and nature itself had seemed to turn on the planet. Humanity had finally pushed the healing ability to no return, finally pushing the Earth too far. LifeSpan atmosphere tower technology turned around the unstable ecosystems threatening to destroy the Earth. LifeSpan brought order. Today, carefully structured rain schedules were maintained. Currently, the rain was a slow drizzle. Nimbus knew it would pick up later in the day, just what the schedule called for. Everything was on a schedule, and Nimbus knew there was no other way. LifeSpan was responsible for not only the weather, but all of humanity.

Yes, he thought, *they must never forget how much we have saved them.*

Humanity had been on the brink of disaster, the dark days of the twenty-second century, and LifeSpan had been there to show them the light.

Nimbus reached forward and held his hand over the balcony edge, letting the rain collect in his cupped palm. *Everything runs together; LifeSpan is intertwined.* He internally recited one of the most popular LifeSpan slogans. *Everything runs together; LifeSpan is intertwined.* Nimbus looked down at the fast-building pool of water. "Everything gathers here in my hand first, and I choose to let them have it." Nimbus turned his hand over, and the water emptied and fell far below. Still holding his damp hand out, he turned and a servant ran forward with a towel to gently pat his hand dry.

His many servants were buzzing with activity, he knew, many still cleaning his room and preparing his outfits for the day. Just as the weather was on a schedule, so was Nimbus.

This afternoon in science class, we all said goodbye to Johnnie. His time had come at 2:52, and he expired in front of us all. Of course, the Collectors came and took him away just like they did for my uncle last week. After Johnnie left, I found a red marble in my desk he had let me borrow. Now that he's gone, it's mine now. I used to tell my teacher everything that I thought of during school. Why do the Collectors smell weird? He just sends me to the LifeSpan counselor, like everyone else. So, I sit in detention and type nonsense and give them what they want. I hate to type. My Momma has a real book at home, which she has kept for a long time. So I can write now. I can write my real thoughts, not what they want to hear. Momma says it's good for me. Momma says don't tell anyone. As long as it doesn't interfere with my chores. Oops, almost forgot, I should go wind her fireplace clock. Goodbye diary, I'll write you soon.

GATEWAY

The rain was not very heavy today, just enough to glaze the sidewalks and have a person second-guessing the absence of an umbrella. Jon reached into his back seat, looking for something to cover his head just as the storm passed, relinquishing control of the heavens to the sun and blue sky. Jon shrugged, exited the fleetliner and walked around to the passenger side. Looking into the flip-down mirror, his wife begged him to go ahead of her; she would eventually catch up. Regardless, Jon continued to wait, holding the car door open as he stared at the woman he loved and patiently waited for her final makeup touches.

Ever since he first met her, years ago, he knew she was the one for him. The following courtship was a whirlwind of work and play as they planned their lives together. Finally, their relationship profiles were approved by LifeSpan, and he proposed. Jon had never been happier.

Today's appointment was prescheduled with their marriage paperwork. It was the fifth of November. Their one-year wedding anniversary. That special day still felt like it was yesterday.

Bringing his jacket collar closer to his cold neck, Jon's mind drifted back to that blessed day, surrounded by family and friends in the Great Chapel.

The chapel was filled edge to edge, with barely a vacant seat. Those seated composed a symphony of various sounds: some were weeping, some were laughing, and continual whispering was broken only by the occasional cough. Suddenly, floating through the air like a cloud, a soft melody quieted the crowd. All eyes turn to the rear, waiting for a glimpse of the bride . . .

His palms were clammy, her eyes were glistening, and their hearts were full of hope.

"Do you promise to have and to hold . . . ," the chapel director's ceremonial voice boomed through the audience. The subtle sounds of sobbing and creaks from those who couldn't sit still for too long replaced the earlier talking.

"I do," Jon whispered.

"I do," Mary whispered in return, smiling.

The director looked up from his digiscreen. "Do you plan on including children in your life spans?"

"We do," the newlyweds replied in unison.

"And have you filed the proper digifiles with the LifeSpan parental offices?"

"Jon! Were you daydreaming again?" Mary asked. "Sometimes I feel like you're a hundred miles away when I need you right next to me. Now, for the third time, how do I look?"

"I was just thinking about the day I gave up my real name," Jon laughed.

"Yes, yes, officially a Jenkins. Are you still complaining newborns are no longer named after their father? Don't worry, we are a welcoming family. Now, don't change the subject! You still haven't answered me."

"You look like a beautiful woman, about to fulfill your greatest wish. Now, let's get moving, Buttercup," Jon replied with his nickname for her as he extended his hand. She smiled, checked her lipstick one last time, took his hand and finally emerged from the car. Mary was barely able to reach Jon's shoulder, despite her heeled shoes giving an extra boost. Her hair was dark brown, flowing to her shoulders and curling back slightly. Mary had always been impeccably dressed, paying careful attention to fabric colors, feel and fit. Next to Jon's disheveled appearance, she could easily turn heads wherever they went.

They turned together, their gazes climbing upward to the massive structure before them. Wide, gleaming stairs rose higher than any surrounding building, cresting to a blazing-white arched gate. Amidst the rather ordinary, bland buildings to the left and right, this lone structure seemed incredibly out of place. At first glance, the stairs and gate appeared to be smoothed stone, but further examination showed not a single seam or structural post apparent. This gave the entire structure a smooth plastic shell.

This was a great day for the couple, and this place was the gateway to the LifeSpan grounds. Jon and Mary were eager to begin climbing the stairs, one step at a time, hand in hand. They passed under the gate, going into the main courtyard of LifeSpan, known as the Core. People were everywhere, walking in groups, talking about their day or what they were planning this evening. Mary noticed that everyone had a smile, some even laughing aloud as they shared stories with friends.

LifeSpan was the largest corporation ever formed, renowned as the savior of mankind, bringing order from chaos and structure to citizens' everyday lives. It was no wonder the Core would be full of optimism for the future.

"I still can't believe we are here," Mary remarked.

"Uh, yes, me too," Jon replied absently. His neck was craned to see the tall walls surrounding this inner sanctum. They were easily ten stories tall, the sun reflecting off a ribbon of silver running horizontally across the middle. This gleaming metallic band ran the entire length of every building, with no beginning and no end.

Sitting inside the imposing walls were massive buildings, each with its own insignia above the doorframe. Jon knew from their previous interview at home, they would be passing every other building today and proceeding to the most important structure at the end of the galley: the Birth and Development Building.

Set in the middle of the Core, he saw the LifeSpan clock. With its four massive clock faces, visible from any direction, this was the center for all of the timekeeping at LifeSpan.

Jon stopped and checked his digital wristwatch. He compared the time to the towering clock face in front of him. Exactly correct, minutely in sync. He expected as much, but was still amazed at the level of continuity. While everyone was issued a LifeSpan pocketwatch, there were still normal digital watches to tell the time. This only made him even more aware of the fast approaching appointment.

"Come," he said, reaching for Mary's hand. "We haven't much time." And they picked up their pace while still gaping at the structures.

School was a little boring today except for a visit from some LifeSpan guy. He was talking to us about the little computer bugs in our body. They were placed there to help us when we were babies, and stay there our whole lives. I don't remember what he called them, but he had a machine that could make them move closer to our skin. I saw them! Moving slowly under my arm and in my hand, like jelly. He told us they were there to help us be healthy and only LifeSpan has the controls for them, for safekeeping. Gotta run now, time to wind mother's silly clock. She says it's very old, and I am the only one she would trust to take it down from the fireplace and wind it everyday. The clock was carved from trees. I keep telling her to get a LifeSpan digiclock. At least they never need winding. Being perfect and all. She said not everything needs to be connected.

SCI

The plasteel room was cold. Not the temperate cold that tickles your skin, but the cold that sets you on edge. The lack of ambiance in this room was due to its extremely sterile environment. Completely void of any porous surface, the room was outfitted entirely of translucent plastique and solid plasteel. There were no plants hanging, no animals curled under the chairs looking for companionship. There were no elaborate decorations. Infrared light cast a pale orange glow through every plastique surface. Overall, this particular setting was suited for only one purpose: a laboratory.

The entire room was seamlessly built around an enormous tube—a massive, tilted telescope pointed not at the sky, for there was no gap in the ceiling of this smooth egg, but to a small viewing screen just inches off the floor. The laboratory ceiling, over four stories tall, was a web of wires and connecting scopes, feeding into the next level of even more highly powered magnification; this microscope was built for viewing the extremely small. The eyepiece was actually built into an aerial lift. An elevated chair was connected at this end and held aloft with a series of beams and arms. Although the seat was solidly built, it sagged in protest with the bulky figure filling its bucket. Sci Tym sat hunched over in this room of stillness, completely at home above the high-powered microscope.

Encircling him were small tables, each attached to elongated snaking arms. There was no need for him to remove his eyes from the goggle helmet of his own design. The tables responded to the subtle waves of his hands and his mental will.

Sci Tym was wearing another invention of his own, gloves that were outfitted with a connector at each finger, running to the center of the palm and powered by wires running down from the ceiling.

He stared down into the microscope, trying to calm his nerves as he applied the finishing touches to his latest breakthrough. Not only was Tym one of the greatest scientific minds at LifeSpan, he also received numerous mental downloads, each unlocking another digital subject matter, helping him achieve the esteemed Senior Scientist rank from LifeSpan.

Sci Tym was on the verge of his next great development. He designed nanotechnology biological robots. They were the true driving force behind the success of LifeSpan and the collective health of the globe. For the past 250 years, generation after generation of mankind had been infused with nano models coursing through their bloodstream.

Tym was the current scientific mind constantly working to upgrade the most recent series of nanos. In fact, the previous four versions of nanotechnology improvements had been due to Sci Tym's hard work.

Tym was finishing another improvement on the motors of the nanobots. After all these years, he was still amazed at the effective little machines. Tym worked on the medicinal end of the advancement of nanotechnology, more commonly referred to as Nanomedicine.

There were many types of the tiny robotic workers flowing through the bloodstream of every citizen of the world, effectively all citizens of LifeSpan.

Sci Tym lived within the nano world, which consisted of the manipulation of molecules, on a nanometer scale. This was his world, the world of the very small. Tym helped build tiny nanomachines that consisted of groups of atoms, each aligned and manipulated into gears, bodies and arms to build a nanobot.

Each of these nanobots was created for a specific purpose. Some were able to harness infrared light and destroy cancerous cells. Many extracted and delivered valuable nutrients to the body. Others were simply repair bots, used to transport nanotubes and repair broken bones or degenerating marrow.

Sci Tym also excelled in molecular manufacturing, with his inventions redefining how the replicators built these complex machines. LifeSpan created the first fully functioning nanobot for the human body. Each nanobot colony consisted of thousands of nanobots and was no larger than a single grain of sand.

Just a few more modifications were needed today. Tym worked well under this pressure, completely focusing on the job at hand. Through his movements, the giant mechanized arms minimized each of his muscle reactions down through the four stories across various gears and into the nano world. So, if Tym were to pull his arms out to the side while holding the machine arms, that movement would follow a series of connecting arms and follow a series of smaller arms, allowing the nanobots to place a single atom for fusion.

Finally, the last carbon atom was connected to the propulsion end of the nanobot. Tym blinked rapidly to adjust to the wider world within this room. Each blink refocused the goggle lens, pulling back each magnifying disc, refocusing every slide to bring Tym's vision back to his base spectrum. He moved the closest tables away from him, sending them back along the wall, each cascading into a neat holder like horses in a stable, their mechanical arms still attached. He dismissively waved away hundreds of digital projections and holographic screens, and tech readouts blinked away. He began unbuckling his gloves and stepped out of the seated chamber for the first time in over ten hours.

Sci Tym rose slowly, his short arms settling onto the rolling folds of bulk on his sides. He was built like a roiling water balloon, his body shifting and resettling with every movement. It was hard to distinguish if the shifting was caused from his bulk or by the many trinkets and tools he insisted on keeping attached to his person. Indeed, Tym was a walking tool chest, carrying many assorted gears and techy devices whose purposes were known only to him. Each was connected by a series of buckles and pouches to a many-pocketed vest he always wore. Now that his day's work was finished, it was time to check in at the Holowall, the digital link to LifeSpan.

He stood in front of the electrified wall. Light spectrums shifted along the surface. Occasionally, a figure would appear or a room would come into focus as the Holowall searched for communication requests. Sci Tym stood at the designated spot, crossed his arms behind his back and announced to the wall, "2774.85 Sci Tym reporting from Sky Post Nine. Accounting for work completed on special project Mech Seventeen."

Tym waited for the response. He knew they could hear him, he knew they could even see him, but he waited to be polite. Some days Tym felt like yelling at the wall, but that wouldn't be very polite at all.

"Sci Tym, have you completed another breakthrough?" The wall color faded away and was replaced with a clear image of another scientist in LifeSpan's employ. Tym knew her well, and he smiled. Tym hoped he wasn't blushing; she did that to him.

"Yes, Trina, I have." She was too beautiful to sit behind a screen all day long. She needed to be out under the sun; she needed to be here with Tym and laughing at his jokes. Or so Tym thought.

"I have added an extra propulsion engine," Tym updated.

Trina was shocked, her expression clearly impressed. Tym bowed his head and blushed.

"Most of the Sci Community worked for years just to move one molecule into a slightly better spot, usually with hardly a noticeable difference at all. You are reporting an entirely extra engine construction? That doesn't seem possible. For over a hundred years, the current schematics showed there was no room for another engine without making the entire molecular machine too large. This will have to be checked and—"

"It works, Trina! I'm telling you, it works, and it will increase the speed of any nano by over thirty percent. This is it; finally the public will be able to take—"

"Nimbus will decide how we will use this development," Trina interrupted him.

It was a response all too familiar to Tym. He had expected the same phrase from anyone at the wall; it just sounded ever more disheartening to hear it from Trina. Every instance of success Tym had achieved, every breakthrough invention, every minute change to molecular theory, nano development and scientific gadgetry met with the same response. *Nimbus will decide how we will use this.*

It was at this moment Tym decided to make a stand.

"No, Trina, this one belongs to the populace. It is too significant of a change, too important to our growth as a species." Tym could hardly believe the words as he spoke them. Even now, with the room dead silent, he could hear them repeating in his head, over and over. Trina stared at him, mouth agape.

Trina looked as if she were encased in ice, unable to move. Slowly, she became more animated, shaking her head furiously in disbelief, looking over her shoulder for any passersby that may have heard this blasphemous statement. She was at a loss for the proper protocol in situations such as this.

"Sci Tym," she whispered, leaning closer to the screen in front of her. Although the vocal sensor wasn't near the Holowall, she felt that if she inched closer, they would somehow be isolated from her laboratory. "You know that kind of talk can find you trouble."

Tym did indeed realize this. In one ridiculous statement, with his guard down, he could have thrown away his entire career. He would probably be monitoring the automatic street cleaners after this. But Tym knew he was right; he felt it in his heart. This advancement was for the betterment of the globe. Everyone alive had nanobots coursing through their bodies at this very moment. They had to.

The Great Pestilence, over ten generations ago, had ravaged the population. It was an unknown disease, carried on the wind, circling the globe in less than forty-eight hours. Clouds were poisoned, and when the rain fell it poisoned humanity. LifeSpan stepped forth and became the savior of mankind once again. After decades of nano research, LifeSpan had figured out how nanobots could prevent any disease particle, including that which caused the Great Pestilence, from attacking healthy cells. Following this, they required nanobot integration into every living human being. Millions chose to receive the infusions, and many who decided to turn their back on LifeSpan eventually perished. Humanity was thinned very quickly, and those who remained knew they owed their lives to LifeSpan. The nanos remained to defend against other diseases that everyone feared.

As technology improved, the nanos decoded humanity at the molecular level and discovered a digital revelation. Through a series of genetic testing, a point of maximum development was revealed. This point differed for every person. For some, it could be at age 5 years. For others, it could be at 97 years. LifeSpan decided any time spent beyond this genetic summit was wasted. Thus, the expiration date was revealed.

Order was restored; progress followed. The Scientific Community was established for increased developments.

"We should be able to share our discoveries; they are, after all, our discovery." Tym was already losing heart, mumbling the response, his shoulders sinking a little further.

"Thank you for the contribution to LifeSpan, Sci Tym, and your digiscreen upload will be expected before the end of your shift. Nimbus is proud of you and your work. The future of LifeSpan will be forever recorded in . . ." Trina recited the same response she had given to Tym over a hundred times.

Tym wondered if she even realized what she was saying; it was such a quick monotone reply. So much protocol — why couldn't she just talk with him as a friend? He waited for her to cease the endless bureaucratic congratulations.

When she stopped, Trina stood silent, waiting for the proper sound off from Tym before ending the transmission.

"Human nature was flawed. LifeSpan is the cure," Tym halfheartedly mumbled.

The wall video faded away. The last image was Trina smiling. Tym imagined she was smiling at him and not about the tech innovation. Tym shuffled back to his workstation, replacing his glove and powering the fingers to respond to the eight wall screens before him. He was uploading his day's work. If anything, he was diligent in his research and loyal to LifeSpan.

Tym sat and gathered every screen of data, the video recordings of his time in front of the microscope, his notes, journal and loggings. He literally plucked the digifiles out, stacking them in a holographic image, floating in front of him. Each file stacked on top of the digital grouping, compiling his research. This was a great breakthrough, and he wanted to present it to Nimbus in a perfect package, worthy of all his praise. Tym was finishing the task, his hand moving through the screens of data, while his mind was wandering back to the conversation with Trina.

It didn't seem that bad to Tym, to want to share. That was the driving force behind all of his work. Nanotechnology was a global engine, with the entire population thriving from the nanobots in their systems. Tym considered any information about the machines a global issue. Therein lay his dilemma.

Did Tym's genius belong to LifeSpan, or did it belong to the people?

He stopped gathering the digifiles and looked around the room. For so many years, he was allowed to work in his laboratory without interruption. The globe probably didn't even know he existed.

Uncharacteristically for Tym, he stared at the finalized report files hovering before him, held aloft by his glowing glove. The package was awaiting upload to LifeSpan. He could easily send it off, go home, and resume his life as a successfully unknown scientist, somehow working for the people but going through LifeSpan to do it. Tym placed his glove over the upload screen, but did not complete the transfer. He pulled his hand back, removed the glove and laid it on the counter. The digifiles absorbed into the glove.

He needed some air and a little time to think. He knew LifeSpan was the same as the people, and eventually they would receive the improvement. Or would they?

Tym exited the facility, squinting in the bright sun. He leaned his bulk against the outside wall, high atop his hillside, looking at the lights below, the weather towers dotting the countryside, millions of people bustling around in the city far below. This was where he was at peace. Alone to contemplate.

The outpost was a Sci Laboratory, inhabited by Tym, and no

one ever came up here. Well, nobody except that man walking up the road.

"Hello, friend. You must be lost. Can I direct you to the right path?" Tym greeted.

The man stopped walking, his hands at his side, obscured by the loose fabric of his sleeves. His jacket was dark charcoal gray, cut at seemingly random angles to meet across his chest with buckles and straps holding it firmly to his body. A hood was pulled over his head, hiding his face in shadow. He stooped in his posture, which Tym found odd, for his personal nanobots would have compensated for any muscle fatigue.

"Just walking home, thank you," the man replied peacefully.

Tym laughed, hugging his belly. "You are a long way from any home. I can assure you that much." He moved his bulk, extending his arm in a comical sweep to emphasize the vast empty lands around them.

"Home is with those who share your dreams and desires," the man responded, and lowered his hood. His hair glistened in the sun, silvery white, with a matching beard and mustache that was trimmed under a nose too large for his face. His skin was weathered, with every contour accented by clusters of wrinkles. His eyes were full of stories from a lifetime of events. Tym was confused. The man was old; that was evident. However, he seemed much older than his outward appearance let on.

"I understand your riddle. Very clever, in context, but I do not understand why you are spouting your prose to me. I have a home. I upload my dreams. Ha ha!"

Your dreams fall on deaf ears, the elderly man thought.

The old man looked at Tym very closely. He walked a few more steps, so he was within arm's reach of Tym.

"Home is with those who understand your . . . *frustrations*," the old man said, carefully emphasizing the last word after easily reading Tym's body language.

The stressed word wasn't lost on Tym, and he carefully backed away from this stranger. His first reactive thought was that the old man could be a LifeSpan employee. Quite possibly a new division started to check up on scientists like Tym. But that was too convenient. Tym had always been a perfect employee, a Sci of the highest ranking. Today was his only lapse in judgment, ever. Besides, he didn't really do anything wrong. He had only backed away from his update, but as soon as he returned to the lab, he would send the transmission. It wasn't worth the risk to throw it all away now.

"Uhh, yes, well, thank you for your time," Tym said, careful not to say too much in case the man was an administrator. "I should get back to my work. I hope you find your way home, Mr. . . . ?"

"You are very talented, Tym." He mispronounced the name.

"Very close. My name actually rhymes with slim. Although, I am far from it. Ha. Wait, how did you know my . . . ," Tym started.

"You should be using your talents to help the people in need, not the ones who would hoard your special gifts and keep them for their own use."

Tym was intrigued, that much was true, but also on guard. He still felt this was a test from LifeSpan.

However, there was something in the stranger's eyes he found calming. There was a tranquility there. Tym's heart told him to trust in this old man. He was wise of mind, he could already tell, but worldly wise beyond Tym, for sure. Sci Tym decided to take a chance.

"What if I told you I had a breakthrough capable of helping the entire population?"

"I would tell you to share it with the entire population," came the honest reply.

"Do you work for LifeSpan?"

"No."

"Have you *ever* worked for LifeSpan?"

"That is a very convoluted question. You would have to come with me to hear that story. You would have to leave this all behind, never to return."

"What security would I have?"

"I will be your family now."

"You still never told me your name."

"You can call me the Father." And with that, Tym knew he had made the right decision. He motioned for the Father to stay where he was, on the road, and Tym did something that surprised even himself. He ran back to the lab.

Tym rarely ran anywhere. His bulk alone, pushing 300 pounds, was enough to keep him living a slower lifestyle. On top of his body mass, there were the many numerous inventions, gadgets and trinkets bulging from every pocket and strung around his neck and arms. His appearance was more like a bouncing ball wrapped with wires and chain.

When Tym ran, it was only for extremely exceptional occasions. Lucky for them both, this was a matter of urgency.

Tym reached the entry pad, and placed his hand on the identification plate outside. The door swished open, sliding into the frame, and a metallic voice chimed, "Welcome back, Sci Tym."

He knew this would be the last transmission anyone would receive from him. Tym walked over to the long plasteel workspace and scooped up his glove. The wires connecting to the wall and ceiling far above were easily detached from the electronic sleeve, and Tym stuffed it under his arm. The information he had uploaded previously, including his most recent breakthrough, was safely stored in the glove memory.

Tym tried to move fast. He knew if he allowed himself one

moment of rest, he would rationalize what he was about to do, and possibly change his mind. He was committed to fleeing with the Father, but his lab had too much information to leave behind. The trick was in the retrieval.

There were a series of monitors lining the far wall, each a connection point to different sectors within LifeSpan. His laboratory was networked with many other labs, each compiling and storing data, constantly trying to improve upon the latest incremental change. Tym also knew that each network was connected because of the technology chain from the previous laboratory.

If he unplugged from the web of labs, he would be disconnecting almost a third of the other labs across the globe. Surely, someone would notice and send word of his breach.

He would have to leave it all behind. A life's work of technological breakthroughs. Unique access to the combined minds of the world's top scientists. It would all be left behind.

Tym gripped his glove even harder. At least they wouldn't get this. Not even Trina would see his groundbreaking design for the three-part nano engine.

Trina. He should let her know. He should tell her in privacy, in trust.

Suddenly his knees were weak, and he wanted nothing more than to call her up on the wall screen and pour his heart out, to divulge everything about her that he held dear. She was working within LifeSpan, but she was a treasure unable to shine in her dim box. He couldn't leave without saying something to her. He couldn't leave without telling her.

He tumbled over to the interlocked screens and started a new document, entitled *Three Parts to Engine Propulsion*. It only took him a minute to update her on his epiphany. He sent the file for her eyes only.

Tym backed away from the screens, lingered for one last view of his laboratory, and ran out the door. The swishing panel closed behind him. This was a final goodbye to his life as a LifeSpan Sci.

He was relieved to see the Father still standing on the road. He gave Tym an approving nod, and began walking back down the road. Tym lurched to catch up to him, and they walked in silence for some time.

"What's the glove for?" The Father broke the stillness.

Tym looked down at the crumpled glove cradled in his arm.

"It's for the people," he replied truthfully.

The Father patted him lightly on the arm, raised his hood, and they walked toward the town, neither saying another word.

> Three Parts to Engine Propulsion.
> Step 1: Tingle of a flame,
> Step 2: Combustion of affection,
> Step 3: Burning of desire.
> I will miss you, Trina.
>   Sci Tym

Mother says I should be outside playing with the Collectors at the park. It is, after all, Saturday. A group of the "white clouds," as everyone calls them, give toys and sweets at the field across our street. Usually, they laugh and run with us. They are so fast! We never have a chance to catch up. Sometimes I think they are testing us. I don't want to go out and play, because I don't trust the Collectors. I shouldn't be writing such nonsense, but I was questioned by one of the white clouds. He asked me if I told anyone about my ideas, he asked me if I share my stories and all my questions. He seemed angry at my next question for him. I only asked where they take us when we expire.

LINEAGE

Mary reached the front steps of the Birth and Development Building before Jon. As he shuffled along behind her, the doors came into view. What was once a solid white plasteel wall transformed into a door and swished open.

Jon now stood next to Mary as a representative of LifeSpan emerged. He wore an ivory coat, slim fit, with a stiff collar sticking up high above his shoulders, ending just below his earlobes. He moved stiffly, unable to turn his head without his shoulders following suit. He bowed in greeting to Jon and Mary.

"Welcome. I am Dr. Dehmer. We have been looking forward to meeting you," he said. "Please, if you will follow me inside, all is prepared for you both."

Jon nodded, smiled, and let his wife lead the way. The three of them walked down the seamless white plasteel hallway. The only sound was their own footfalls. They continued on for many minutes. Finally, unable to take the silence, Mary asked, "Are there any children in the facility today that we may see?"

"No. None you may gawk at, since that is your intention. During the gestation period, the fetuses are in a strictly controlled environment. They are initiated and matured to full development in a condition tube."

"That sounds very technical. Will I at least be able to see *our* child during the process?" Mary pressed. "I would think the parents are able to be involved in the process."

The Doctor stopped walking and slowly turned toward Mary. His eyes looked uninterested, but contained an intensity that could not be ignored. "No, Mrs. Jenkins, you will not be able to view your child until he or she is handed to you. Your involvement begins and ends in the donor room. After that, we can handle the rest. The growing fetus is regulated constantly; pumps remove toxins from the subject and simultaneously dispense drugs. Growth hormones further the process; antibodies ensure the assimilation. I assure you it's quite a science, not a single drop too much, not a single pump too little. The machines respond to each minuscule change. Finally, freeing the organism from all the impurities we naturally attract upon conception.

"Removing the mother's body from the equation allows the fetus to focus solely on itself and naturally grow at a quicker rate in the gestation tubes. The child relies on us to adequately develop its body, instead of relying on an outdated, organic womb."

"It's a boy . . . um, will be a boy," Mary meekly replied, shrinking slightly under his gaze.

"Precious." The word rolled off of his barely cracked lips. He began walking again and stopped. Sighed. "Do you have a name chosen?" The Doctor had been informed that small talk helped a conversation.

"Yes, yes, I was thinking of naming our boy Cole," Jon replied, stepping in front of Mary.

"You were thinking, or you are doing?"

"Doing, uh, yes, we are naming him Cole," Jon clarified.

"Well, congratulations on making one decision."

"Thank you?" Jon didn't know if that was a compliment. He looked over to Mary, but she was staring off.

Mary was thinking of what life would be like three months from now. There were still so many details to finish at home. What would be his favorite toy? Would he act like his father, a daydreamer? Hopefully, he would take on his mother's more creative aspects.

"If you will follow me to the donation room, we can begin our process, furthermore allowing you to go back to your home and finish making decisions on wall hues and playful trinkets," the Doctor finished with a scoff.

The three of them walked slowly down the glossy hallway. Mary and Jon glanced around nervously, palms sweating. Dr. Dehmer was singular in focus, his eyes half closed with boredom. Not a word was said among them until the Doctor stopped at a door marked simply with three horizontal dashes.

"Please, allow me." The Doctor opened and swung the door inward, waiting for the couple to enter first.

Surprisingly furnished with comfortable plush seating and soothing colors, the room was a stark contrast to the facility seen thus far. Mary noticed the calming wall color, the coordinated furnishings and the slight aroma of lavender. The couple sat at the edge of the couch, obviously tense. A silver swiveling chair was set against a small plasteel desk. The only silver furniture in the room was in such contrast that it could only be assumed the Doctor's seat. They had assumed correctly, as he lowered himself into the cold, hard seat, looking right at home.

Mary looked around the room again, and relaxed her shoulders a bit.

"We are honored to be here. This is great. It actually reminds me of home." Jon turned and smiled at Mary. "Isn't that right, Buttercup?" Sometimes he tried so hard to cheer her up, with little effect.

"Yes, well, obviously, it is made for you to enjoy. I need to finish a few more questions before we continue. When you were a child, was there any —"

The Doctor was interrupted by the door abruptly opening, and a young nurse poked her head around the corner. Her eyes darted around the room and she looked at the floor. Her voice quivered as she quickly delivered her message.

"Excuse me, Dr. Dehmer, this could not wait," the nurse apologized.

She handed him a digiscreen. He read it over, and Mary watched him closely. She read his body language, his behavior, and noticed a very small, imperceptible raise of his eyebrow. He glanced quickly at Mary and Jon and again at the nurse.

"There are robes folded behind you. Change into them. Leave all of your personal belongings in this room. You will not need them for our next stage."

Dr. Dehmer swiped his finger across the screen, moving the message to his private files. Locking the digiscreen, he excused himself from the room, leaving the digiscreen behind.

Immediately Mary hopped off of the couch, and walked along the wall towards the door.

"I have a bad feeling about this, Mary. You have that look in your eyes. What just happened?" Jon was looking around, feeling eyes on him as Mary was stalking around the room, listening and eventually working her way over to the digiscreen. Staring down at the thin silver screen, she knew there was something in there that turned the Doctor off of them. She wanted to have a child so badly, she didn't want anything to jeopardize that.

"Mary, what are you thinking?" Jon knew she was in one of her *question everything* moments. *She gets that from her mom*, he thought. Jon removed his clothing and changed into the robes.

Mary picked up the digiscreen and the screen displayed a

locked status. As with any digiscreen, it will only unlock when the registered owner is touching the device. She knows one trick, though, that by turning the digiscreen off and back on, it will display the last message it was open to, a failsafe in case the power abruptly failed. She turned it off, then back on, and left it on the counter, waiting for the Doctor to return and touch it again. Mary changed into the robes.

The door swished open, and Dr. Dehmer apologized for the interruption. As the door was closing to the hallways, Mary noticed two men were standing on either side of the doorway, their shoulders visible around the doorjamb. Did the Doctor need escorts for Jon and her?

As the Doctor reached for his digiscreen, Mary conveniently dropped her clothing pile. She stooped to pick it up and looked at his screen at the same time. The last message pulled up instantly, and she was able to read the opening sentence before he swiped his finger across the screen and scooped up the pad.

"Now you will follow me to the birthing facility and we will finish what you came here for," the Doctor said.

Mary was shocked, and only glanced at Jon, wishing she could tell him the message as she saw it. She was second-guessing herself even now. Did she read that correctly?

The screen read, *Possible members of the Movement. Exercise special caution when . . .*

Jon walked over, took her hand in his, gave a nod to the Doctor and followed him down the hallway. Their "escorts" followed closely behind, pretending to read their own digiscreens and talk to each other about various patients and procedures.

The Doctor led them farther into the vast complex that was the LifeSpan Birth and Development Building, finally arriving at an oversized plasteel door. As with every wall and doorway in the LifeSpan complex, there were not any noticeable seams. In fact,

Jon barely noticed a doorway, until the Doctor raised his hand and removed his glove.

He waved his exposed hand in a counterclockwise motion once to the right, and again to the left. The doors opened with a small hiss, revealing a well-lit room, with attendants standing around the edges and two chairs in the middle.

"Please have a seat." Dr. Dehmer nodded to the vanilla-colored chairs. "Jon in the left chair, Mary in the right."

As they sat, flexible mechanical arms lowered from the ceiling and the attendants attached suction points to both Mary's and Jon's left wrists.

"What are they doing to my wrist?" Mary asked, and tried to sit up.

"Please remain seated; you are being cleaned for the transfusion." Another attendant stepped forward and lowered Mary back into the seat back.

The suctioning continued, slowly moving up and down their forearms. Mary was staring at the tubes, wondering how clean she needed to be for whatever they were preparing. She looked over at Jon and noticed he was squirming in his chair, his feet wringing into each other. He was more ticklish than she was, but he kept very still even though his face betrayed him.

"We need three crucial samples from you today, all of which will be taken while you remain in your seated position. You will not experience any discomfort. Please do not try to rise out of your seat again." Dr. Dehmer's voice drawled out in the quiet, sterile room, like he had repeated the same litany too many times to make it sound interesting anymore.

"The first extraction will be the basic cells from your body. Red blood cells and white blood cells. Of course, oxygen plays a huge role in the development of proteins and nucleic acids...," the Doctor droned on in the background.

Mary was thinking about the future. A huge weight was settling onto her shoulders, and she knew Jon was just as worried. How would they be as parents? Actually being allowed to have a child was one thing, and she knew from her friends' lighthearted heckling that a child was a tremendous amount of work. How would Jon handle the extra responsibility, and would he be jealous of the attention their child would take away from him?

"The bones are another factor when growing a new infant subject. You can't just string together calcium-rich supplements and hope the rest will fall into place. You need to start with a base, and nurture a chain reaction within the marrow and increase the density of the bone mass over — "

Mary looked down at the cleaning tube and was shocked to see it was no longer cleaning the surface of her forearm. Rather, it was *under* her skin, slowly pulsing without causing her any pain.

"Doctor!" Mary cried out, reaching with her free hand to grab at the tube.

"Please, just sit back, and quit overreacting." The second attendant was now standing over her chair. Mary tried to look over at Jon, but her view was blocked by the nurses.

"It's alright, Mary, trust them," Jon spoke softly, but with a command that calmed her immediately. *If he is making it through, then I can*, she thought.

Just as Mary leaned back, another tube snaked down from the ceiling and attached itself under her robe, between her legs. She felt pressure as the machine snaked in. The nurses stepped back and unlocked a release bar under Mary and Jon's chairs. Mary could see another tube attached between his legs. The nurses pushed their chairs together, as the tubes stretched to compensate.

"For this next part," the Doctor began, "the process has shown further positive results if you are in proximity of each other. Please hold hands, and stare into each other's eyes."

Still sitting in their chairs, Mary reached out and was comforted to feel Jon's hand covering hers. His hand was cold and clammy, verifying that he was also feeling nervous and awkward. Surprisingly, Mary was further comforted with this knowledge.

"I would like to completely remove the human psychological element, but the stimulation you feel has a driving force, helpful for conception . . ." The Doctor's voice seemed like part of the room, like an air filter, another dull drone in the background.

Jon looked over and smiled at Mary. She knew he was trying to be strong and supportive at the same time. Jon pulled her hand to his lips and lightly kissed her knuckles.

"So, this is what they used to do, years ago, to have a baby." He rolled his eyes, wondering if it was worth the hassle.

"No, Mr. Jenkins, this is a much safer way to conceive. The nanos have blocked your natural reproductive organs. As you know, conception is a privilege given from LifeSpan. You are stimulated right now, are you not? Mary's body is also preparing to receive. The barbaric ancestors of yours would rampantly spread viruses and diseases, and then wait while a baby slowly grew in the mother's womb, inviting an infinite number of defects and abnormalities. Our method removes passion and injects science. The way I prefer to run my laboratory."

"So you want a life without passion?" Mary couldn't keep herself from chiming in.

"Sometimes safety overrules the heart." And he turned to the wall chart, examining the results, occasionally glancing at his pocket watch.

The room quieted. Jon and Mary never took their eyes from each other. The machines pumped, their bodies pulsed together. Hands intertwined, they craned their necks to be fractionally closer together. Mary desperately wanted to be in his arms. It seemed the right thing to do, the natural thing. She found herself breathing harder. Jon's chest was rising and falling as his ankles crossed and he closed his eyes. Mary clenched her teeth and her eyelids shut.

She imagined herself floating endlessly across the ocean, Jon bobbing along with her, intertwined, lips locked together, washing out to sea. She imagined herself many places, far away from this room.

She was jolted back when the machines stopped pulsing, and the room fell quiet.

"Very well, then. All done now." The attendants and the Doctor began disconnecting wires and tubes and helping the Jenkinses out of their chairs.

Slightly disoriented, they made their way to the door leading back to the hallway.

"Dr. Dehmer," Jon began.

"Hmm?" The Doctor looked up from his screen, and his eyes bored into Jon, suddenly making him feel very small. This experience was very odd, and he felt cold. Jon couldn't suppress a shiver running down his back and fizzling into his toes. He felt like something was taken from them today, something sacred, and was replaced with an irreplaceable sense of loss. Jon wanted to make his thoughts known to the room of scientists, especially the Doctor, but his mind couldn't form what his heart was feeling.

"Well, umm, thank you for your time." Jon tried to think of something more, and was again stumped.

"Yes, very well, then. Come back in three months to pick up your infant specimen." Dr. Dehmer dismissed them both with a backwards wave of his hand as he walked away.

One more thought. I don't know if I'm supposed to write these kinds of things in here, but I heard Daddy whispering in the kitchen. He didn't know I was on the stairs. He was telling Momma there was something he found, but wasn't supposed to find it. He said there is a problem at work now, his research brought up questions. He told some people, and they got mad at him. Really mad. I've never heard him like this before. He sounded worried and walked around the house throwing things and scaring Momma. Goodnight diary.

Jon continued cleaning after their early dinner. Mary had run upstairs to prepare for her guests this evening; she had told him she was meeting with a group of friends she had met a few weeks ago. It was good she was extending herself to make friends. Sometimes Jon was concerned about her, hanging around the house all the time.

He had finished loading their dinner plates into the refuse reclaimer and setting the various cleaning bots to begin their roving of the eating area. He stood back, watching each small rambler leave its charging dock and go about its task. His favorite was the edge sweeper, no bigger than a tennis ball. It slowly made its way around the wall edge and suctioned any dirt into its tiny container. Later in the night, it would deposit its waste load into small chutes placed around their home, ultimately leading to a recycler for extra energy in the home. It really was an amazing system.

Jon was thinking about the scrubbing bot on the counter when he heard the door monitor chiming. Their guests must have arrived.

Jon called upstairs as he made his way to the door. "Hey honey, they're here."

Jon raised his hand and the door swished open. He was surprised by the sight in front of him. A squat man, chubby beyond his frame with an oversized jacket, pockets stuffed to their limit, was standing between an older man with a soft expression and a striking woman. Her head was held high, and her features were sharp and powerful, like a hawk.

Jon was struck by the nature of these three, complete opposites on every spectrum you could compare them. "Come in. Glad to meet you." Jon stepped back.

"Your invitation to share the splendor of your home is most appreciated," the old man responded, and motioned to the tall, glamorous woman in a flair of ladies-first geniality.

She moved not a muscle, but her eyes looked left, then right, blinked once, and then she took the first step into the entry of the house. Once inside, she began walking around the front foyer, looking into the corners, noting windows, exits, corners. She even dragged her finger along the edges of the digiframe currently displaying a classic painting.

She stared at the image, stepping back and crossing her arms behind her back, admiring the digital representation.

Jon was shaking hands with the men, gently guiding them to the kitchen with his open palms on their backs. "My name is Jon, in case you didn't know."

"How polite, but we already know. I'm sorry we overlooked the greetings. My name is Professor Lander," the old man said. "This is Tym. He's a bit shy, but one of the best people you could ever know, and a great techmind to boot!" Tym attempted to bow in acknowledgment of the introduction, which only served to topple him forward as his center of gravity was disturbed. Professor Lander calmly reached out and resettled the blustering Tym, who shrugged his shoulders when settled, settling his gadgets back into place, his cheeks blushing a deep red.

"Yes, well, the exquisite art buff is Gretchen," Professor Lander continued. "She —"

"Does not need an introduction, thank you." Gretchen turned from the frame. "Interesting choice of work to be displayed today. Did you choose it for our visit?"

"Actually, my wife chooses the lineup. I am not that involved with the classics. I understand the need for decoration, but didn't think it mattered . . . Well, art matters . . . The house looks great because of her. My wife is responsible . . . Thanks to her . . . ," Jon mumbled.

"So, let's review your rambling. Your wife chooses the artwork, and you are ignorant of the possible ramification of the works displayed in your home and accept them without an intellectual comment," Gretchen teased.

"Gretchen, please. He is our host. We are not here to judge. There are many important issues we need to discuss," the professor said, obviously trying to defuse the situation.

Jon was uncomfortable, that much was certain, but he steeled himself against Gretchen's accusations. "I'm sorry. I guess I never thought much about it. Would you care to enlighten me and explain the 'possible ramifications' this has reflected about my home?"

Gretchen turned toward the digiframe. "This is a painting by Rembrandt van Rijn. He was widely considered one of the greatest painters of all time. The image is titled *Abraham and Isaac*. It is an old story of a now defunct mythos. In the story, Abraham has a son named Isaac. In a test laid out for Abraham, God tells him to go to the mountain and sacrifice Isaac."

"That's terrible," Jon commented.

Gretchen, irked by the interruption, continues after a steely look at Jon.

"Yes, but it was a ruse. When Abraham raised the knife and plunged it towards Isaac, an angel swooped down from Heaven and stopped the blade at the last possible moment, effectively saving Isaac, but leaving Abraham with the guilt of what he almost accomplished."

"So, this painting is about testing your faith?" Jon pieced together.

"Yes and no, Jon. This story shows that it is not the *act* that is necessary, only the *will*. If you can impose your will, you have already prevailed. The action is not important, for without *will*, there *is* no action."

"And that is precisely why I wanted to meet with you," Mary announced as she descended the stairs into the room. "Jon, if you could excuse us, I would like to catch up with my friends here. We have been working on a project together, the details of which would quickly bore you."

Jon was all too happy to let his wife try her hand with this group. He grabbed his jacket, said goodbye, and made a quick exit as the front door swished open.

When it was clear they were alone, Professor Lander quickly approached Mary. He took her hands in his own, excitement clearly showing.

"We've done it Mary. We have the tank." He looked to Tym and Gretchen. "It works. We can finally hold those little buggers. We have set the base in Bangalore."

"This is great news! Thank you, Father," Mary replied.

BIRTH

The birthing room was shaped like the inside of a large egg. Walls stretched up and around, seamlessly merging into a high cusp without a ceiling break, then flowing back down to the floor. The wall surface was made up of tiny digital pixels, cycling through the prism of rainbow colors, pulsing in various levels of brightness. The visual display was mesmerizing. Located in the middle of this shell was a small plasteel table, surrounded by a stretched white fabric connected on all sides. The fabric sealed around the oval table and ran tautly back up and around the curved walls. At the far end of the table sat two digiscreens, an oblong metal helmet, and a pair of measuring calipers. A child lay naked on the table. Minutes ago, he was pulled from the growth tubes, and now he lay kicking and waving his arms in the air.

"Subject 7759-03 ready for nano infusion, vial 6692. Post," a low voice droned out to break the silence.

The baby merely lay back, captivated by the color-changing walls around him, completely unaware of the rigorous testing about to begin that would shape the outcome of his new life. The fabric surface surrounding the table began to swell as objects were rising up from underneath the material. At first indiscernible, shapes that became evident as heads and shoulders rose, the material shrouding the upper body of the LifeSpan Doctors. The Doctors were seamlessly connected, with only shoulders and heads stretching the fabric so thinly that they could see clearly through it. From an outside observer, the scene was similar to ocean waves gently rising and falling during a hectic storm. The bodies pushed and pulled the tumultuous ocean surface. The Doctors raised their arms, pushing against the fabric, reached for the baby, and slowly forced him to a prone position.

"Ready vial 6692," a voice projected across the table, but it was impossible to discern the origin of the voice, let alone single out the contributor. "Commencing with infusion. Post."

An additional Doctor swooped forward, pulling the fabric and the others connected with him. He pushed his hand against the mesh and raised the boy's foot. He pulled out a measuring device and began recording data on a digiscreen. As the boy's foot was hoisted, another Doctor took his head and slipped it into a round metallic helmet, covering his ears and shoulders, restricting his chin and halting all neck movement. Still, the child did not cry out.

From the left side of the newborn's miniature neck, a small needle lowered into the helmet housing, advancing gradually forward, holding barely a hair's breadth away from his skin. The needle waited without a sound and suddenly plunged into his skin. The walls abruptly changed to a dull gray color.

The boy cried out.

"Infusion has begun," a deep voice echoed above the infant.

With that final statement, an army of tiny robots, each no larger than a common bacterium, emptied out of the needle tip and began swimming through the young child's bloodstream. They streamed through his system, some staying behind to bond with the heart, lungs and liver. Platoons of nano soldiers were infused through each valve, vein and artery.

The walls of the infusion room revealed various charts with each advancement, showing cholesterol readings, heartbeat recordings, blood pressure data, red and white blood cell counts. Relentlessly, the nanos swam through the boy's innards, dodging individual cells, tiny molecular motors propelling them into every corner of his system. The walls were covered with stacking data, graphs, readouts and statistics.

"Systems report. Nano introduction twenty-one percent complete," an emotionless voice droned out.

And so the process continued, Doctors bobbing throughout the room, reading and recording data. The walls became crowded with graphs, charts, and numbers. The screens began to overlap as new data came pouring in. The data displays showed a hundred holocards, shuffling with increasing speed.

"Systems report. Nano introduction eighty-two percent complete."

The entire room was alive, tossing and churning with hurricane-like ferocity. The fabric connecting the Doctors was glowing a fierce blue, heating the air above.

"Systems report. Nano introduction completed. Full system online. Processing data. Processing completed. Expiration date confirmed." The room activity halted, every cowl frozen. The diagrams and charts grew fainter, receding into the distance. The walls cleared as a series of digits slowly emerged into view.

18980.13.8.3

"Subject recorded expiration: eighteen thousand nine hundred and eighty days, thirteen hours, eight minutes and three seconds."

"Induce tranquilizers."

The baby's crying came to an immediate halt.

The ceiling shifted to reveal a color-changing tapestry once again. The heads and shoulders stretching through the continuous fabric began to sink down through the floor, and were seen no more. The room returned to a still lake of water as the fabric stretched tautly again to the walls.

Jon opened his eyes as the auto-tint windows dissolved from black, letting the sunlight fill the room.

He sat up in bed and turned to see his wife beginning to wiggle out of the covers, stretching her arms and legs at the same time. He loved her most at this early time. Her mind was free from worry for a few fleeting moments before the day began. The covers were their own barrier to the outside world; this was their safe haven.

Mary had moved on to rubbing her eyes, and as the sunlight filtered into their room, her mind snapped into today's schedule.

There was really only one thing that was important today.

Mary quickly turned her head to him and smiled widely.

"It's today, Jon! Today we are finally parents. I can't believe he's here already!" Mary shouted and leapt out of bed with a renewed vigor.

By the time Jon swung his legs down to the floor, Mary was already in the next room, activating the shower with a cheerful, "Pressurize, please." He let his feet linger in one spot, and crunched his toes. Today was an important day, a day that would change everything. Jon looked around the room, trying to imagine a little boy running up to the bed, waking him up, brightening his day as much as the sunlight did. He laid his head back down on the pillow. Mary would be in the bathroom for a half hour at least. No rush for him to get out of bed just yet.

"Jon, in the shower! Let's go!" Mary poked her head around the corner, startling him back to a seating position. He looked over at Mary standing in the doorway with only a towel held in front of her naked body. Her hair was still dry.

"I thought you were in the water!" Jon was dumbly blinded by her exposed beauty.

"There isn't time for us to take separate showers. Now get up and get in!" Mary ran back into the shower room.

"Your order is ready for pickup," Jon mumbled, and walked to the hall, unbuttoning his nightshirt.

"Welcome back, Mrs. Jenkins and Mr. Jenkins." Dr. Dehmer acknowledged both of them with a nod, and began walking down the hall.

"It was a long three months, but we think everything is ready at home," Jon responded, thinking this was a conversation.

The Doctor stopped walking, turned back to face the new parents and dispassionately said, "Good for you. I trust his room is full of digilights and darling baby items." He finished with a sneer.

"Yes, as a matter of fact, we started his room thinking he would like the red—"

"How precious. Well then, if you would like to follow me, we can go wake up our newest subject." Dr. Dehmer was already a few steps ahead.

"Cole," Mary threw in.

"Yes. The subject baby Cole."

Cole was resting in a high-walled crib, wrapped in a white blanket with the LifeSpan logo embroidered on the front. Next to him sat a few empty bottles, a LifeSpan rattle, a change of clothes and a smooth white timepiece.

Jon picked up the LifeSpan pocket watch, lacking seams and decoration except a small engraving on the back.

Cole R. Jenkins
No. 7759-03

He knew from the identical timepiece in his pocket that the only person who could open the lid and view the interior regulator was Cole himself. Eager to see his son's expiration, he lifted Cole's white robe and placed the clock onto Cole's tiny stomach, his squirming threatening to knock the timepiece off of his naked flesh.

Recognizing Cole's unique technological signature reading from his nanos, the clock opened and revealed a series of dials. They were spinning in unison, driving the dials counterclockwise. His march towards expiration had already begun. Jon quickly counted the dials and totaled fifty-two years.

That's my boy. You will live longer than I will, Jon silently congratulated.

"Your son is ready for you to take home. The nano infusion went as planned, and he is one of our best subjects," Dr. Dehmer disclosed.

"He looks like me," Jon commented.

"Of course he does. The genes are still intact and passed on. Hair color, eye color, propensity to be thin or obese, expressions, skeletal structure. These still develop outside of the nanotechnology. Unfortunately, we are all still very unique."

"I know the nanos keep him healthy," Jon chimed in. "Cole will be everything we wished to be. My boy will be hungry for knowledge, and maybe a bit of a daydreamer, like his dad. But I can't wait to teach him to walk, and tie his shoes and—"

"You will not need to teach him any of those mundane activities more than once," Dr. Dehmer interrupted. "The nanos are instilled with the knowledge of generations. Your simple tasks mean nothing."

"How can you be so callous?" Mary started indignantly, pushing her way to the Doctor. "How can you not see a child as a new beginning? The start of a new life to learn and to grow beyond the limitations of the parent—"

"He is already beyond you," Dr. Dehmer interrupted again, in a droning, lecturing monotone. "You will show him one time to tie his shoes. The nanos will take over from there. They already know how to fasten those laces better than you. Actually, even better than I. Every new generation learns and perfects these tasks, these muscle memories. They are nothing more than that."

"I'm teaching him. I am the one showing him how to do that in the first place, right? He doesn't know at birth how to ties his shoes. He doesn't know how to walk or run when he's just a child!" Jon was becoming agitated.

"Of course he can't walk right out of the tube. That's ridiculous. There are muscular limitations. For example, as a newborn, his neck muscles cannot hold his head up. The nanos release their information at appointed times. No sooner, no later. You will show him these things, these tasks that somehow fulfill you as a fatherly figure. How cliché. You show him once, and the triggers release. You go ahead and play the good daddy. He already knows everything you will be telling him. He just doesn't believe it yet," Dr. Dehmer scoffed.

"I know when your profession is chosen, the knowledge of the craft is unlocked so you can add to the successes. Why not unlock everyone? Why not have everyone know everything? Wouldn't that be better? Isn't that possible?" Jon asked.

The Doctor looked at him with an incredulous expression. "Mr. Jenkins, would you need an ocean ship captain to understand how to build a city structure?"

"Then Cole can choose for himself. We will support him in any area he wishes to pursue," Mary joined in encouragingly.

"Again, he does not *choose* the profession. There is still an anomaly we cannot seem to weed out. There are still the right choice and the wrong choice for each person. I would rather assign the needed craft to each new citizen. However, there is a skill set buried deep with the genetic code. One day we will find the strain and even the playing field."

"This is still our free choice. We all have talents," Mary replied.

"Yes, of course. So very talented we all are . . . ," the Doctor trailed off. "Good day to you." The Doctor turned and walked away, returning to his duties.

Nimbus stood with his arms clasped behind his back, pacing the long reporting room as the reports came flooding in. Weekly, he received updates from across the globe. The global land masses were split into sectors, with each sector controlled by a Praetor. Industry, Economy, Agriculture, and Population Control were among the many reports from each area. Nimbus reviewed the endless stream of reports. He read at a blazing speed. He was power, he was the decider.

"Sire, we have a report from the solar fields of the East Hemisphere. Specifically, in the village of Bangalore, twelve degrees fifty-eight minutes North by seventy-seven degrees thirty-eight minutes East. The report states a decline in the energy intake from their solar panels. The decrease seems to be from outdated technology, not from arcane devices."

"Are the solar fields working at their maximum output?"

"No, sire, they are still capable of increasing by twelve percent. The only impediment is that the next level of technology needed is locked away in the LifeSpan Pro Dev vaults. Do we have permission to unlock level eighteen?"

Nimbus sat down in his high-backed chair, slowly folding his hands in his lap, over his knees, and pondered the question. The Progressive Development vaults were the heart of his power. Knowledge was power, and the vaults were the culmination of hundreds of years of knowledge, slowly collected from the nano responses of the world population.

The problem facing him was twofold. First, the solar arrays across the globe were positioned in areas of maximum sunlight, allowing the solar cells to charge fully and distribute the energy to the growing populations.

Second, software upgrades for the entire system would not only increase the input, it would give extra power to the surrounding communities. This upgrade could spur development in the area. The larger issue was why the power was needed.

"Tell me, has the population expanded so quickly they are in need of this extra energy?" Nimbus inquired.

"No, sire." The messenger flipped through his digiscreen. "That is the peculiar data. There has been a marked increase in new births, but no more than the allowable limit."

"Yet they are suddenly draining the grid?"

"Yes, sire. Forty percent higher energy drains are reported within the last quarter."

"Alert the Praetors," Nimbus ordered. "I want to know why."

"Yes, of course." The messenger bowed. "LifeSpan is the path." The messenger turned to leave.

"One final item." Nimbus leaned forward. "*Reduce* the current power in Bangalore by twenty percent. I suspect we will flush out the real cause here."

"A wise choice. It will be done."

I can see the birds waiting in the tree, looking for the morning light. The sun moves slowly over the mountains that ring our town. Momma says instead of sitting inside watching the sun move, I should be outside at the park with my sister and the other kids. My neighbor always goes to the park. Their whole family goes to watch the Collectors play with the children, allowing them to hang off their arms and racing them across the fields. I never really liked them, there's something in their eyes. Something behind their eyes if that's possible. I call them Montgomery's Mumblers because if Dr. Montgomery made them, you would think he could help them talk better.

THE DAWN

Mary stood in the front doorway, waiting for the sun to rise. She always waited for the sun. It felt refreshing, and today she needed to bask in the rays and clear her thoughts.

"Honey, soon it will be 5:05 a.m.," Mary started. "And you'll want to—"

"I'll want nothing. We have prepared for this very moment, and all is going as planned," Jon hastily replied.

Mary stared back at him and could not think of a rebuttal. She crossed her arms and glanced outside to check the sky again. She looked down the cobblestone walkway, lined with marigolds and leading to their porch. It was true, Jon had known of this day even before they met each other. He would be the first taken away. Then it would be her, and much later, their son Cole.

Looking at her husband, with his hair perfectly set and his blue pinstripe suit purchased just for this occasion, she was actually filled with a sense of wonder for the LifeSpan system. However, there was a hint of . . . *something*, just under her skin. An emotion she thought was lost, but suddenly forced to the surface. She desperately tried to place this feeling. Was it melancholy? But why should she be feeling this? Today's date was registered and verified by the LifeSpan Department of Records.

"Hello, Cole," her husband called out to the back room. Mary turned to look.

Peeking around the corner was their nine-year-old son. He bolted into the room with a handful of choco-sticks, his father's favorite way to ruin his dinner. Cole threw his arms around Jon.

"Father, it should be time soon, right?" Cole asked.

"Yes, and I wanted to ask you one last favor before they arrive," Jon said as he lowered himself to one knee and took hold of Cole's hands.

"Take care of your mother, remember all that I have taught you, and always hold your head high. You are the son I always wanted." He glanced at his LifeSpan timepiece. "Now, the time is almost upon us." Three of the five dials had stopped moving, leaving minutes and seconds spinning away.

"That is it, Father. Time to expire," Cole explained.

As Jon stood, the Collectors arrived.

The morning sun rose over the horizon but was blocked by a wall of three imposing men, standing shoulder to shoulder. They moved in unison, capes billowing behind their physiques, the strong wind whipping against them, stirring their cloaks and hair but having little effect on their focused gaze. Their traditional garb was pure white, the finely woven, shimmering threads reflecting in the sun. In full light, it was difficult to stare at the clothing for any length of time. They were the angels of LifeSpan. As their legs were obscured by the long flowing robes, they appeared to float forward.

Wide eyed, Mary slowly stepped away from the doorway, walking backwards, until she backed against the wall under the staircase. She glanced around, looking for her husband and son, eventually finding them: her husband fixing his tie and standing a bit straighter with a smile on his face; Cole standing tall, watching the approaching Collectors. He was proud, and so accepting of the LifeSpan way.

Mary moved her arm behind her body and felt the wall, then half turned and was caught looking at the mounted digiframe. Images and video of the three of them were cycling through the screen. Her family, looking back at her. Images of Cole as he grew up these last nine years with them.

Three of us. Complete. Soon to be two, Mary thought.

PLATEAU

Nimbus sat back in his chair. Alone. Deep in thought over his most recent series of tests. Every year, he was tested on his developing performance, measured in many areas ranging from athletic performance to intellectual prowess. He had been minutely improving each year, barely measurably, but consistently. However, for the last five years, he had not shown any improvement. His body levels and muscle mass had stayed exactly the same. Nimbus planned on finding the reason his body was not further developing, at any means possible. After all, he was supreme, and nothing would change that.

Nimbus knew he would have to remind the assembly of Doctors of that crucial fact.

The entrance chime came precisely on time.

"Enter. Your prompt arrival is noticed; your voice will be heard. Come, be my guest," Nimbus formally declared.

The door slowly opened and the meek Dr. Powell came forward.

"I don't want to drag this out any longer than I have to." Nimbus stood and walked closer to Dr. Powell. "At my last session, there was no difference in —"

"You have attained greatness," Dr. Powell adulated.

Nimbus abruptly stopped talking. He folded his hands in front of his waist, slid his feet farther apart, and stared deep into Dr. Powell's eyes, squinting and clenching his jaw.

Dr. Powell saw this movement and knew he had made a grave mistake.

Powell had interrupted *him*.

Powell had offended the perfect being.

"I see you have become comfortable in your new position," Nimbus hissed. "Perhaps you are merely forgetful of the path shown."

"No, sire, I had a momentary lapse of judgment." Dr. Powell was shaking, feeling his knees grow weak. He thought quickly and raised his hands. "How can I repair the damage? I am nothing without LifeSpan, I am nothing!"

Nimbus waited, reconsidering this meeting or planning for Dr. Powell's sudden disappearance.

"As I was saying, at my last session, there was again no difference in my micro development. So, I have decided to take a new direction. In two day's time, I will be calling a meeting of the Extractor Sciences Board. During this meeting, you will have your chance to step into my favor once again. Your decision will ruin your career, your friendships, and all of your future research will be at risk. I do not ask this of you; I command it."

"You command, I follow, sire," Dr. Powell conceded.

He listened as Nimbus laid out his plan.

The Collectors walked through the threshold and into the front foyer. Immediately they began looking around, scanning for people, exits, and assessing the situation. The lead Collector pulled a digiscreen from under his white cloak. Raising it up before his face, his mouth cracked open and, in a slow drawl, he read the screen. "Jon Jenkins. 16477.5.5.4. Confirm your presence and submit to expiration."

Jon looked down at his timepiece. "I am Jon Jenkins. Thank you for arriving . . . You are early?" He looked over at his son. "I am ready, anyways."

A Collector looked over at Mary. "There she is," he stated as he glanced down at his digiscreen. "Subject Mary Jenkins. Stay where you are."

"Why would you tell her that? She's alright. She is just worried about caring for our son. Isn't that right, Mary?" Jon watched his clock tick down.

"This is all going as planned. Why are you crying, Mom?" Cole questioned her.

Immediately in front of her was a Collector, looking down at her. She looked at him as the room was fading from view, the edges of her vision turning black and out of focus. He was very tall, muscular, and his features were cut harshly, like a chipped stone. His skin was drab, colorless, uncooked bread dough. His nose protruded and took a quick hook down. His lips were a thin line held tight by a constant pressure from his clenched teeth. Her mind was yelling at her not to react, while her arm suddenly raised and swung for the Collectors throat. Before her arm straightened, the Collector caught her wrist and shoved his face inches from her own. She didn't even see him move! Mary stared into his charcoal-colored eyes.

Out of options, Mary began to struggle. She was not able to move before her hand was engulfed in pain. The lead Collector had her left arm in an iron grip, and as Mary glanced down, it was twisted enough to bring her to her knees in submission.

"Listen to me very carefully, woman. It would be *unwise* to provoke us," the Collector spoke, slowly and with clarity. His voice had the sound of chains dragged over gravel.

Between gritted teeth, Mary stared at the ground and could smell an acrid stench she only assumed was the Collector's breath. She wasn't aware of anything quite so vile. Heavy with ammonia, it burned her nostrils. Sweat beaded on her brow, collected above her eyes and fell the distance to pool on the floor. She could only nod her head in submission.

Then she was standing again, and the Collector wore a blank mask of emotion. He stared at her, not showing any signs of their recent one-sided struggle. Mary, however, was panting hard, rubbing her wrist and barely able to stand.

"Mary! What has gotten into you?" Jon cried. "It is time for me to go. I have lived the life I was given. Please don't do this!" Jon turned toward the other two Collectors as he depressed the side button again; the cover flipped open revealing the second hand making its slow, final lap. "Gentlemen, please take me away. I am ready." He walked over to the staircase. The Collectors waited in the doorway.

"Not now, not this way with . . . ," Mary began in a rambling protest, to no avail.

Jon bent down to one knee, glanced over to Cole, a proud smile creased his face. He managed to slump onto the stairs, resting in a lifeless heap, expired.

Cole nodded, complacent with the outcome.

Mary wailed.

The Collectors advanced.

Nimbus walked slowly and deliberately along the glass wall running the length of the conference room. Situated at the highest floor of the LifeSpan Extractor Sciences, it offered an expansive view of the surrounding city. Usually, he was filled with power and pride when he was scanning his city, his world. However, today he was disgusted. He raised his hands and waved them across the windows, once, twice and a third time. Each wave tinted the windows down another shade, effectively plunging the room into darkness. Sensing the lack of sunlight, automatic lights started to fill the room with a soft, pale orange glow.

Nimbus approached the head seat of the gathering table. The entire LifeSpan Extractor Sciences Board sat before him. They specialized in the absorption and reassignment of nano data, making them some of the most important men and women on the planet. Nimbus had gathered these great minds to give them an ultimatum.

"Welcome, colleagues," he greeted. The lights shining up from the tabletop were reflecting under his chin, giving Nimbus a surreal, firelight glow.

A few heads nodded in recognition, and a scattered verbal reply of "Hello, Sire Nimbus" rippled around the table. It was obvious the Doctors were nervous. Their last meeting with Nimbus had not gone so well, leaving them in a serious scientific predicament.

"Recollecting how our last meeting ended, I understand the insecure thoughts you show openly on your faces. I would like to readdress my current situation. Although you have failed me time and time again, I still believe you are my only hope."

This helped to lighten the atmosphere.

"You believe my body has succumbed to a natural plateau. I am telling you this is false. You will find a resolution through an in-depth investigation into how we currently handle my extractions, and why they have failed."

"Perhaps you are at the highest level . . ." A meek Doctor in the back of the room tried to squeak out a comment, only to let his remark fade away, running out of courage.

Nimbus answered loudly and clearly. "I have not reached the full potential of the human race! I have only reached the potential of your mundane machinery and your subpar minds!"

The Board members snapped into silence. Everyone was frozen in their seats, unsure of how to react. Many of them had never seen Nimbus this upset. He rarely raised his voice.

"Dr. Zander." Nimbus motioned toward a pale Doctor on his left. The Doctor had raven-black hair and eyebrows that jumped out on his face, his skin taut and gaunt, stretched across his cheekbones. It was a wonder he could move his mouth at all. "The nanotechnology coursing through our bodies is regulated through the lifetime of each recipient. This is based on a combination of nanomemory and muscle memory of each donor. Correct?"

Dr. Zander was unsure of how he should respond. Nimbus was fully aware of the intricacies of nanotechnology, especially the memory features inherent in each tiny nano.

"Yes, sire. The nanos are evolving with each recipient, and the internal nanomemory is built from strictly motor responses, muscle reactions and related physical responses."

"For example, when a subject swings a hammer, the muscle reaction is recorded in the nano and stored in its memory, only to be replaced if the hammer swing becomes more efficient, correct?" Nimbus prodded.

Again, Nimbus knew the answer, but now the Doctor caught on that Nimbus was leading him somewhere, leading them all towards a series of questions and answers. "Yes, sire, the nanos are constantly tracking the response, searching for a more efficient completion of any task, no matter how minuscule. This information is stored for later use, of course."

"When a client expires . . . ," Nimbus led. "My question is, who is given control of the memory in the body? Is it the brain that remembers how to do the task, or is it the muscles that remember the task?"

"Yes, sire. While it is true that every memory and perception is formulated with the bias of each individual, it is at least *recorded* correctly in the mind and motor functions collectively. However, each memory is flawed, primarily for one reason: our perception of recollection." The Doctor was gaining momentum as he turned to his colleagues, taking on a lecturing tone. "The power of each individual to recollect what has transpired carries with each circumstance an immense amount of variables. For instance, returning to the hammer example. Although it is a rather mundane process, hammering a nail differs slightly from one individual to the next. While everyone is capable of hammering a nail, there are certain unique differences in the muscle mass, strength of the tendons, length of the arm, and an innumerable amount of smaller factors, of course.

"Thus, the nanos automatically adjust for each individual and employ changes as upgrades when the subjects are created. This, of course, is the foundation by which we have become so efficient. Each generation of nanos has become more superior than the last," the Doctor finished.

DEVELOP

Nigel had been staring at his digiscreen results for over a half hour. He knew this would be considered his greatest work to date, and the other scientists would have no choice but to finally acknowledge his intellectual prowess.

For years he had been among the leading scientific minds on the planet, even being promoted to sit on the board of Nimbus's prized Doctor Panel. However, he was shunned for being caught somewhere in between professions. With the mind of a Sci, as he was a genius in the lab, and the heart of a Doctor, since his passions also drove him to help his fellow man, Nigel had become the punch line for many jokes inside LifeSpan's elite. Both the Sci and the Doctor circles rarely used his full name. Instead, they snubbed him professionally, and he was known only as Nigel.

He was working on building a central hub for the nanos in the bloodstream to pass through and immediately deposit their information on muscle memory and developmental processes throughout the life of the host. In other words, he had created a mini checkpoint.

This would allow the LifeSpan Extraction team to collect

memories, feelings and emotions before they were filed away in the unreachable subconscious. In effect, Nigel's checkpoint would become an electronic subconscious.

Nigel had the finishing touches in place on this amazing machine, with results to prove his invention. This would be the one that would elevate him above all the other sneering scientists. They walked past him in the hallways and looked down at him. While it was true he was significantly shorter than most of the Doctors, he was also the youngest on the team. A mind years ahead of his own generation, Dr. Walter Nigel wanted the admiration of one man only, Nimbus. That was his true goal in life: to work alongside the great Nimbus as his right-hand man, above all the other patronizing Scis and Doctors.

Nigel was preparing his files for submission. No matter what the breakthrough, no matter the urgency, there was always protocol. He walked over to the light-shifting Holowall and turned on the connection point.

"Hello, Trina. Dr. Nigel ready for Experiment 67338 to be submitted for review and approval of Nimbus."

"Thank you, Nigel. How do you think it went?" Trina came into focus.

"Very well, Trina, very well indeed. This is the breakthrough we have all been waiting for. Nimbus will be happy with this one, I know it." Nigel beamed with excitement.

"Let's not jump to conclusions, Nigel," Trina warned. "He will review your information, and I will update you with his decision."

"Of course. Thank you, Trina. I'll be leaving for home after the submission."

"Please submit now, while we have an open connection."

"Yes, well, of course." Nigel tapped the plexi screen a few times, dragged over an image and tapped in a submission code that was the secure line to Trina and her offices.

Within seconds, the reply came. "Thank you, Nigel. Please be patient for an answer. I will be in touch."

The Holowall powered down.

With his work finished for the day, Nigel packed up quickly and went home. His house was humble and barren of most furnishings. His walls and counters were covered in plaques, awards of recognition, and the occasional digiscreen of new and retired technology models. He had always thrown himself into his work, reserving little time for anything else, except a few plants. Unfortunately, even those had suffered under his intense research schedule.

He sat down on his floor, cross-legged, and felt the small disk hiding in his Doctor's robe. He glanced around the room, not sure why he had even done this in the first place. He had gone against the protocol. Nigel had made himself a backup disk and removed it from the office.

This was a very serious breach. He was not allowed to bring anything into the outside world. This was not for any "ignorants" to read. He doubted they even could decipher the elevated physics contained within. But the fact remained: he made a copy of his nano-checkpoint data before he sent it to Trina. There was no excuse for his actions.

He wanted a piece of it for himself. This was his child. All scientists were required to send the entire process and files to Trina. It was a one-way trip for the information. Nobody was allowed to "go back to the drawing board" if Nimbus didn't like it or need it. Someday it could be revisited, by his express request only, but that rarely happened.

Nigel stuffed the disk into the dirt of a neglected house plant and went to bed.

Jon's body was carried between two Collectors on a stiff plastique board, his arms folded over his chest, eyes closed. They marched across the Jenkins front lawn, leaving Mary and Cole behind with the last Collector still blocking Mary.

Their transport hatch opened with one panel expanding upwards onto the roof and two out to each side. A plasteel bed lowered from within and the Collectors loaded Jon onto the platform, which swallowed him up as the panels moved back into place. The two Collectors swung themselves up into the cabin compartment, one at the wheel and the other ready to assist. The third Collector left Mary's side and walked across the lawn to their vehicle. He sat with Jon's body in the back as the vehicle sped away.

"Unfortunately, that is only a basic memory response. We can build worker bots to perform the same task, infinitely more efficient than any human. It's when we have human ingenuity that true advancement is possible. You cannot build a worker bot to be a scientist; there is too much passion needed in scientific undertakings," another Doctor chimed in from the back of the room. His name was Dr. Powell, one of the newest scientific minds to join Nimbus's inner circle. Just because he was the newest didn't mean they trusted him less.

As soon as Dr. Powell finished, the other Doctors moved to object.

Nimbus stood, to cease any further interjections.

"Gentlemen, that is where we are falling behind. We can no longer rely on basic muscle responses to advance humankind. The *memories* of an individual are the next frontier. That is why I have gathered you together today. We will be traveling beyond the motor reflexes, and delving into the human mind." He held up his hand once more, for the Doctors were beginning to voice the expected response. "I know we have already looked into the development of the various sectors of the brain."

"Sire, there have been . . . *complications* in the past; that much is true. Unfortunately, we are still unable to pull a specific memory or emotional response out of the human mind. Although the mind has carefully catalogued an event and filed it away deep in the subconscious, we have never been able to jump in there and retrieve it," Dr. Powell said.

"That is because we have always tried to retrieve a *single* memory, to no avail. Therefore, I see only one path we can take to achieve our goal." Nimbus was directing this debate, guiding the Doctors towards his plan now.

"Sire, the problem is, for us to dig anything out of a specimen's subconscious, the entire mind must be open to us. This would utterly destroy the specimen completely," the Dr. Zander said, his eyes widening. He began slowly shaking his head, finally realizing where Nimbus had been leading them all along.

"There is only one circumstance where I can see that would not be a problem." Nimbus looked around the room. The understanding that Dr. Zander had come to was finding its way through the assembled men like a wildfire. As Nimbus planned, the first to voice his stance was Dr. Powell.

"The most logical time for an entire memory download would be at a specimen's expiration date. When we are extracting the nanotechnology reports, we can drain the memory at the same time," Dr. Powell recited from the carefully planned script Nimbus had given him.

The whole of those assembled were aghast at this possibility. The Doctors erupted amongst themselves, vehemently defending their moralistic duties as caretakers to the expiring individuals. Shouting at each other about limitations, need for further testing, not to mention the act of draining the entirety of a human being.

They would be called monsters of medicine.

"Can it be done?" Nimbus asked.

The room fell silent with the various scientific heads looking at each other, unsure of how to answer their leader.

"*Can it be done*?!" Nimbus leaped from his seat and banged his fist onto the table.

Dr. Zander held his tongue.

Finally, the predictable Dr. Powell, who had tried so desperately to be in Nimbus's good graces tonight, gently replied, "Yes."

Slowly, the remaining Doctors nodded their heads, a clear moral burden settling on their shoulders. Some looked back at Dr. Powell with disappointment.

"Then do it. The next extraction specimen, I want sapped. I want *everything*. Muscle reaction times, calculations, memories, dreams, desires, feelings, psyche. Everything. Am I totally clear?" Nimbus vehemently made his stand.

"Yes, sire. If I may interject one crucial point: Due to the obvious risks involved with downloading another specimen's mind and completely merging with another, may I ask who the test specimen will be?" Dr. Zander implored, even as he knew the answer.

"No test. This inherent ingenuity that you spoke of is what my body needs. If I have to drain every expiration from now on, so be it. I will not be stalled in my progress." Nimbus bore down with a gaze so intense, Dr. Zander found himself nodding before Nimbus had finished talking. "The next expiration will be downloaded directly into me. I understand the hazards, but you shall not fail me. Is that understood?"

"Yes, sire, of course. There are expirations today." Dr. Zander checked his digiscreen, scrolling through expirations, the countries and towns of their locations, eventually finding one in their current city. "There is an expiration moments away. We can use him. His name is Jon Jenkins."

"I don't care what his name is, I just want him drained. You are all dismissed."

Nimbus turned his back on the Doctors as they shuffled up from their seats and let themselves out. The gentle swish of the automatic door sliding shut was the last sound Nimbus heard before he settled down, cross-legged, and began his deep meditation.

THE GATE

"We are here. Charge him up," the Collector at the wheel said over the speaker. The Collector across from Jon responded, opening hidden panels in the transport and connecting wires to Jon's head and chest. The walls hummed and the compartment filled with white noise. Building into an electric crescendo, the wires danced with power directed into Jon's body. With a final pulse, Jon leaped into a sitting position and opened his eyes.

"What is happening here?" Jon blinked, panicked, and searched for a way out of the vehicle. The Collector said nothing and began pulling wires off of Jon, returning them to various compartments that blended back into the wall. Jon sat and stared at the Collector. The vehicle stopped. He heard doors swishing open from the front and the back hatch unfolded again, lowering his table down.

"Time to go." The Collector finally spoke, and motioned for Jon to exit first.

As Jon stepped out, he realized he was in a familiar place. Very familiar. The LifeSpan grounds were as he remembered, back when Mary and he were here to pick up Cole. He turned and faced south, looking down the galley to LifeSpan Birth and Development, remembering Mary standing on the front steps, filled with wonder and excitement to start their lives as parents.

"Mr. Jenkins, come with us." The blonde Collector gently guided him off of the bed.

"I expired. Where are you taking me?" Jon was confused, and tried to pull away.

"You are very important. You have been chosen."

They walked towards the smallest building in the grounds.

The three Collectors approached the door, removed their gloves from their right hands and placed them in unison on seemingly random panels of the door. Each hidden panel glowed briefly, and the door popped open.

"Time for you to continue alone, Mr. Jenkins," the lead Collector said softly.

Yes, because I am very important. This is my destiny. Jon turned to face the doorway once again, its gleaming surface catching the sun's rays with a blinding reflection. He steadied himself, and stood a little taller as he walked through the portal.

It's like I'm walking into the sun itself, Jon thought.

He looked down at the smooth floor with a small black line running along its center. As the Collectors closed the door behind him, Jon focused on the black line and continued down the hall. He eventually left the door far behind and saw another light source a short distance further.

He stumbled into a small, white room with one plasteel table in the middle. A booming voice echoed throughout, telling him to lie down and wait.

Jon lay back on the table, waiting for his destiny to be fulfilled. *We are lost. LifeSpan is the compass.* He began to recite his morning litany as the floor around him slowly rose, revealing it to be a tightly woven fabric attached to the edge of the table, without a break from the walls. He turned and began to sit up as a figure emerged from under the fabric, arms raising slowly.

He could barely make out a face as the fabric stretched and spread tightly around the head. The figure had the appearance of a stretch-wrapped doll from the waist up.

"Hello, Jon. We have been waiting for you. Please lie back and we will begin. You have served the human race well. You will be rewarded." The Voice sounded distant, ethereal, and soothed Jon immediately. The Voice had no source, emanating from the entire room, muffled slightly by the fabric. He couldn't tell if it had come from this fabric face. Regardless, he lay back, his head suddenly feeling very heavy.

"You have lived a long and fruitful life. You have been a great help to your community. You have been a worthy father and dutiful husband." With each droning exclamation, Jon was slipping more deeply into a hypnotic stupor, only vaguely aware of how close the figure was to his table.

Jon looked up at the ceiling, which was slowly convulsing from every spectrum of color . . . His mind was caught up in the color storm while the fabric hands cradled his head. He felt himself enmeshed into the shifting colors, and unexpectedly he felt a growing pressure in the back of his head. The colors on the ceiling weakened in hue and were replaced with full-color images from his life. The room enveloped him with a video transmission of the world according to Jon.

Playing all around him in rapid succession was every moment of his life. Some brought a smile to his face, remembering when he met Mary: she had been seeking shelter under an oak tree in a rainstorm. Jon had walked over and offered his umbrella to her.

The images shifted to watching their first date and when he met her parents. His thoughts wandered back to a familiar oak tree, but now he was alone, holding an umbrella. His recollection was fading. Suddenly, he couldn't remember meeting Mary, just that she was his wife. What was before marriage? They were always married. They were never married.

As the images kept flooding onto the screen, Jon was unable to keep up. The scenes transitioned from his work, to his home, to his son Cole. No home, just work. His parents were there, both of them staring down at Jon. Then, he only remembered his father. He had no mother. They were shown, and forgotten. Jon began to panic, and tried to sit up on the table and was forced back down. He arched his back, thrashing his head from side to side.

"Those are my memories! Why is this happening?" He reached over and grabbed the hand away from his head. He grimaced as his head was weighed down in the back, and electrical jolts shot through his spine.

"Those are mine!"

"This subject was the daydreamer," Dr. Zander said. He was high above the chamber housing Jon in an observation dome. Appearing as no more than a small dot in the high ceiling, he watched down on the proceedings. His low-lit room was surrounded by touchscreens, projections and a multitude of dials and switches.

Dr. Zander leaned down to talk in a desk-mounted microphone. This transmitted over the earpieces of the floor technicians.

"Limit his left hemisphere," Dr. Zander said.

"We cannot. We are in too deep," came the reply.

"Then shut it down. We have already entered dangerous territory," Dr. Zander ordered.

"Negative. We will be keeping the subject at full capacity."

Dr. Zander was taken aback at this reply. The floor techs did not have the authority to disobey his request. There was no call for this gross insubordination, nor the need for further suffering from the subject.

"You will not disobey this order. I assure you, I outrank you, and I will shut it down from here and remove you from your post." Zander reached over to limit the amount of information flowing through the transfer subject.

"I'm sorry, Dr. Zander, your booth has been disabled." A new voice responded to his order.

"Impossible. What is your name, technician?"

"Dr. Powell. I will take it from here." One of the cloth-stretched technicians turned to look up at the aerial booth. Indeed, it was the Doctor; he was down below next to Jon, watching the memories play out and fade forever from his mind.

In response, every screen blinked away in the booth and the door locked. Dr. Zander sat helplessly as the subject, Jon, was drained.

Jon was moving frantically now, desperately trying to remember his parents, the first time he brought Cole home, his acceptance into college. Nothing was coming back to him, and as he saw his life playing in fast forward, he became more anxious with each passing frame. As he felt his anger mounting, suddenly it dissipated, like a light switch turned off. His mouth sagged down, facial muscles completely lax. His eyes drooped and he sat back, tongue swelling against his lips, opening his mouth enough to release a small pocket of drool. Jon looked up at the screens and calmly watched the rest of his life in rapid speed, not aware this was the last time the memories would be his own.

Every ten days, Nimbus was subjected to the Absorption. Depending on the amount of data, it could last two minutes or it could last two hours. He knew from the debriefing that this would take the better part of the afternoon. He had never absorbed an entire consciousness before, but he was desperate.

Regardless, Nimbus entered the Absorption room in good spirits. He knew today would be a landmark event, a pivotal moment in the history of LifeSpan and a stepping stone to the future of individual betterment. Nimbus watched the scientists checking one last time for any fault in the machine, readying his chair.

Dr. Zander was in a heated exchange with Dr. Powell. Nimbus cared little for their squabbling, and was not surprised to see them disagreeing once again.

Nimbus settled in with his team working all around him, connecting anodes, testing screens and strapping his arms and neck.

"Begin, already!" Nimbus was impatient. "Commence sequence!"

And so it did. The room burst to life, intense colors and images splashed to every corner.

Nimbus lurched as his mind flooded with new information. It was an intense sensation he had never felt before. Every past Absorption paled in comparison.

Nimbus was empowered. Intense cognition overloaded his mind as he absorbed Jon's memories.

He was running through the park. He was reading reports at Jon's work. He was falling. He was climbing. He was a child Jon, an adult Jon. Married. He was in his home, opening the door to a trio of wildly different individuals. Completely opposite on every spectrum of comparison. A squat man, a hawkish woman and an old man.

Nimbus was shaking hands with the men, gently guiding them to the kitchen with an open palm on their back. "My name is Jon, in case you didn't know."

"How polite, but we already know. I'm sorry we overlooked the greetings. My name is Professor Lander," the old man said.

Nimbus was shocked to see that Alexander was alive. "That man! Find that man!" he screamed. "Alexander! He is with Sci Tym!"

"So, let's review your rambling. Your wife chooses the artwork, and you are ignorant of the possible ramification of the works displayed in your home and accept them without an intellectual comment."

"Gretchen, please. He is our host. We are not here to judge. There are many important issues we need to discuss."

Nimbus was thrashing about, flailing his arms in the purest rage. "That man!"

The Doctors tried to hold him down as the alarms sounded. The walls were colored in deep shades of red and purple, pulsing in reaction to Nimbus's emotional swing.

"Sedate him! If the connection is broken now, there will be irreparable damage!" Many of the Doctors looked blankly around the room, unsure of how to handle Nimbus. He was, after all, no ordinary patient, and this was no ordinary transfer.

Nimbus continued to scream and gnash his teeth, barely able to control his own feral response while his personality collided with Jon's.

"Back it out! Take the transfer back!" the inexperienced Dr. Powell suggested.

"We cannot! That could tear him apart! How can we distinguish the memories from one man's to the other's? They are merging!" Dr. Zander yelled back.

"This is a disaster!"

"We have no choice. He cannot continue like this!"

The assembled Doctors were shouting over the screaming Nimbus, each giving his own opinion.

"We can retrace the process and . . . ," Dr. Zander found himself yelling in a suddenly quiet room, their ears left ringing.

All eyes went to Nimbus.

Indeed, Nimbus was no longer screaming, for he was slumped over in his seat, unconscious, as the transfer continued on.

HOMESTEAD

Cole shook his head, snapping his mind back to the present. He was about halfway home, leisurely walking along the paved walks. Cole got his bearings and set off due north. He actually enjoyed spending time outside, letting his thoughts take their course. Daydreaming seemed to run in his blood, so he was never short of crafting stories in his mind while he walked. Most of his co-workers owned fancy, expensive vehicles with voice recognition driving programs. They preferred to end their day with a high-speed drive around the perimeter of town, music blasting while they escaped into a virtual reality playground, with the vehicle driving itself; indeed, that was the only arrangement any car was allowed.

During the last quarter of the previous century, dignitaries were gathered at the Summit of Minds for the greater world peace negotiations. As they drove away in a single motorcade, a mysterious explosion destroyed almost every building and car within three miles. Known as the Royal Crash, almost every major president, chancellor, king, queen and other powers of state were killed. This allowed LifeSpan to step in and create the

Restricted Transportation Act. Every vehicle was equipped with an automatic driving navigation chip via LifeSpan. This mandated a totally computerized network of tracking and regulated travel, so accidents like that tragic multiple crash would never happen again.

Cole turned onto his block and paused. A few houses down on the left was the house he shared with his mother. The one with the large pine tree out front, constantly dropping needles and keeping the automated lawn bots very busy.

The last ten years had been very hard on Mary.

She was withdrawn, constantly making excuses about her inability to leave the house or stay in contact with her friends. She said there were projects to work on, futures to plan for. Cole never saw her working on anything important, just sitting at the kitchen table, mumbling to herself. Her digiscreen sat by her side. She never used it to check the local news feeds or sports schedules, or anything that could be considered a hobby. She used to love tennis, her eyes lighting up whenever he would ask her a question about who would possibly make it to the championships.

He stopped at the mail screen at the end of their driveway, lifting open the lid to reveal a flat screen about the width of Cole's briefcase.

Current Status: Five new digipost messages.

These could be forwarded on to any of the registered digiscreen handhelds, including his mother's, but he knew she would tell him to ignore any from her sister. Scrolling though the messages, there was indeed one from Aunt Hester.

Glancing back at the house and carefully checking every window for his mother's spying eyes, he opened the most recent post.

Dearest Mary,

Please respond when you receive this. I know the last 3,652 days have been hard for you. I also realize what today is, and beg of you to step out of the house, feel the air on your skin, smell the flowers, realize there is still a world growing and thriving. There is a place for you, but only if you let it come. Cole needs you now more than ever. He is a 19-year-old man. He would never admit it, but there are days I look in his eyes, and there is a hardening, a distance that gets further every day. When you . . .

The screen abruptly went dark as Cole deleted the post from the view screen. *If that is what Aunt Hester thinks of me,* he thought, *that I am retreating, then she can keep writing to herself. It's best Mother doesn't have that on her shoulders too.*

Cole turned his back on the house. He was half-tempted to continue walking but he knew his duty tied him to his mother, so he turned back towards the front door.

His attention was diverted to the silver car that just pulled up to his neighbor's house directly across for their own. Mr. Adams was returning from a long day at work. Cole knew he was coming home to a perfectly run life. Mr. Adams was gathering up his coat and briefcase as the silver fleetliner was autodocking into the recharge station. The car slid into position as a panel released under the vehicle, lowering a recharge pipeline, and connected to the solar energy grid snaking through the city. The car would be awaiting Mr. Adams's commute to work, fully charged.

The vehicle door slid along the outside of the driver's side panel and Mr. Adams stepped out, jacket slung over his crooked arm. He swung his head over and smiled at Cole, lifting his chin in a friendly hello.

Cole started to yell a greeting back, but was cut short when Mr. Adams's daughter ran out of the house and wrapped her dad in a hug. He scooped her up and walked to their stoop, where his

wife was waiting in front of their red door. Cole thought red doors
meant love. There was love in that house. Almost everyone on his
block had red doors. Well, all of the houses that had love, of course.

Cole turned and walked up the front steps of his home. He
did not have a red door. At one time it was painted a dark green,
back when his father was still there. Mother never had a knack for
painting, and Cole always had other things to do. So the door was a
bland, weather-worn green, about as far from red as you could get.

Cole stopped and compared his house to the neighbors'. His
house was dark, cold and a far cry from how it was before his
father's expiration. Of course, he knew it was because of his mother.
She had been visited by the LifeSpan workers on many occasions.
After they left, she would improve. She floated around very happy
and was a pleasure to be around, but that would wear off.

The door swished open at his advance, and Cole stepped in to
the dark house and turned on the lights. Mother never turned on
the lights anymore. She just locked herself in her office under the
stairs. She said there was research she was conducting and should
not be disturbed.

"Welcome home, Cole." Mary was standing in the doorway. "I
will have dinner ready for you soon. Would you like that? I'm sure
that's what you were wondering about, is some food, right?" She
always rambled. Without waiting for an answer and still continuing
to ask about dinner, she retreated to the kitchen, mumbling all the
while.

Cole fell onto the couch, arms limp at his side. Cole already
knew what his night would be. His mother was working on a
meal she only half thought through. They would sit at the table
and have a strained conversation. She would leave the table in a
melodramatic show and tell him to figure out the rest of the day
without her. Then Mother would leave. And be gone for hours on
end.

"Cole, come in here please. I have the table ready for us," Mary called.

"Here we go." Cole rolled his eyes.

He walked into the room, and could have accurately described the exact settings and probably the food before entering. The table was set exactly the same way every meal. Cole's plate was in front of his father's chair, now as the head of household, whatever that meant, with his mother to the left, facing their window overlooking an unused yard. Mary turned off the lawnbots when she thought Cole wasn't watching, and the yard had become a mismatched image of perfectly trimmed spaces, overgrown vines, and color-faded equipment.

Cole sat, grabbed his silverware and moved his lips in a silent mockery of Mary's first predictable question.

"How are you doing at LifeSpan?" Mary asked.

"Great, Mom, just fine. Always doing great," Cole snapped back.

"Well, you don't have to be so grumpy. I am trying to talk with you, about the things that you like. I have things that I like, and you never ask me about them."

"Really? Well, Mom, how was your day today? Did the walls move? Did the floor shift?" Cole immediately shot.

"What is that supposed to mean?"

"I know you sit here all day, staring at this place. There are real people outside, Mom, going about their day, making a difference."

"I see what you are doing." Mary pushed her plate forward. "You think the only people that are capable of making changes in this world are the ones you know. The mindless goons walking around out there, waiting on the next big LifeSpan announcement."

"At least they have tasks!" Cole found himself shouting. "They wake up with purpose to complete LifeSpan's work."

"They have lost the ability to dream!" Mary screeched. Her

eyes were wild, and she was talking under her breath as Cole was yelling back at her.

"I know you leave at night," Cole revealed. "I've seen you running along the yard's edge, hiding from walkers and traffic."

Mary sat back down.

"Where do you go Mom? Who are you visiting? Why won't you tell me?"

"I don't know what you are talking about," Mary denied.

"It's time to stop the lies. After ten years, it's time for us to be a family again!"

"It's too late for that, Cole." Mary hung her head, hair falling over her face. "I should have acted sooner, when Jon was still here. You have been sleepwalking. We have all slumbered, as the storm rolled in."

"Well, then, it's time for a new awakening!" Cole screamed.

Mary snapped her head up, an old memory sparked from Cole's phrase.

"Yes, yes . . . ," Mary began mumbling. "You are right. I think this is the time. It has dragged out long enough . . . There really was no other . . . ," she continued, and Cole stopped listening. He knew they were done for tonight. She would pace the house, talking to herself, and he really didn't feel like following her this time.

Mary rounded the table, walked over to Cole, cradled his head in her hands and looked him eye to eye.

Well, this is different, Cole thought.

"You are so much like your father," Mary said, and she leaned forward and kissed Cole's forehead. "Always the daydreamer."

She left the room, leaving a dumbfounded Cole, and started climbing the stairs.

HAMEL

I had to leave Cole out of this, Mary thought as she closed the door to her private bathroom. Mary stood there for a short while, pressed her ear to the door, waited a little longer and finally stepped back. This was the barrier to the outside world. She knew there was no turning back now. Cole wouldn't understand; he was too caught up in the lies of LifeSpan. Today she would act.

Mary knew this deed could be done. She knew it was possible. Unfortunately, she has never heard of anyone in the last ten generations or more even attempt it, but she had a secret weapon: the truth.

Cole stood at the bottom of the stairs looking up to his mother's room. The door was closed. He knew she would be in there a while; she always locked herself in her room for hours on end. Sometimes he heard her talking to herself, mumbling. Cole had enough. This time he was going to find out what she was hiding under the stairs. Cole pulled back her door; there was no hand plate. There was no swish. Only a small room, void of light. *I know this isn't a storage room. There has to be something important for all the secrecy.* Cole pressed on.

He patted the floors, shuffled clothes to the side, and pushed back piles of mismatched dishes and containers, revealing a small desk.

Working his way up to the desk, he closed his hands around a peculiar rectangular object. Thinking it was an outdated digiscreen, Cole brought it out and into the light of the living room.

Mary reached under the sink and slid a false back aside, revealing another few inches of cupboard space behind the piping. She reached into the darkness and pulled forth a bundle, wrapped in an old t-shirt. Slowly, with it held close to her bosom, she settled back onto her knees and began to unwrap this mystery bundle.

Cole was looking down at a book. He didn't even know anyone had books anymore. His mother often told him of a time before digiscreens. The museums had a few books in their collections on display as old relics from a more laborious past, when people used to write things by hand. Yet, here it was, a book. *The Queen of Hamel*. The weight of it settled into his lap as he sank down into the couch. He opened the front cover and saw a handwritten script note on the first page, written at an angle.

Dearest Mary, Hopefully this will reveal the answers to you during this new movement in your life. You will know when it is time. Lovingly yours, Alexander.

Cole's brow furrowed in thought. Who was Alexander? More importantly, why would he give his mother a book?

Mary opened her eyes, now bloodshot, her vision blurred with tears waiting to be released. She looked down at the opened box, containing a jagged shard of plasteel, sharpened along one edge, with the handle wrapped in linen and bound with rope.

Cole cautiously looked up the staircase, and then began flipping through the book. It was filled with large color illustrations and a few poetic verses under each image. The story looked to be centered around a serving woman who fell in love with the King of Hamel. Cole began to read the pages.

She knew they were destined to be together forever, and the king felt the same bond. He dismissed his other mistresses and told the serving girl he would break tradition and spend his life with someone his heart chose, not the nobles. They married, bringing prosperity to the kingdom. The common folk loved them because the queen was one of them.

Mary sat on the bathtub edge, now thinking about Jon. He had worked so hard to make her happy. He could have been with any woman but he chose her. "Love at first sight," he always told her. He would do anything for her, no matter what the odds or consequences. Everyone thought he was lacking his own willpower, because he usually let Mary make all the decisions, but Mary knew he just wanted to make her happy. She felt like she was the only one who truly understood him.

Unfortunately, the neighboring provinces were ruled by very jealous men who craved power over everything else. They believed themselves far above the normal populace, and berated the king and queen of Hamel for their relaxed grip. In secret, the four kings of the adjacent lands met and staged an uprising, determined to destroy the land of Hamel and distribute the bounty between themselves.

Mary's eyes began to swell with the thought of LifeSpan controlling everything she held dear. Was this the price to pay for living a secure life? Did we all trade our free will for a pocket watch and punctual deaths? LifeSpan did more than manage a utopia; they manipulated the opinions of the population, slowly imposing their hold. Why would nobody listen to her? *LifeSpan has taken us hostage and we don't even realize it.*

The new queen jolted awake to a clap of thunder. The rain was ferociously falling outside and beginning to blow in through the open windows around the room. She found her king was gone, possibly out for a walk before he tackled the many daily duties of a ruler. The queen hoped he wasn't too far away; he'd be soaked and likely to catch a chill. She rolled back the covers, rising from bed, and ran to the window to scout for her husband. She saw the mountainside pouring with men, some on horseback, screaming and killing anyone in their paths, and they were headed to her castle . . .

Mary stood and began to unfasten her pants, kicking off her slippers. She solemnly unbuttoned her shirt, slipped her arms out, folded the blouse and placed it on top of the pants. Finally collecting her slippers and setting them on top of the clothes pile, she looked into the mirror.

She saw her king defending himself in the courtyard. He was furiously swinging his brilliant sword, fending off three men in white robes. He rolled under and dived to the side of their thrusts. He took a moment to glance up at the queen on her balcony, and in that brief second, their eyes met as he was fatally stabbed through the heart by one of the invaders. He reached for the queen, and fell. She screamed. The men looked up at her and their eyes widened with bloodlust. They charged for the stairs at the base of the tower, the last man pausing to wipe his bloodied blade on the fallen king's robe. The stairwell was filled with the sound of their clanking armor and their howls.

Mary paused for a moment at her reflection. The woman staring back at her was hardly recognizable as the hopeful Mary of old. Her skin and features were as vibrant as ever, a product of the efficient nanos coursing through her body, keeping an outer shell of falsehood for all to see. However, the eyes did not lie. Her eyes were sad, defeated. They lacked all glimmer, her mouth hung in a continual frown, and her shoulders slumped. Mary turned in the mirror, observing her naked body, trying to connect her psyche with this sham. She was beautiful, but it was false, only skin deep. Unable to bear her counterfeit image any longer, Mary reached for her robe hanging on the wall hook, tying the purple sash tightly around her waist. She sat back on the tub edge, staring down at the plasteel shard in her lap.

The queen ran into her quarter, diving across the bed, and reached under the king's pillow, grasping at his hidden safeguard. She spun just as her door was reduced to splinters, the frame falling inward. The three white-robed men stepped over the debris, lewd expressions painted on their ugly faces. Upon seeing the queen conveniently kneeling in bed, they smiled in unison.

Mary turned to the tub, held her arm over the interior, and rolled up her sleeve.

As the men cried out and rushed the queen, she raised her husband's jeweled dagger and struck it across her wrist.

Mary took a deep breath, raised the weapon and quickly slashed her left wrist, spraying the wall and tub bright crimson. She had never seen her blood before, and was quite surprised.

The queen fell forward, dead before the first scoundrel reached her.

CYAN CLOUD

The lone watering hole for miles in any direction was especially busy today. Zebras, alligators, gazelles, waterbucks and a vast selection of smaller scuttling birds were united for a brief moment to bask in the refreshing waters so rare on the barren continent.

High above, a low humming filled the air, incredibly faint but nevertheless detectable to sensitive animal ears. They raised their heads from the water's edge, on alert, and slowly dug in their feet for a hasty retreat. As the humming increased intensity, they peered from side to side, realizing the noise was coming closer to them instead of retreating. The animals decided the risk was too great to linger in face of this unknown threat. Starting with the nervous gazelle, the animals scattered, each of the species forming into their own protective herd, trying to distance themselves.

If they had looked skyward, they would have noticed a pale blue cloud. This was a familiar sight to the world population. For the cyan cloud was the trademark sign of the enormous LifeSpan carrier. Floating high above the land and encircling the Earth in a seemingly constant journey, the carrier was a symbol of the power from LifeSpan.

The carrier was beyond the scope of any flying machine in existence. Much more than a public transport, many likened it to a floating city in the clouds. The carrier spanned such a large amount of sky, the very engines that kept it afloat were enormous cold fusion devices, burning a silvery blue as the condensed matter threw off massive amounts of atmospheric steam, thus trapping the turbulence under the carrier. From the ground, it was a slow-moving cloud, independent from any other formation, fading and appearing with each alteration in the sky's color.

It was from this carrier that Nimbus stared down at the animals running across the plains. He was sitting cross-legged, arms gracefully resting on his thighs. He spent a great deal of time on his carrier lately; meditation among the clouds stilled his mind. More importantly, it stilled the *other* mind absorbed into his subconscious.

Nimbus looked down and replayed the last ten years since he and his Doctors had drained that man's entire rambling nonsense of a life into his head. He had lain in a coma for over two weeks. Every hour, he was swimming in the subconscious mess the merge left in him. He was reliving that fool Jon's pathetic life. Lately, it had become harder to suppress the thoughts overlapping Nimbus's own memories.

The Absorption did not solve the plateau that stalled his improvement, and as much as the Doctors had tried, they could not extract Jon's thoughts without damaging Nimbus. Just as they tried to explain to Nimbus, the dual subconscious was even farther beyond their reach. It was locked away, far from access unless they drained his entire mind, which, of course, was not plausible.

Therefore, he had lived a decade while slowly losing control of his formerly focused mind. Now this Jon was always on the edge of his thoughts, interjecting some rambling nonsense about the beauty of the changing seasons or wondering about any number of possible outcomes with any project imaginable. A daydreamer indeed.

Meanwhile, the search for Alexander had been inconclusive. Despite the immense resources available to the LifeSpan company, it seemed global influence had been for naught.

In his mind, Nimbus replayed Jon's memories again and again. Watching the Jenkins family had amounted to nothing. Following the fool woman Mary revealed a life of boredom, and Nimbus could not stand more than a few hours of updates on nothing. From Jon's point of view, Mary was always involved with their boy, and ran a seemingly perfect home. Then how did Jon mastermind anything without Mary suspecting?

Nimbus knew Jon was connected somehow. He had to be the catalyst. Hidden from everyone, even his wife Mary. Jon must have led quite the double life.

"Sire. It is Dr. Powell," an emergency transmission interrupted.

"Continue." Nimbus granted permission to finish the report, only half listening to the insufferable Doctor.

"There has been a . . . disconnect," Powell paused. "On Moling Way. The Jenkins residence, sire."

Now they had his full attention.

I had to do this. Yes, this is the only way. Mary shook her head repeatedly from side to side, her knuckles white, still holding the shard of plasteel. *The men in white robes will not take me away, not like everyone else.*

She continued to hold her arm over the tub to drain out her life, thinking it should be hurting more than it actually was. Mary slowly looked down at her hand, and turned her wrist to glance at the wound.

Incredibly, there wasn't a mark on her skin. She had the blood running into small pools of her cupped hand, but it was the original strike's aftermath. The bottom of the tub had only a few small drops.

Frantic, Mary took the shard up in her hand and again slashed her wrist . . . only to immediately watch the cut open wide, run off some blood and begin to close again. She could not hurt herself! Every time she tried to cut her arm, it repaired instantly. Her mind raced, and she stood up quickly. Desperate, she realized there was not much time, and *they* would be coming.

"What have I done? Oh, Cole, I am so sorry." Mary dropped the makeshift knife, gathered up her clothes, hastily throwing on her pants and shirt and dashed for the door.

Throwing wide the bedroom door, she fell into the hallway and looked to the front foyer.

They're not here yet, but there's not much time. I must get to Cole, Mary told herself as she stumbled down the stairs. Cole jumped up from the sofa, book held behind his back. Upon seeing his mother's state, he dropped the book and rushed over to her. She was breathing heavily and mumbling about going into hiding.

"They were right. I should have taken you to them . . . into hiding. We could have made it. Away from this madness. Now what have I doomed us to become? Who can live anymore? Is there no release from our suffering? Never in control—"

"What happened? Why are your arms stained?" Cole stepped back, eyes widening as he took in this desperate figure of his mother, red stains covering the arms of her shirt and smeared across her pants. Cole could not conclude this was blood. Who would have so much blood on themselves? *How* could that be?

"Cole, listen to me. We have to leave. *They* are coming. I tried to free myself . . . We haven't . . . Oh, Cole, I have failed you. I've failed us all—"

Mary was interrupted by an electric chime, announcing guests at the front door. Cole jumped to his feet and started for the foyer.

"Don't answer that!" Mary shrieked. It was a desperate call from someone who suddenly realized that all of her options had disappeared. Mary looked around, wide eyed, trying to focus on the room, seeking exits, strategies, possibilities of escape. As each option played out in her mind, it was just as suddenly dismissed as an impossibility.

Cole took her head in both his hands and roughly pulled her face within inches of his own, forcing her to focus on him.

"What is going on? *What happened to you?*" Cole spaced the words clearly, with emphasis on the last question.

She heard nothing but the alarm in her mind. *I'm found. It's over. I have to find Cole; I have to give it to him. He has a right. He's not ready. It's his to have* . . . Mary ran off to the kitchen, screaming, "I know it's not my time to expire! They shouldn't be here. We are leaving, we are getting away. Don't you see this is wrong?"

The door chimed again. Cole shook his head and turned, bounding for the door, trying to stop the chaos, trying to sort out what exactly his role should be. The door was the obvious choice. Whoever has been waiting must be here to help, or invited by his mother at the very least.

"Do not open the door!" Mary's voice was drowned by the deafening sound of smashing glass, as if the entire kitchen was coming down around her. "I have something to retrieve, just need some more time. More time . . . That's the spot. Time."

Cole placed his hand on the scan plate. The door swished open. Cole was facing three Collectors. He had opened his home to them, without an expiration scheduled. This was highly irregular. So were their expressions. Cole could see a hint of . . . irritation?

The Collector closest to Cole put his hand on his shoulder. "Hello. We are here for subject Mary Jenkins. Tell me now: where is she?" His teeth were too large for his mouth to contain their bulk. Stretching the lips into a skeletal grin, this Collector was intimidating.

However, Cole wasn't frightened in the least, just more confused. He trusted the Collectors, but why would Collectors be looking for his mom?

"I think you are mistaken. We still have time. We are —"

"We have urgent questions for the subject. I only ask this final time. Where is Mary Jenkins?" The Collector removed his hand from Cole's shoulder and stared at him.

"She's breaking the kitchen." Cole lowered his head and pointed behind him. The two Collectors broke their stance on the porch and stepped into the house, brushing past Cole and headed towards the ruckus.

Cole thought back to his schooling. The daily admirations of LifeSpan, the ever vigilant, the everlasting. Here was a Collector, out of place, still staring at him. Staring through him, coaxing his secrets. Coaxing his mother's secrets.

"I have to show you something. Something of my mother's. Something secret," Cole confided, and led the Collector to her spot under the stairs.

Shortly after, Mary was roughly dragged out by the other two Collectors, kicking her legs to no effect on the Collectors. She was screaming to see Cole one last time, to hug him.

Unable to ignore her pleas, Cole rushed to her side.

"They are going to help you. I'll take care of myself now," Cole tried to calm her.

When Cole came in close for a hug, Mary quickly whispered in his ear, "Wind the clock, from the inside." Mary desperately exhaled in a frantic breath. "Do you understand? Wind your grandmother's clock *from the inside.*"

With that, she was pulled away again. Cole stood and stared.

"What is your name, boy?" the last Collector to leave his house asked him.

"Cole, and I'm not a boy. I'm nineteen, and I work at LifeSpan." He looked around to see his mother loaded into a long white van, just like the one his father expired in.

"Is that right? Well, you should be given a promotion," the Collector congratulated Cole. "Your assistance was very helpful in apprehending this subject."

"She's not just a subject. That was my mother." Cole knew he shouldn't contradict a Collector.

"She was a liability. Goodbye, boy."

After a short time standing on the lawn, Cole watched the van drive away. Another vehicle pulled up, this one bearing the LifeSpan logo on its side. A shapely woman stepped out and handed Cole a digiscreen notification.

His mother's sister had chosen to have Cole relocated to her house.

"I can take you there right now if you would like to leave all this behind," the LifeSpan worker offered. "Is there anything you need inside the house?"

Wind the clock, from the inside, Cole mulled.

"Yeah. Just one thing. Then this place can implode, for all I care," he said.

Cole returned to the house, passing the hidden room under the stairs. He could see the Collectors had already torn it apart. His mother's belongings were thrown out and around the room. He ran on to the clock. His mother would never let him touch this old clock in the past. Why would it be so important now?

Terrible old relic, if you ask me, Cole thought.

He found it would not wind, and flipped it over. A fabricated piece of plasteel was covering the back. Cole pried his fingers around the edge and popped off the panel. He discovered another book, this one well used and titled *Diary.* Intrigued, Cole flipped through and randomly read a journal entry. *My neighbor always goes to the park. Their whole family goes to watch the Collectors play with the children, allowing them to hang off their arms and racing them across the fields. I never really liked them, there's something in their eyes. Something behind their eyes if that's possible. I call them Montgomery's Mumblers because if Dr. Montgomery made them, you would think he could help them talk better.*

He had only heard one person EVER call the Collectors Montgomery's Mumblers, and that was his mom. He realized with astonishment that this was her handwritten diary. He tucked it under his arm and quickly collected some of his more personal objects throughout the house to throw into his bag.

A chiming blip came out of his digiscreen. He took it out of his inside pocket. The message was from LifeSpan.

```
Cole   Jenkins:   For   efforts   related   to   the
apprehension  of  known  threat  at  455  Moling  Way,
you  have  been  selected  for  immediate  training  and
clearance  in  LifeSpan  Division  Four.
Report  in  48  hours  to  your  new  post.
Confirm  Message  for  acceptance.
```

The digiscreen sounded an ending ‘blip’ indicating a response was needed.

Great, Mother would be so proud. The irony was not lost on Cole. More importantly, why would his mother keep a diary from him all these years? Cole flipped through the pages again. *Jon is the most caring man I have ever met. We talk about marriage . . .*

```
Confirm Message for acceptance. 'blip'
```
. . . I have followed the Collectors. They joke. Their guard is down. We know their methods.

```
Confirm Message for acceptance. 'blip'
```
. . . finally accepted by the Movement. Jon would never understand

```
Message Confirmed.
Welcome to Division Four.
```

Mary was totally defeated in body and spirit as the vehicle pulled away from her home. She knew it was the last time she would ever see Cole. There was no help coming from LifeSpan. They knew her role now.

Her mind was replaying the past few years. She remembered Cole and her husband, Jon. Their time together, all three of them, was the best time of her life. How did it come to this? Cole resented her more than she planned for. He wouldn't understand the truth, so she kept it from him. This was a moot point now. Her future was not important. The Movement must endure.

Mary focused on her surroundings, trying to weigh her options, as slim as they may be. She did not risk moving her head, and only looked from side to side in her peripheral vision. She was in a smooth vehicle, traveling quickly. She was kneeling on a bench. Her hands were bound behind her back and attached to slots built into the plastique walls.

Well, let's not forget one of them *are in here with me*, Mary thought. She could feel his anger pouring into the cab, washing over her.

Mary raised her head, and met him eye to eye.

The Collector was disgusted and did not back down, his rage growing even more heated from her insolence. He smashed her head back down.

Finally, the transport stopped. Mary assumed they had reached their destination, and hopped off of the bench, trying to stand as best she could. The Collector was upon her, throwing a fibersteel bag over her head, which began shrinking, constricting her ears and pulling her lips tightly to her teeth. Mary's eyes shut on instinct, convinced this bag was crushing her. The bag continued tightening over every plane, inside her nose and under her chin. She tried to scream out, and the bag wrapped into her teeth and pinned her tongue at an awkward angle. Mary could breathe through the fabric, but could not see or hear.

The Collector dragged her by the front of her shirt, and when that ripped, he carried her by the waist of her pants. She kicked at the ground, trying to find a foothold. The Collector continued along with his human suitcase, using Mary's body to push obstructions out of the way.

He ripped off the bindings at her wrists and placed his hand against the side of her head. A small electric charge pulsed into the bag, and it fell slack against her face. The Collector tossed her onto a marble floor, and Mary slid, unable to see, before she hit hard against a solid pillar. She tore the bag off and squinted against the sunlight, raising her free hand to block the light and get her bearings.

"Sire," the Collector announced, "this is the variant. She has been disconnected."

"Very well. You may leave us."

Mary could feel the power in that voice. This was *him*.

Not good. Get out of here, Mary thought. *Get up, and get away.*

She leaned heavily on the pillar for support, gasping at the pain still in her side. Her body felt terrible. How could she still be hurting? It felt like the nanos had abandoned her.

"I don't care what you can do. You don't scare me. We are on to you." Mary tried her best to sound convincing, and then she saw him.

He moved with a deadly grace, each step carefully chosen and in perfect balance. He rushed for no man or woman. He watched her, calculating, no doubt ready to strike at a moment's notice. Mary realized she was grossly overmatched. If she tried to run he would catch her, she knew. She was mesmerized, as prey is entranced by the hunter.

Nimbus stopped a few paces away, his silk clothing settling around his impressive frame. Mary shrank back, letting out a breath she only now realized she had been holding in.

"Please, continue," Nimbus prodded.

"We will win," Mary forced a whimpering reply. She desperately wanted to believe her own words. She wanted to scream out, but had no courage for such an action.

"You are here before me, after a decade of observation. I have you in my house. Therefore you have failed. I will not . . ." Nimbus staggered back, slumping. He wavered, and raised his hands to his temples.

What is happening? Mary was shocked. *I didn't know he could stumble.*

She watched as Nimbus leaned back, and then lurched a few shaky steps towards her. His jaw clenched and fell slack. His eyes widened, softened, squinted. His mouth smiled, then grimaced, and settled half open. His shoulders slumped, his hands raised palm side up and he stared at Mary.

Nimbus looked . . . misplaced.

"Hello, Buttercup," Nimbus said, his voice soft. His inflection was unmistakable.

"*Jon?*" Mary asked.

PART TWO: THE FATHER

For the third time, Cole checked the number on the digiscreen that LifeSpan had given him and stood before room 1462 on the fifty-second floor. The small nameplate on the plasteel door stated simply, "Mr. Stratus, *Scheduling Director*." After a deep breath to still his nerves, Cole raised his hand, palm open, and set it on the plate next to the door. The door chimed and swished open.

"Hello, Cole. Thanks for meeting with me today." Blocking the doorway and standing before Cole was Mr. Stratus. He was a squat, greasy-looking man with unkempt, wispy white hair. His mouth hung lackadaisically as he spoke, the words only seeming to project from the back of his throat. His hand moved in a wide sweeping gesture and he stepped aside for Cole to pass by him.

The success or failure of the entire Scheduling department sat on Mr. Stratus's shoulders. He orchestrated the employees, time schedules and flow of the offices. More importantly, he scheduled the Collectors.

Despite the power and wealth of his position, Mr. Stratus smelled like overheated electronics and cologne as Cole walked by and entered his expansive office. Briefly glancing around the long room, Cole noticed an almost complete lack of furnishings. The room was completely devoid of artwork or plants of any kind.

Since only a desk and a couple chairs attempted to fill the room's space, the office felt cold and unwelcoming.

"Thank you. I understand you are a busy man," Cole nervously replied. "I, ummm, I think you have an impressive office here. Great view." Cole looked around, eager for something to comment on, to make up for the awkward reply. Truthfully, the office was giving him a stale taste in his mouth, but as his gaze fell to the huge windows, he could see his entire neighborhood spread before him.

There was Norway Park, where he learned to ride a bike. His parents would walk him down to the park after he had finished his homework, which was usually pretty quickly after school. He never had trouble in his studies. They seemed to come easily to him, which afforded him more moments outside of the house. He smiled, remembering his dad spinning in the field with him, mother watching on, always so cautious. Finally, when they were both dizzy, they would come spinning to the ground, lying there, looking at the sky twirl around them. Like the entire universe was orbiting around Cole and his Dad. That was the . . .

"*Cole* . . . ," Mr. Stratus emphasized.

Cole blinked, and realized it wasn't the first time his name had been called.

"I was informed of your daydreaming," Mr. Stratus calmly stated from a few paces away. He walked over to stand behind a large desk with one chair pulled up to the front. Mr. Stratus motioned for Cole to take the seat. As Cole approached, he jumped as he noticed they were not alone in the room. Standing at the corners on either side of Mr. Stratus were two Collectors. At first, he thought they were robed statues, and as he continued to stare, he could see their eyes move to him. Cole immediately dropped into his chair and noticed a silver pen standing straight, balanced on its tip. Opposite Cole stood Mr. Stratus, holding a digiscreen. A few moments passed as he swiped through the information on screen.

"In reviewing your personal information, I am very impressed with the speed in which you have climbed through our company. It seems your attention to detail is unsurpassed among your peers."

"Thank you, Mr. Stratus. I have always placed LifeSpan ahead of my own schedule," Cole replied with the truth. He was quiet among his coworkers and rarely spent time with anyone after his shift.

"Your commitment to sensitive materials and the secrecy involved is . . . admirable. Our staff can entrust you with any amount of detailed work and you finish the task." Mr. Stratus leaned back and grinned. "Now, there is no question about your work ethics, but it is no secret you have begun to show signs of boredom. What are we to do about that?"

"I apologize if that is reflected on my record. I have a . . . problem, daydreaming," Cole admitted, feeling anxious. Was this meeting making a turn for the worse?

"Relax, my friend, you are a company man." Mr. Stratus rounded the table.

"Then can I ask why you have brought me here?"

"We've had our eye on you, Cole. How would you like a *challenge*?"

"Yes?" he nervously replied.

"How much do you know about Division Four?"

THE NIGHT

Contrary to popular belief, the night was an active time for the city. Animals and insects came out to start their day after the lumbering humans ended their own. An easy sleep came to those who felt safe. After all, why would the populace feel anything other than total safety when their lights turned down?

The moonlight stretched the buildings' shadows, and the night took on the silhouette appearance of a large spider's web, ready to catch those who did not know how to move between its weavings.

Luckily, Emma knew how to keep to the shadows. She knew where people would look, what would cause second-guessing. *With time to react, most of the population will flee*, the Father told her. She constantly replayed his many lessons over in her head. Every night, every mission. She walked with a practiced gait, like a coiled spring, ready to move in any direction at a moment's notice.

Emma frequently went on scouting missions for the Movement. Most often, her missions were conveniently at night, which didn't bother her at all. She was more comfortable in the dusk hours. She easily dodged the dreamy-eyed couples out for a nightly stroll and the exhausted late worker, squeaking in a midnight jog, dog loping beside him as reward for so patiently awaiting his master. These busybodies of the night were never aware of their surroundings.

The truth of the matter was Emma never understood how people could be so oblivious. How they could be so self-absorbed that they hardly noticed her until she wanted them to see her? For the last few months, she had been walking the streets, memorizing the land, the people and the cars, and always ended her night staring at the same building. The LifeSpan office of Division Four.

Emma kept to the shadows, just as she had been taught. *"Stay hidden. Stay smart."* She could hear the Father's voice. A quick glance skyward helped her judge the advance of nightfall. Perched in the treetop branches, she watched the entrance to LifeSpan about fifty yards away, just as she had watched every night. After tracking the man for weeks on end, tonight she would confront him.

Last night, the Father told her to act on the next phase in their plan. Not entirely sure of how the other Movement members felt about his actions behind their backs, she knew the real reason he was ready to begin. Cole was in trouble.

The LifeSpan offices began emptying. She kept her eyes tuned onto every face, every haircut, to spot Cole. Finally, his shaggy brown hair came into view as he walked down the street. She remained in the tree as he walked under and beyond her perch, gangly traipsing home, oblivious to her green eyes boring into him. He went directly home, just like he always did, never joining the other employees for a party or a drink. The same route every day.

You would think he could change it up once in awhile, Emma thought.

Ultimately, he would make it home, but tonight she had to talk with him first. Slowly arching her back and lowering her right leg, she felt for the branches below her. Lowering her weight onto her leading leg, she alternately grabbed and reached down the tree, careful not to disturb a single leaf. Never taking her eyes from

Cole, she descended branch by branch, working her way to the ground, as silent as a shadow, avoiding detection. *Stay hidden. Stay smart*, the mantra repeated in her mind.

Cole hung his head, thinking as he was walking. It was a wonder he didn't bump into fences and trees. He failed to realize someone else was on the sidewalk in front of him until he slammed into her.

"Oh, I'm so sorry! I didn't see you there!" Cole reached forward in a poor attempt to pat at the stranger's shoulders, realizing it was a she, not a he. He lost his nerve, and took a step back. "Are you alright? Did I hurt you?"

Hardly, she thought.

"I am fine, thank you." The girl wasn't blinking, only staring intently at Cole. "I was just out for a walk. You should be more attentive."

"Oh, no, I was just thinking about . . . ," Cole began. "Are you out here alone?"

"I prefer it that way."

"Well, then. You could walk with me, if you want, not that you have to, or if you prefer to stay . . ." Cole stopped to actually look at her.

She had long, waist-length red hair, haphazardly thrown into a loose braid that rested over her left shoulder. Her clothing was of a cut more popular a few years ago than any modern trends. Most likely some sort of hand-downs. Cole noticed the mud stains around her boots and unpainted fingernails cut short like a man's. He imagined her as some sort of nature biologist. Despite her rough edges, Cole was mesmerized.

"On your way home?" she asked softly. "My name is Emma."

"Well, Emma, it's very nice to meet you, and, umm, I'm Cole."

"I see we are going opposite ways after all. How about I come find you tomorrow?"

"I would like that very much. I work at Division Four. Meet you out front, say 19:00?"

"I'll be there," Emma replied.

As Cole walked away from her, she called back to him "By the way, Cole, Happy Birthday!"

He stopped mid-stride and turned back to face her. "Happy *what*?" Emma was nowhere to be seen.

Cole continued along the street, trying not to look as obvious as he checked over his shoulder every few minutes. He had a feeling Emma was still following him. Maybe he was hoping she was still there. *Who was that girl?* He was definitely intrigued.

He glanced one last time over his shoulder as he arrived at his aunt's front gate. Her house was two stories and in a great neighborhood. Compared to his mom's house, Aunt Hester's looked brand new. Her husband had expired almost twelve years ago, but she fancied herself quite handy. Cole tried to take up most of the basic duties, but he became so busy with work, there never seemed to be any progress from him.

He stopped to check the mail screen on the street side. *Current Status: No new digipost messages.* Cole had thought if today was his own birthday, someone should know about it other than a girl on the street.

Crazy Emma. That brought a smile. *At least I can't forget her name. Maybe I just need to meet more crazy people in my day.*

Entering his aunt's house, he was greeted by the permeating smell of beef stock, vegetables slowly roasting and gravy thickening. His aunt was still one of the stubborn cooks who preferred to make dinners by hand. *Culinary dinosaurs,* he called them, unable to really quit the habits of home cooking and replace it with LifeSpan's ready-to-heat meals the rest of the city used.

"Cole?" Aunt Hester's raised voice called from the kitchen. "Are there any digipost messages?"

He took his time removing his jacket, hung it in the front closet, and made his way back to the kitchen. His aunt was standing with her back to the door, dropping scraps from a laser slicer into the compactor. Turning to face Cole, she was wearing a red and white polka dot apron tied over her crisp outfit. Cole thought she looked ridiculous. Something out of an ancient digiscreen history lesson.

"No telemail today." Cole carefully watched her reaction at his next statement. "Nothing to tell me Happy Birthday."

Aunt Hester looked up slowly, her eyes meeting his, briefly widening, and returning to normal quickly. It was there: the reaction he wanted.

"Who wished you a Happy Birthday?"

"Nobody *wished* me, I just heard it. Never mind. It's nothing," Cole lied and ducked out of the kitchen, eager to end this conversation. He already had the answer from his aunt's expression.

"You heard it today? Someone said it today to you?" Aunt Hester called to him.

"Yeah, I just heard it from some girl, some crazy girl with wild eyes." Cole bounded up the bottom step and ran up to the second floor, two steps at a time.

"Just never mind, I'll never see her again," he called down from upstairs.

Aunt Hester was left standing and thinking about an old song her dad used to sing to her, whispering as she fell asleep. Something they were forbidden to teach in school.

Happy Birthday to you,
Happy Birthday to you,
Happy Birthday, my sweetheart,
Happy Birthday to you.

It was early. Emma walked quietly along the edge of the street, with her head hanging low, hands in the pockets of her hooded jacket. If anyone was watching her, it would appear she was out for a morning stroll, taking her time to stop and watch a squirrel as it ran across the road, skittering around the wheels of a fleetliner, narrowly avoiding another squirrel, only to run up the same tree it dived down from.

While she was watching the little animals or smiling at a bird pecking the soft ground, Emma was completely aware of her surroundings, listening carefully for any approaching steps, vehicles out of place or, especially, anyone looking out their windows. Emma rarely trusted anyone, and she had good reason.

Emma made her way back down the street, passing the same houses she had just walked in front of. Confident that nobody was around but still not taking any chances, she walked in between two properties, reached into her pocket and pressed a small button sewn into the inside of her coat. She knew the button would alert the house in front of her. Three more presses of the button in quick succession alerted them to the north window of the home.

Emma stooped below the side window frame, pretending to look at the flowers planted along the house's edge. She spoke without looking up.

"What time does the sun set tomorrow?" Emma asked, waiting for the correct response to let her know one of her men was listening.

"The sun sets after it rises," came the correct response.

Emma liked this riddle. It was in reference to the sun setting across the world. When the sun rose in the east, it set in the west. Emma also thought this was a poignant question, while the majority of the population were so focused on themselves, they thought the sun rose and set only in relation to themselves.

Because he was able to answer correctly, Emma was comfortable divulging her report.

"Everything is as we discussed. He is our inside man. I'll be gaining the knowledge we need in short order," Emma said.

"Does he suspect?" the voice responded.

"Never," Emma replied a little too quickly. It was a good question, and rightly asked. But was that her ego speaking? After years of assignments, she was confident in her ability to hide her emotions.

The downtown square was bustling this bright spring day. Cole was waiting for Emma. She told him to meet her across the street from B's Bouquets at 16:30. So, here he was, on time. Emma was late, as usual.

Cole was drawn to the flowers and was debating whether he should walk over and purchase a selection for Emma.

They had progressed quickly in their friendship over the last few weeks. Emma had met him outside of Division Four almost every day, and then they walked to Aunt Hester's home. Cole asked her to come inside and meet his aunt, but Emma always declined. Although they grew up in separate cities, they found that they had many of the same dislikes, which, in a way, made them closer.

He started walking across the street to the florist, but changed his mind and came back to his waiting spot. He still didn't know what his true feelings were for her. She was beautiful in her own way, interesting to be around, and seemed to be getting along with him just fine. While there was a need to register with LifeSpan on any permanent engagement, there was no protocol for dating, if they tried to take that route. He just didn't think Emma would like him in that fashion.

Cole glanced at his watch again, for the umpteenth time, and peered up and down the block. Even compared to her habitual lateness, she was very tardy. Maybe she changed her mind. Another ten minutes slipped by, allowing Cole to attempt to cross the street once again to purchase flowers, and once again changing his mind for fear of being embarrassed by his boldness. She probably had more important things to do. But Cole had been looking forward to their meeting all day.

"Psst. Hey, Cole, down here," a familiar whisper rang out.

Cole turned and saw Emma leaning against the interior wall of the alleyway behind him. Her body was set at such an extreme angle, it looked more like she was holding the building up instead of the other way around. Her arms and legs were crossed, a half smile on her petite face.

"What are you doing back there? Why are you by the refuse chutes?" He was unsure of actually going into the alley. After all, people didn't regularly find their way into alleys, especially if they didn't want their clothes dirty. There weren't many places in town that were dirty; LifeSpan kept a pretty clean house. More than enough maintenance bots were roving around. As if to prove his point, a tiny, wheeled sweeper bot nearly clipped him in the heel as it continued along the building's edge. Sweeper bots were only about the size of a dinner plate, with a domed surface and the LifeSpan logo stamped into the middle of the chrome peak. Cole knew it would have stopped and waited for him before continuing on, but he always seemed to trip over the roving bots.

"Are you saying I'm garbage?" Emma teased.

Cole did not pick up on her lighthearted tease. "No, what would I say that for? I'm sure you were in the garbage for a reason. I mean, why would you . . . ," he stammered. "I wasn't calling you garbage, you just happen to be with garbage, well, you know what I mean."

"No, I don't," Emma smirked. "In fact, I kind of like it in here. It's private. Like another world within our world, away from the rules. More primitive." Emma looked off, as if imagining a different place, far away. She snapped her eyes over to Cole, and left her dream to fade away. "I'll let it go for now. I suppose I'll come out of the garbage and join you on the clean side like everyone else. Got to be like everyone else, right, Cole? Y'know, I was watching you while you waited for me."

"Well, I was looking for you down the block, but you were late." He looked at his wristwatch and held it up for her to see, as if to further prove his point. "Can't you tell time? Where's your watch?"

Emma reached into her pocket and produced a pocket watch. The cover was dull and worn. At one time it appeared to have a silver finish, but the coating was tarnished. The timepiece was decorated with a relief of planes, boats and a large bird swooping to the foreground, a fish in its beak.

Cole had never seen anything like it before, and was amazed by the old-fashioned timepiece. Just about everything nowadays was newer, constantly updated. Very rarely did you find anything that was more than five years old, let alone as old as this timepiece.

Emma popped open the cover to reveal a single clock face, with the hour and minute hands slowly making their way around the circle. Small red gems were placed at the hour markers. Behind the scratched glass, the clock face was perfect, a flawless white background with very distinct lettering. It seemed out of place to Cole in the tarnished and dented watch covering.

"Did you think I wasn't coming? Were you going to go home, just say the frag with me? Going to do better things?" Emma asked.

"I have things to do. I'm a busy man." Cole laid on the sarcasm pretty thickly.

"Oh, really, like what?"

"Actually the thought never crossed my mind," Cole teased.

"Then why did you attempt to cross the street twice?"

Cole didn't realize she was standing there all *that* time. Did he give something away? Did she suspect he was going to buy her flowers?

Emma pressed, "How long would you have waited for me?"

"For anyone else, I would have left after two minutes. For you, I would wait a very long time just to see you again," Cole mumbled, slightly embarrassed at the wording and what it implied.

Emma seemed very happy with his response and skipped a little closer, smiling, still holding her old timepiece.

"Can I see that?" When she handed the item to him, he was surprised at the heft of the pocket watch, easily twice the weight of his own.

"What is the dial on the outside of your pocket watch?"

"Well, that's so you can wind it. This is my family heirloom timepiece, long before LifeSpan issued their own. I think it belonged to my great-great-great-grandpa. The boats are on there because he was a fisherman, right on the ocean, with nothing to worry about, just catching fish every day, eating what he caught, selling what he didn't eat. My mother used to tell me all sorts of stories about everyone in my family. That was when there were no expirations, and people cared about genealogy. What do you know about your grandparents?"

"Nothing on my mother's side," Cole lied. He didn't feel like getting into the journal. After all these years, he still read passages from the carefully hidden diary. His mother wrote very briefly about her parents, and it wasn't too favorable. Thinking of her diary brought him back to the pocket watch in his hand. His mother was always writing about her time winding the clock on the fireplace. The same clock he found the journal in. That was probably one of these family heirlooms. For a moment he was sorry he left it behind. But it reminded him of his mother too much and he wasn't about to wind it everyday.

"Well, you need to wind it or something. It's three minutes behind."

"Behind what?" Emma asked.

"The LifeSpan time, the global time." He fished into his pocket and once again brought out his LifeSpan timepiece. "Where is yours?"

Emma started walking away, "I left it at home."

Cole had never heard of anyone being without their timepiece. There was no requirement to carry it, but it was a significant part of an individual's identity. It was issued by LifeSpan, to count down remaining time.

Tracking expiration dates was the measure by which everyone lived.

"Well, how do you know what time it really is? The exact time, in sync with everyone else."

"That's the great thing about time. It moves differently for everyone, if you let it," Emma said.

They walked along in silence for some time afterward. Cole was digesting her enlightening statement. They reached the end of the block and watched the maintenance bots drive into a small dock, releasing their payloads to be sucked away and recycled. Everything that fell on the sidewalk was recycled. The fallen leaves, food wrappers, dropped items, sand, dust.

"Alright, Cole, see you later," Emma said as she began digging in her bag.

Cole glanced over at Emma as she took his picture.

Cole was surprised. "What was that?"

"It's a camera," Emma said as she looked up from the screen, "to take a picture of someone or something. It saves an image of your surroundings," she finished sarcastically.

"I know what it is. I was wondering why you would want an image of someone," he said. He walked over and held his hand out to see this camera. It was lightweight with a large glass dome protruding from one side. Made out of metal, it was worn, dented, and looked like it could barely hold together, let alone capture anything.

"Well, that's a silly question. Mainly to remember them I suppose, to keep, like you would a necklace or ring."

"Why would you want to remember anyone if they are standing here, talking to you? You can't remember me talking to you?"

"No, Cole." Emma was getting frustrated with his lack of nostalgia. "It helps me remember someone when I can't see them or talk to them anymore."

"You mean after they expire?" Cole attempted to clarify.

"Sure, after they die. That seems to be taking it to the extreme. How about when you go home, or someone wants to know who I've been hanging out with? Not everyone has a number. Everything isn't scanned. You need to open your mind to feelings we all share."

Cole stood there for some time. His brow furrowed with thought. He finally walked away, mumbling under his breath, "I don't know why you would want to remember anyone after they expire."

Emma jogged lightly to catch up.

"Cole, where do you think we go after we die?"

"Well, I suppose whoever takes the body —"

"That's not what I meant. I mean, what happens to our core. The essence of our personality, our inside being that makes us all different and unique."

"Emma." Cole looked away, thinking of a response. She always caught him in these discussions. He thought she had a game to see how fast he could be caught off guard every day.

"You always find something to make me think, don't ya?" Cole looked up, deep in thought.

"Don't think about what I want to hear, just say the first thing that comes to your mind."

"Hmmm, well, I would have to say . . ." He knew she was looking for something intensely emotional from him.

"Say what are you thinking! Just go!" Emma poked him.

Just when he wanted to be profound, he replied, "I guess I never really thought about that. I always figured it was LifeSpan's job, not mine."

"That's the problem with you. Everything is someone else's responsibility. Even free thought is better left for someone else." Emma held her hand out, the other sternly perched on her hip. Cole placed the camera in her waiting hand and she abruptly turned and walked towards the Central City Market. She was walking very fast.

Oh man, she is fuming, Cole thought.

He always felt like an uneducated lump when talking with her.

I've never met anyone like her, that's for sure. Cole knew he never would again.

"Hey, wait up!" he called and ran to catch her.

The Central City Market was filled with many different types of vendors attempting to sell their crafts, competing with new technology being introduced to the public. It was an odd combination of old-fashioned meets modern innovation.

Emma stopped at a stand filled with different pieces of jewelry. Cole finally reached her side and saw her excitement as she was looking through a particular set of necklaces. Red and purple wires were tightly wrapped around natural stones and tied in a crossing pattern across the necklace.

Nobody else was at the stand, and the owner sat in the back, hardly caring who looked at her trinkets. Indeed, the owner looked slightly surprised by Emma's interest in her crafts.

"Cole, look at the intricacy of the wrapping, the careful

handling of the stones. Look at the holes drilled into each rock. It's so different from one to the next."

Cole was used to the more popular designs available in the city, those produced by machines, expertly assembled, with crystals grown exactly symmetrical to the next.

Most jewelry and clothing were entirely created by machines. Huge factories were another testament to the efficiency of LifeSpan engineering. There was never a stitch out of place, never a color error, and most certainly, nothing like the mess of a necklace Emma was holding in front of him. It was no wonder there wasn't anybody else looking at this lady's jewelry; it was a disaster. The stones were very different in size and shape from one another, and the wire-wrapping held no symmetry.

"Did you make this by yourself?" Cole asked the owner.

"Yes, sir, I did. Every part of it is hand-crafted. I even found the stones and polished them," the artisan replied sheepishly.

"Well, that was time consuming." Cole thought it was common knowledge that people were supposed to be time efficient. Why would anyone want to sit around and wrap stones? He thought Emma would agree with him, and as he turned to her, she was staring at him quite disapprovingly.

"Well, I think it's beautiful. Do not listen to my friend here. He is a stubborn mule." And she turned to storm away.

"Do you really like it?" The woman stood up and caught their eye. She had moved away from her seat and forward into the sunlight. She was older than Cole had seen in a long time. Surely by now her expiration was right around the corner. What did she have left to contribute to society? These baubles?

"If you really do like this piece, I can give you a deal on it. Half price. You are the only one who has complimented my work. It would mean so much to me if you could have it."

The lady in the stand reached under the counter and produced a flat disc of frosted glass. These finance regulators were a part of everyday life. If someone would like to purchase anything throughout the city and even beyond, it would be through a finance regulator. Emma shied away from the disc, and suddenly became very disinterested in the necklace.

"I would love it, really I would, but we have to go now. C'mon Cole, I didn't realize how late it was." She turned back to the shop owner, who now seemed like it was her fault, pushing too hard for a sale. "You really do have a great gift when it comes to crafting. Do not ever give it up."

Cole was confused about what had transpired, but likened it to the unusual nature that was becoming part of everyday life with Emma at his side.

"We'll take it," he said.

"No, that's alright, Cole. Really, I don't need it."

"Fine, then *I'll* take it. You can charge me full price." He turned to the frosted disc and placed his right hand on the disc, fingers extended, palm flat. It lit for only a second. He removed his hand and with his left hand tapped the surface of the disc in a sequence only he would know. Index finger, thumb, ring, index again, pinkie and thumb. Having entered his personal code, the transaction was completed and he picked up the necklace and held it up to Emma, ready to hang it around her neck.

Mr. Stratus stepped back from his perch. Something was odd about the girl. She hid herself when Collectors walk by. She was always turning her head, pulling her hair across her face, or lifting her collar over her mouth. Cole had been mixed up with her for long enough. He was asking questions at work. Too many questions. Mr. Stratus knew it was time to report back to his sector's Praetor.

Ultimately, Nimbus himself would need to know of this one.

VISITOR

Cole fell into his high-backed swivel chair, sinking into the plastique-covered lining, and looked around his corner office. Light streamed in through window slits along two walls, intersecting its rays in the center of the room, creating a crisscross pattern on every surface. Cole connected his fingers, stretched and cradled the back of his head as he spun his chair. As he had everyday, he marveled at his success in the LifeSpan Corporation. This office was in the upper levels of Division Four, responsible for the collection of recyclable products. Here he was, heading the department that started the human race on the track towards renewable living.

LifeSpan was a globally spanning corporation, and the collection of waste was no longer a human responsibility. However, human oversight was needed. Robotic tracking, computer statistics, and redistribution were organized through teams and divisions of hard-working employees. Cole directed over thirty teams on a daily basis, which usually became very challenging, but he had a knack for keeping track of separate groups, all working towards a common goal.

Indeed, Cole was in a high position for someone his age. He had had great success with LifeSpan, and no regrets.

Outside of work, he led a pretty boring life, until Emma came along. She had changed him and given him purpose, it was true, but she was a distraction, too. She was always in the back of his mind.

Cole looked around his room at the gleaming plasteel walls without seams as if the the room were built in one quick oozing metal coating.

Cole watched the last few assignments fade from his screen, and his digiscreen powered down.

Finally, Cole thought, and smiled ear to ear. He kicked out of his seat and stepped out of his office and briskly passed the other employees at their desks. In the past, Cole never rushed. However, today he had plans with a crazy girl who had been showing him the world, although the last time Cole asked her about her family, Emma did not have the warmest reaction. She changed the subject almost instantly.

Still, she would be waiting outside, like she always did.

When Cole exited the front foyer, Emma was sitting under the ash tree across the street. Her hood pulled low, she appeared to be sleeping, but he knew she was watching everyone pass by, studying them.

I don't know why she does that. She's always making it seem like she's not interested in what other people are doing, but then it turns out that's all she's interested in. Cole shook his head.

Emma looked up from her spot even before Cole had a chance to call out to her. *She never ceases to amaze me.* He jogged across the street and over to Emma's tree.

She had pushed her hood back, letting her hair fall down to her shoulders.

"Hello. Have you seen a crazy girl in need of some exceptional company?" Cole joked.

Emma smirked. "Birds of a feather flock together." She hopped to her feet and swung her satchel over her shoulder. Without another word, she spun and set off at a quick pace, confident Cole would keep up with her.

She thinks I'm her puppy. Well, maybe I am. With that, Cole scrambled to fall in line with Emma, who was already ten steps ahead of him. Finally, when he caught up to her, he only had one question in his mind. It had been tugging at him all day, distracting him, to say the least. Well, one of his distractions today.

"Where is your home? Can I see where you live?" There. It was out. Let the backlash begin.

"Why do you keep asking that? Is it that important for you to witness my past instead of focusing on our future?" She stopped walking so quickly, turned and smiled at Cole. She was messing with him, wasn't she? He forgot his next question, so dumbfounded by her flirting.

"I guess that's the truth of it. Everyone comes from somewhere," Cole began. "You know so much about me, even a few things I have never told anyone before. Will you stop for a minute?"

Emma did stop, and she turned to Cole.

"It's just, if we are really serious about each other, then we have to be honest too," Cole stated. "I don't even know where you work. You are just here, and that's usually enough for me, so everything else can just fade away. My old questions just get overlapped by new questions and you are always introducing these weird little things about how we look at the—"

"Cole. You are rambling again," Emma interrupted. She took his hand up in hers. "Just be patient."

They continued walking side by side at a slower pace, saying very little, until Emma steered him off the main road. She was heading to an area of the city with primarily single residences, houses of smaller stature. Cole never had reason to venture this route before. The neighborhood was built for those of the population who had no care to greet each other at the corner parks or coffee shops. This was a place for those who kept to themselves.

In other words, perfect for Emma.

"Well, then, would you care to enlighten me on exactly where we are going?"

"We are going to my home, of course," Emma shot back. "I was always planning on bringing you here today."

"Why did you just give me a hard time about it, if that's where we were headed anyway?" Cole threw his hands up in frustration.

"Oh, Cole, quit whining. I can assure you, when I want to give you a hard time, you'll know it. Now, here we are."

Her home was quaint. Surprisingly well kept, with blooming flowers of every color and a path leading around the house, complete with a natural archway covered in ivy. The house was very different from anything Cole would have expected from Emma.

"So. This is it. It's so . . . very . . . welcoming. Not what I expected from you," Cole said.

"You always have such a way with words," Emma replied. "This is my home now. My friends are here, and that's good enough for me."

The door swished open. Emma jumped up the steps and entered. Cole was right behind her. The inside was just as warm throughout. Cole was about to take a seat when he noticed they were not alone.

"Cole, these are my friends." Emma began the introductions. "A great scientific mind, Sci Tym, and a great philosophic mind, Professor Lander."

"Nice to meet you, Cole." Sci Tym was the first to hobble over and pull Cole further into the room.

"We have heard so much about you from Emma," the professor revealed.

Emma smiled, and Cole relaxed and sat down next to Tym. The two of them immediately struck up a conversation about digiscreen tech models like old friends.

I knew they would get along, Professor Lander thought. He set some breads and sliced meats, iced desserts and whole fruits onto the table. He also passed around shallow cups and a bottle of juice for everyone to share. He then joined up with Emma across the room.

Cole was sitting with his back to the entry, and turned to look over his shoulder after Tym's eyes narrowed slightly.

Standing in the doorway was a tall, well-built woman in a green jacket, various buckles and clasps running the length of her coat. She had short, cropped hair, buzzed so closely to her head that you could see pale pink skin through her light blond fuzz.

She was an equal mixture of beauty and toughness, with eyes like a hawk, darting around the room, observing and calculating. Finally, she settled on Cole, and she craned her neck. He knew she was an authority here.

"My greatest wish tonight was to be graced by your company, dearest Gretchen. Come and greet our visitor," the professor suggested.

"Hey, Cole, that must be you!" Tym commented, bringing Cole's head swinging to face him, breaking his gaze away from Gretchen. He started to rise. "Don't stand yet, it'll look too rushed. Besides, she'll want to control the situation. She always does," Tym warned.

Cole sat back down, whispering to Tym. "I thought you were all friends," Cole shot back.

"We are all friends, sorta. You just have to watch that one. There's something eerie about a person who never smiles." To further prove his point, Tym smiled as big as he could, squishing his food into his mouth, and his drink dribbled down his chin.

Cole couldn't stop himself from laughing full out, an honest heartfelt laugh. Tym wiped his mouth with his sleeve, only smearing the food around to his cheek.

"Yeah, laugh it up. You have food on your face too." Tym pointed at Cole's cheek.

Cole reached up and wiped icing from his mouth onto his hand, and leaned forward to grab a napkin just as he was greeted.

"I trust you are enjoying some revelry with our dear Tym?" an icy voice asked.

He stood quickly and had no choice but to wipe his hands on the front of his jacket and attempt to stand straight enough to make an impression. When he turned to look at Gretchen, he was even more impressed than before.

She had removed her jacket and wore three necklaces of alternating precious stones and fine chain earrings dangling down from each lobe.

Her lips were wide, plump and creased into a continual frown. If Cole hadn't just heard her talk, he would assume she hadn't opened her mouth in years. Still waiting for his reply, she gently raised an eyebrow.

"Yes, Tym had some food on his face. Well, in his mouth, running down his mouth. We were talking too . . . Conversations . . .," Cole stammered, and knew he sounded like a fool.

"I assume his conversation was as interesting as his lack of table manners."

"Gretchen, no need to start so early picking on Tym," the professor interjected.

She sneered at Sci Tym and leaned against the wall.

"See, Cole? One big happy family, just like you wanted," Emma laughed.

"Tell me, Cole," the professor began. "You work in LifeSpan Division Four, is that correct?" Cole nodded in agreement. "What groundbreaking projects are you working on to better the lives of your fellow man?"

"Well, I plan renewable resources. Our last meeting was about the ocean floor, by the lower Eastern Continent, and how LifeSpan is working to develop the deepest part of the ocean," Cole continued on, completely unaware of losing his audience. "It would turn the ocean into a furnace capable of heating long tubes that would be brought to the surface as a regulatory inst−"

"Cole, I think what we are asking is for any local projects." Emma finally stepped in, before Cole made a fool of himself. "Hasn't LifeSpan ever given you an update on how this city is doing?" Emma directed.

"Well, hmmm . . . ," Cole thought long about his response. "No, I suppose they haven't mentioned any local improvements, just what good they are doing−"

"Halfway around the world," Gretchen finished.

"Doesn't it strike you odd? The only information we ever hear is how great everyone else is doing? Are these updates coming from Mr. Stratus?" the professor interjected.

"No, he works in a different sector now."

"But he was the one who promoted you," Emma said.

"Yes, that's right." Cole realized he was the only one sitting down. "I don't understand where this conversation is going. There's nothing wrong with this town, there's nothing wrong with my job. I'm happy, really I am." Cole looked at Gretchen again. She gave him the creeps.

"Of course. Please relax. We just didn't want you to lose our reasoning." The professor patted his hands in the air and sat down. The others followed his lead.

"So, what is the point?" He was looking at Gretchen when he said it.

"The point, my dear boy, is you will never see the bottom of the ocean. You will most likely never visit the lower Eastern Continent. However, you take comfort in knowing these far off lands are doing so well. You also are comforted that the reason for their success is LifeSpan, and coincidentally, you work for LifeSpan. How wonderful you are doing your part, however small that is in these many global achievements." Gretchen spit every word in response to his glare.

Cole stood and looked around the room.

"Thank you all. It was nice meeting you. Emma, I have to go now."

"Cole, we are just playing around. Stay a little longer," Emma pleaded.

"I would like to, but it's getting late. Thanks again. We should do this more often," Cole lied, and he exited through the front door.

When Cole was a safe distance, Emma erupted at Gretchen. "You didn't have to lean into him so hard! He's a good man. Yeah, he works at LifeSpan, but that's not his fault. He has never —"

"You care for him," Gretchen determined.

Emma stopped.

"If he can help us build the case against LifeSpan, you can continue to see him," the professor said. "Is your mission still attainable?"

"Yes, Father, it is," Emma confirmed.

"Try to keep lover boy on track," Gretchen threw in. "Stick to the plan."

THE ASSOCIATE

The warm summer air was humming as the weather towers filtered and expelled gases into the atmosphere. The towers were everywhere, and Emma was talking about the possibility of the towers taking on so many different duties. *How could one tower control the weather, filter gasses, run reports, and make the rain?* Cole let her run from one topic to the next, nodding and throwing in what he could, usually pushing her into another stream of criticism. *How could she think about so much? Why not just let it be? Who really cares about the humming of the towers? They have their purpose.*

To be honest, Cole was just glad to be out with Emma, alone. Anywhere but at her house. He had returned a few times after the first visit fiasco. They discussed LifeSpan history, expirations they have witnessed, even Mr. Stratus. Cole was building a strong relationship with the professor and Sci Tym, not as much with Gretchen. Emma had been with them for years now. The night usually ended as Emma intensely disagreed with Gretchen and Tym unveiled a new invention or two.

There was far less excitement when Cole brought Emma to his home. Aunt Hester had immediately bonded with Emma, and they talked for hours, jumping from one topic to the next while laughing and pointing at Cole. He was just happy to see Emma enjoying herself.

Today, it was just the two of them sitting in the Howland Park fields for over two hours now. It seemed the whole city was outside today, enjoying the perfect weather.

"Hey, I'm exhausted. Wake me when it's your birthday," Cole teased.

"Funny. I'll wake you when you have to go back to work. How about that?"

"Nah, I don't need to go back to work."

"You don't need to, or you don't want to?" Emma challenged.

"Is there a difference?"

Emma thought about it. "Well, I guess not. Night night, Cole." She smiled in an almost motherly way.

Cole thought about curling over and laying his head on Emma's thigh. He could justify the move for a thinly veiled excuse of comfort. Instead, he took his jacket off, bunched it up and stuffed it under his head as a makeshift pillow. He had no trouble taking a quick nap as the trees swayed in the breeze, the birds keeping a long-strung melody. Emma unexpectedly ran her hand through his hair.

"Don't answer that!" Mary shrieked.

The door chimed.

"Cole, don't open the door! I'm your mother; you need to listen to me!"

The door chimed.

The door chimed again and again, more and more loudly.

"Cole, why don't you listen to me? Why would you do this to us?"

Chime.

Cole looked down and he was covered in blood. He knew it was his mother's.

He didn't want to open the door, but he did, and they were waiting.

Cole jumped awake, sucking in breath and groping for something to grab onto, inadvertently pulling out a few blades of grass in his fists. He hadn't had a dream like that in a long time. That one was strong. Emma was staring back at him, her legs pulled up, a small notebook resting on her thighs.

"Rough sleep?" Emma sounded like she could sympathize.

"Yeah. Wait, what are you doing?" Cole asked.

"Observing you while you sleep," Emma answered. "What else should I be doing?"

"Not that. Wait, you are *observing* me? I'll get back to that." Cole sat up and crawled closer to her, aware she had moved a few feet away from him. Wasn't she rubbing his head just a moment ago?

"You are *writing?*" Cole was very confused. She was writing on pages with a pen. Actually writing. "But, nobody does that!" he said incredulously.

"Why don't you come over here? I'll show you how," Emma offered.

"How time consuming! Wouldn't you want a digiscreen? I don't think I've ever seen you with one," Cole responded.

"True. I leave it at home. Besides, I don't want anyone to know what I'm writing." Emma winked.

"If you typed it into the digiscreen, it's yours. Who would read your entries without your permission?"

"Oh, Cole, you are so naïve. Digiscreens are connected; they are part of the grid. There's always someone punched in to your signal. They always have a way." Emma seemed paranoid.

Cole sat back. The park had emptied during his dozing.

"I just thought everyone learned how to read and type. I didn't know there was anyone who even wanted to use a pen."

"Well, then, why don't we start from the very beginning? Come closer, and I'll show you how to use a pen." She raised her voice into a patronizing pitch. Emma was provoking him now.

Cole took the challenge and scooted in very close. Any excuse to be so close to her was good enough for him. He glanced down and noticed her writing was very fluid. The letters were individual pieces of art. She turned the page and passed the notebook to Cole. The blank page was intimidating. She handed him the pen. It felt awkward in his hand, heavy and unwieldy.

"Well, go ahead," Emma prodded.

"I don't know how to write. I already said that," Cole moaned in resignation.

"You don't have to write, you can draw. The pen is yours."

"So, what have you drawn?" Cole flipped to the front of her book. Emma tried to pull it back. Cole playfully tackled her, rolling while he kept the book aloft. He jumped up, keeping his back to Emma.

Cole dodged Emma's flailing arms, and quickly flipped through her sketchpad.

He saw pictures of the LifeSpan weather towers, measurements of buildings, drawings of the Collectors, a floating city in the clouds, pages full of expiration dates.

Emma pulled the book from his hands, and stuffed it in her bag.

She didn't seem angry, only quiet, which could be the same thing.

Well, that was awkward. This would be a good time for a distraction, Cole thought.

As if on cue, his digiscreen began buzzing.

Cole returned to his crumpled jacket and pulled his digiscreen free. The incoming request was coming from his office.

Emma stood with him and dusted off her pants. As she bent down to check her shoes, she looked around the park, noticing a familiar couple across from them. It was the same couple who had been walking behind her earlier today. They happened to settle at the same spot, with an entire park around them?

Not likely. Emma thought she was being too nervous. Better to get Cole away from here, where she could talk to him, where she could tell him . . .

Tell him *what?* The truth? He had seen her notes. Maybe it was time.

It was worth a shot. She turned to take his hand. Cole was talking to the digiscreen, apparently deciding not to ignore his work after all.

"Hello, Cole, this is Associate Cordovan. You are working on the Gordon account, aren't you?" Cole's managing director was on the digicall.

"Yes, I have been assigned to their case for over six months now."

"Well, then, I'm glad I called you. I know today is your absence day, but the Gordon representatives are here and need to review the latest change to their agreement. Can you return to the office?"

"Well . . ." Cole looked at Emma. "I'm kinda busy right now. Could they come back tomorrow?"

"I understand you are enjoying the day, but I see the need to rephrase my earlier request." Associate Cordovan's voice became stern. "Cole, come down to the office. I will see you soon."

Cole removed the curved earpiece and began chewing on the inside of his cheek, thinking about the conversation. He didn't want to end his day with Emma. If he went to work, he could easily get stuck there, with other projects always popping up when he walked in the door. He wanted to ask her about the drawings. He wanted the truth this time. Unfortunately, he was a company man.

"Umm, I have to go to the office, real quick. It's not going to take long at all. We can be back here before you know it. Is that alright?" Cole looked up at her. "Do you want to come with me real quick?"

"No, thanks, I'll just stay here." Emma looked like she was unsure of her surroundings. "Just come back and get me when you're done."

"It'll only take a second, and if you come with me, I can tell them I have to get back."

"The perfect excuse," Emma agreed.

Their walk to the LifeSpan Division Four building was awkward. Emma was looking over her shoulder more often than usual. Cole had questions, but didn't ask them. He was disappointed his perfect day needed to be put on hold, especially to go in to work. Another thing concerned him. Associate Cordovan could easily have pulled their information and uploaded the files for the Gordon representatives. He really didn't need to call Cole. Maybe there was something else they needed from him, which was precisely the cause for his discomfort. He'd rather stay with Emma.

Eventually making their way to his work, there were others coming back from lunch or appointments. The scanners in the doorframes alerted each member entering the facility. "*Hello Michael, you have received three new messages during your recorded lunch absence,*" the robotic voice chimed when another employee walked under the scanner. "*Hello Lisa, your children are waiting in the lobby. They were excused early from institutional instruction.*"

Emma tried to hang back and just wait outside, not comfortable with the scanners.

Cole brought her to the side entrance without the voice alerts, and they entered the lobby.

"Thank you for coming, Cole. We actually need your assistance down here." Mr. Stratus walked up to meet the couple. Associate

Cordovan and his assistant also spotted Cole, and they walked to join the group, watching Emma.

"But all my work is upstairs, my digifiles and passwords."

"You won't need those today. Who is your friend, Cole?" Mr. Stratus prompted.

"Oh, this is Emma." He looked over and she began to back up slowly, glancing left and right.

"Yes, Emma, the pleasure is all mine." Mr. Stratus extended his hand.

She did not take it.

"Do you work here? You look familiar." Associate Cordovan was standing on her left with his assistant on Emma's right side.

The lobby was bustling with employees and workers. The crowds curved around the group. Emma noticed every stare. Some were pointing at her and Cole.

"No, sir, you must have me mistaken for someone else," Emma replied.

"She doesn't work here. I brought her. Can we continue to the problem?" Cole tried to step between the workers and continue to the hall.

"Cole, I need your digiscreen. Just for records, of course. The body scanner has an awfully long line. Is that why you avoided it?" he asked with a smirk aimed only for Emma.

Cole produced his personal digiscreen, unlocked the identification screen, and handed it over to the associate.

Emma felt the hair stand on the back of her neck.

Associate Cordovan reviewed the screen.

Cole R. Jenkins
Subject Number. 7759-03
Expiration. 18980.13.8.3

The other two men closed in around Emma.

"May I see your identification?" Associate Cordovan smirked again, turning to face her directly. Emma raised her chin to look him in the eyes. His breath smelled and his posture was lazy, standing there with his hand stretched to her, palm facing up. Emma didn't like the way he was demeaning her. The smug, ugly, stinking associate.

"Sure, I have it here somewhere." Emma began to slip her backpack off her shoulder.

"I can save you some time." Mr. Stratus pulled out a silver disc from his inside pocket faster than Emma could react, and as she looked up, it flashed a red light over her entire face, burning an after-image in her vision as her eyesight began to readjust.

He scanned my eyes. I wasn't expecting that; I'll give him that much, Emma's thoughts raced. *And I thought this day was going so well.*

She curled her toes inside her shoes, stretched her fingers and rolled her head back and forth, loosening her neck muscles. Her eyes narrowed, teeth clenched.

"*Jennifer A. Jackson. Subject Number 263-551.*" The robotic voice bleeped out the scan results from the silver disc. "*Expired.*"

Mr. Stratus raised his head, mouth agape. Cole didn't have a chance to soak in the information before Emma lashed out.

Emma rocked back on her left heel, snapping her right foot up into the face of the associate to her left. Squatting down and pivoting inside his reach, she sprang up from her crouch and caught the bottom of his chin with her elbow. He was holding Cole's digiscreen and it flew into the air, landing with a snap. Somewhere in the back of Cole's mind, he lamented the broken screen, but it went unnoticed as he continued to stare at Emma's twirling. She was suddenly so graceful, and deadly.

Both men fell back, scrambling to get out of the wild woman's way. These men were sloths. Emma moved faster than they could track.

Cole was frozen in place as he watched Emma move about, springing, whirling and ultimately slamming her fingers into Mr. Stratus's neck, her hand stiffened like a wedge. Two other administrators ran across the lobby, losing heart as Emma spun to them, her fingers locked in the deadly wedge and angled at their heads. Her eyes begged for their attack. They turned back and ran, screaming, "Attack! We are being attacked!"

"A girl lost her mind!" trailed down the corridor.

Suddenly, Emma was in front of Cole, and he didn't know if he was her next target. He barely recognized the look on her face. It was intense, a burning hatred that slowly faded away as she relaxed her hands and posture.

"Cole, we should leave now," she said, pulling on his hand and heading for the door.

He pulled free and stopped walking. "What just happened here? Is your name Emma, or is it Jennifer? What were you—"

"Cole, I know you are confused. I need time to explain, but we have to leave, *now*!"

"Hold on, I need to get my digiscreen."

"It's broken, smashed when the fighting began. Leave it, Cole, you have no need for it anymore." Emma reached for him.

"But you hit them! They're my bosses. You can't do that, you . . . have . . ." Cole incoherently continued mumbling as he surveyed her damage.

She grabbed his arm and dragged him along. Cole tripped over the associate's body, rolling along the ground. Not from injury, Cole noticed. He must have been all nanohealed, but he was trying to get away from them. He was *afraid*.

This could seriously hurt my chance for a promotion, Cole thought. *Although, I don't recall any wording to prohibit employees from chopping*

*the associate in the throat. Well, I never thought I would have to bring
that up in our morning sessions. If it was the —*

"Cole!" Emma broke him from another trailing thought. "Stand
up!"

She was dragging me? When did that happen? Cole got his feet
under him, pulled his clothes straight, pushed back his hair and
shot Emma a hurt expression for his injured pride. A small crowd
had gathered, whispering to each other with shocked expressions
as others told them what had transpired in the lobby. Emma and
Cole squeezed their way through the stunned crowd and out the
entrance, eliciting some dirty glances.

Walking at a brisk pace, descending the front steps, Cole was
numb as he was pulled along by Emma. Other employees had
crowded on the steps, continuing to gawk at the pair, but were
even further stunned when four Collectors came crashing into the
crowd, their bulky white coats a stark contrast from the lightly
dressed workers. A quick scan of the street gave the Collectors
their quarry: a woman pushing through the crowd and dragging a
disheveled man behind her. Their urgency was evidence enough.

"You two! HALT!" Their booming voices erupted through
the air like a thunderbolt. The command was amplified by the
vocal devices worn in their collar. Often used for parades and
stadium events, rarely did they activate this ability near a crowd.
The unfortunate citizens who were standing near the Collectors
grabbed at their ears, ducking away from the blare.

Emma and Cole stopped and turned as the Collectors began
walking down the front steps.

"What do Collectors want with us? It's not our time to . . . ,"
Cole was mumbling, trying to piece the last few moments together,
his mind spinning. Emma was pulling hard on his arm.

"Cole, we have to leave!" Her voice was shrill. "They will not
understand."

"Understand? What is there to believe anymore? I'm not even sure I understand!" Cole pulled away from her grasp. "But I do not intend on going any farther without an explanation."

"I said I will explain later, and I will, I promise, but we need —"

"I'm staying here. I'm not going with you. You lied to me." Cole crossed his arms, planted both feet steadily on the ground and gave a quick nod, jaw set. It was a childish gesture, but Emma would have to laugh later.

A part of her was glad Cole was developing a backbone, but now was not the time.

"Cole, please, believe me." Emma looked over his shoulder and saw that the Collectors had reached the bottom of the stairs and were walking towards them. She had less than a minute, at best. Unless they ran.

"Cole, I know about your mother's journal," Emma revealed.

"How? I've never talked about it." His shock was genuine.

"She worked with us," Emma gave away.

"Nice try, but she didn't work with anybody. She preferred to be alone with her worries and her conspiracies," Cole said.

Emma had no choice but to lay it all on the line.

"Cole, I'm part of the Movement against LifeSpan. They are corrupt; you have to believe me. I will tell you more. Please, trust what I say." She looked over his shoulder again and the Collectors had stopped walking about fifty feet away. They were waiting for her next move, slowly distancing themselves from each other. Spreading out in an exaggerated arc, the four Collectors would attempt to surround them and close in. Emma was running out of time; she had to make Cole trust her, but how could he? She knew he felt betrayed, but they were in real trouble, and she had to find a way out. How did it come this far?

The booming Collector's electronic voice reverberated through the air. "End your discussion. Separate yourselves. Sit down on the ground. You will be questioned," the lead Collector said in a slow voice that sounded like a rusted boat being pulled onto shore. *Boy, is he ugly looking*, Emma thought.

Cole looked back at the Collectors, and knew he should sit down. He glanced at Emma, or Jennifer. He had so many questions, but he needed answers, especially about the journal. His heart made up his mind for him, and he would regret it later.

"How fast can you run?" he whispered.

Thank you, Cole. Emma smiled mischievously. "Faster than you. Follow me."

Suddenly, they both turned their backs on the Collectors and ran full speed. Emma had a quick lead, the wind whipping her hair back into Cole's face.

Cole tried to keep pace with her and it was all he could do to keep up with her long gait. She ran as gracefully as a gazelle while Cole hit the ground thumping hard, feeling like he was making very poor progress. He expected a Collector to grab the back of his shirt and risked a look behind him.

The four Collectors unbuttoned their full-length white trench coats, revealing an X brace strapped across their chest. The straps ran over their shoulders and under their arms, connecting to a metal disc placed in the center of their chest. Turning the disc, the air hummed around them. The lead Collector looked up and across the street to the shimmering line of metal along the rooftops of the city and reached both hands out. In a flash, the Collectors were pulled along the street, easily twice as fast as Cole was running. Dirt, leaves, branches and even gawkers standing along the street were pushed to the side as an invisible humming ozone was left in the Collectors' wake.

Emma looked back and saw them gaining quickly. *Great, they're charged*, she cursed. She grabbed Cole's arm and quickly cut to the right, falling and rolling down a hill, heading toward the park, away from the buildings.

"Hurry, Cole, we have to get out of town," she started to explain. "They use the metal strips along the buildings to pull themselves along!"

Now they were crossing a large field. Families enjoying relaxing picnics were startled to see the couple running frantically across the grass, looking behind them as much as forward. Cole stumbled constantly, not at all used to running for so long. Emma was barely tired and seemed to be running faster as time passed.

Finally they reached the pier leading out to the Titus Ocean. Cole remembered coming down to this pier with his parents, skipping rocks along the shore and feeding swarms of seagulls circling the sunbathers. Today the pier was all but abandoned. Even the seagulls seemed to have found a better spot to patrol, farther down the beach.

"Quickly, Cole, *under* the pier." Emma was shielding her eyes from the sun, trying to look back to the city, squinting with the effort. *Were they still after us?*

"What could possibly be under this pier?" Cole was on his knees, looking under the metal and wood paneled dock, but could only see glittering salt deposits coating the underside, accompanied by the endless lapping waves around the posts.

"No, Cole, we have to go under the pier, into the water." Emma looked back one last time and, frustrated with his continuing apprehension, kicked his rump, sending Cole into the water face first.

With one last look towards the city, she jumped in after him.

PRAETOR

Nimbus sat quietly in his chambers, legs crossed, breathing methodically through his meditation routine. In this relaxed state, eyes shut lightly, he thought of the past, replaying events that shaped his company, seeking insight from his failures and planning new ventures.

The entrance to his study opened slowly, and his assistant's head peeked into the room. Looking around and finally seeing Nimbus on the floor, she blushed slightly and began to withdraw.

"Enter." Nimbus opened his eyes as he turned his head towards the door.

"I'm sorry to interrupt, but there seems to be an urgent message from the Praetor in Sector 655, sire." She stood taller with each word, as if the delivery of important information made her most proud.

Nimbus rose slowly, in perfect balance, and smoothed the front of his loose fitting meditation tunic.

"That will be enough. I shall take the call." Nimbus waved his hand in the air, a gesture of brushing away a small fly. His messenger understood the meaning and instantly ducked back into the hall and closed the door softly behind her.

Nimbus walked calmly from his study to the main chamber. It was a spacious conference room, the walls carved smooth and painted a pearlescent white. The sunlight softly filtered through the shades, accenting the walls and enlivening the color by producing a slight shimmer.

The room was dominated by a huge slab of granite, low enough to the ground that those attending his meetings would be required to sit with their legs folded underneath the table. This made for an uncomfortable setting, but Nimbus didn't want them comfortable. If they were content to lounge around his assembly room all day, nothing would be accomplished. The single grand chair at the end was for Nimbus only. He sat above anyone at attendance, like the sun watching the weeds beneath him.

He sat at the head of the table and tapped on the arm of his chair, revealing a hidden storage box that had opened into the crook of his arm. There was a single harmonic bud that he placed in his ear for privacy.

"Report, Praetor," Nimbus said.

The bald head of the LifeSpan Praetor appeared in the middle of the table. The hologram was a digital representation of the Praetor and did not move but only rotated slightly, expanding from a headshot to the full body of the Praetor in his complete regal clothing. The outfit was not unlike a Collector's usual garb, except his was immensely more elaborate. The edges of his trench coat hems were carefully decorated with images of dark, rolling clouds, and the shoulders were stitched with a golden thread, showing concentric circles running over and under his arm. His lapels were crisp and ran the length of his torso, ending at points just above his knees. At the top of each lapel, there were three concentric rings embroidered, a signal of his ranking. The collar was stiff, standing a few inches off of his collarbone.

"Thank you for a timely response, sire. There was a disturbance

at the LifeSpan Division Four building that was unusually . . .
eventful," his voice droned out. "It appears an employee was
screened with a refugee who dropped off the grid some years ago."

"Please, get to the point, Praetor. I sense you are holding back
some vital information. Is your sector under control?" Nimbus
leaned forward.

"Yes, sire. We have reviewed the digifiles and it was a female.
She *fought* sir. She moved and lashed out in the old ways. Someone
trained her in the Bellicose method." The Praetor's voice was filled
with confusion. His hologram was void of emotion, but Nimbus
heard a slight tremble as he gave the report.

"The boy must have established contact. As we had hoped,"
Nimbus deduced. "Working for us, learning our secrets, but to
what end?"

"Sire? Your orders?" the Praetor's metallic voice rang out.

"Cole Jenkins no longer works at LifeSpan, and as far as
anyone knows, he never has. Purge the records, blacklist him
on every database, flag every form of identification. Destroy his
entire work log. Compile all video surveillance, direct messages,
and bring them to me. Search his office belongings for any useful
information."

"Yes, my sire." The Praetor's voice faded out. He must have
bowed his head in acknowledgment away from the microphone.
"We shall leave no trace of his former existence. Will there be
anything else?"

Nimbus schemed. "Yes, one more thing."

"Sire?"

"Take his aunt in for questioning. Tell her Cole is the leader of
a resistance and by association, she is an accomplice."

SUBMERGED

Emma surfaced for the third time, swimming over to Cole, who was bobbing in the water. His brow was furrowed and his arms were tiring. They had been treading water for close to a half-hour now, and Cole was running out of energy. Cole was still in shock from actually being chased by Collectors. What was he thinking?

He had resorted to hugging the pier's post out of sheer exhaustion, trying to keep his head above the salt water lapping into his eyes and mouth. The seagulls were flying above in lazy circles. A few had gathered on the pier, looking at Cole. He wished they would go away before revealing their location to the Collectors. Emma seemed completely at home in the water, diving down as nimbly as a fish, searching for a submerged doorway. She was in great shape and hardly noticed the water's constricting effects.

She had told Cole there was a doorway grate under the pier, and they should take refuge in the small confines until later that night. As long as he didn't have to tread water any longer, he was willing to stay in the hiding place until it was safe.

As the sun was nearing the horizon line, almost even with the water's edge, Emma's head broke the surface a short distance from Cole.

"I've found it," she said as she was spitting the water back into the ocean. "Fortunately, the safety it provides has not been jeopardized by recreational divers. It is a challenging swim. Are you up for this?"

"I think I can manage." Trying to impress her, Cole puffed up his chest.

"You look terrible," she responded.

"Thanks for the vote of confidence. I'm fine."

Emma pushed herself close to him and removed his hand from the post, pulling it to her shoulder. Cole placed his other hand on her waist, their bodies bobbing as one, their faces separated only because the push and pull of the ocean's waves kept them apart. The seagulls were growing in number.

He looked at her, with the sun dipping into the ocean, beginning its nightly routine, and streaking the sky into deep purple and blue ripples.

Cole was taken by the beauty of Emma, her hair slicked back from her face, beads of water running down from her hairline, glistening on her skin, her eyes reflecting the purple sky.

"You are beautiful," he whispered.

Emma was so focused on the task, and more seagulls were gathering now, with two people now in the water. She didn't hear him. "Well then, here we go. Take a deep breath, and do not let go of my hand."

She didn't have to worry about that. Cole filled his lungs with air, closed his mouth, and Emma pulled them both below the waves.

Cole and Emma swam deep down, periodically feeling ahead in the murk, checking that the pier post was still next to them. Emma was careful not to lose their bearings. The Father had told her of this hiding place in case any one of her group needed a spot to hide and be out of the reach of Collectors. He had known this would happen. He had told her on many occasions she was too brash, moving too quickly. The Father had told her she was becoming too attached to Cole, but she knew that couldn't be avoided. The die had been cast.

Emma had to make contact with the Movement. First, she had to take refuge, lie low for a while, and explain the circumstances to Cole. He deserved that much.

They swam deeper. She couldn't see Cole's face, but he gripped her harder once the light filtering through the surface dimmed. Now they were in darkness, with only the pier post to guide them. She could feel his tension building, through his grip and erratic swimming. The seaweed and moss was thick along the wooden shaft, entangling their arms and legs, but they dared not drift too far from their only guide. It was old that much was easy to distinguish. Most everything made out of wood was replaced with LifeSpan's plasteel. Emma wondered why this was an exception. Probably because the pier was seldom used. Not many people owned private boats, and anyone needing to travel by sea were directed to the larger, main ports farther south. Long ago, mass transit became the preferred oceanic travel method.

This pier was probably used by local fisherman ages ago, with their vessels eventually replaced by the fishing-farm buildings scattered across the countryside. Private fishermen, spending every morning afloat in the sea netting oceanic life, were also stamped out by LifeSpan. There was no need to spend days at sea when the fish were grown in a birthing warehouse.

Cole could barely stand it any longer; his lungs felt like they would burst, but he didn't want to let Emma down. He grabbed her hand harder, if that were even possible, and tried to ignore the pressure mounting in his head and chest. Suddenly, Emma pulled him close to the post, and then rolled into his chest, her back facing him. She wrapped his arms around her neck and swam with him piggy-backed into an oblong chamber. Cole could not see how large the opening was or where it was located, but he felt a sudden pressure change. It was the undeniable effect of entering a cramped space. He didn't need light to tell him they were in a tube. A very narrow tube, with barely enough room to swim.

Finally, their heads burst out of the water, and he felt air rush into his lungs. Their hands separated. Cole gasped, spitting water. He relished the deep breaths he was able to take. His lungs were on fire. He'd never had to hold his breath for so long. He looked around for Emma in the darkness. She must be similarly starved for air. Cole thought he could nurture her somehow.

"Stay here. There is a ledge farther up. I'll be right back." Emma's voice echoed loudly, emphasizing the size of this room, or wherever they were. Cole had the feeling it was a metal enclosure, because of how it reverberated with her voice. It resounded with a metallic undertone.

Cole slowly swam forward, reaching his hands out, trying to find whatever ledge Emma was talking about. He moved sluggishly, head bobbing from exhaustion, his arms barely managing the flopping that propelled him forward. He stopped attempting to swim, worried he was going in the wrong direction, anyway, and expending unnecessary energy, when the room filled with light.

He immediately covered his face, shielding his eyes that burned from the murky saltwater, and let his pupils focus.

When he was able to see through squinted vision, Emma was standing above him, the ledge mercifully only a few feet away. She reached down and extended her hand, grabbing his, and pulled him up. She didn't seem tired at all. Cole wanted to collapse onto the platform, but forced himself to stand up next to Emma. He still leaned over, his elbows on his knees, but was standing on his feet. His nanos were feeding oxygen back into his body.

"What is this place?" He glanced around the room, now clearly showing a metal frame, connecting in a crisscross pattern of silver and gray, with metal rafters running high above. Cascading in rigid symmetry, like the belly of some large whale, ribbed reinforcements ran the length of the walls. Cole couldn't tell how deep the enclosure was, but had a feeling it was massive.

"It was an old military submarine. It must have sunk off of the harbor, embedding itself in the muddy walls and forgotten."

"A submarine? When was the last time a submarine was even in commission?"

"More recently than you know," Emma said mysteriously.

"So where is the crew? Perished with the ship? Still here somewhere?"

"Relax, Cole, from what my people can tell, they must have evacuated. Large sections of the ship's electronics are gone, and there were no supplies except what we have furnished over the last few visits."

Cole walked over and sat down in a chair, a chair that would never have been on a boat of this age, for it was too new.

He studied the room. It was fairly expansive, with doorways and nooks leading off into the shadows. There were furnishings, as Emma had said, with a cooler chest, canned foods, even a bed in the corner, with lighting daisy-chained throughout. This was a hideout in every sense of the word, and that thought brought Cole's attention back to his current situation.

"Alright, now you explain what just happened. Speaking of *your people*, I know they aren't deep-sea divers furnishing underwater hotels. What is really going on here? And how did you know about my mother's journal, and who is Jennifer? Who is Emma? And when you are done answering those — "

"Cole, stop. We'll be down here for most of the night. We should change out of our wet clothes. Your nanos may be able to ward off hypothermia, but I can't."

"What do you mean by that?" Cole couldn't help asking, after her odd comment.

Emma didn't take the bait. Instead she got up and walked over to an armoire. It was stocked with clothing, all neatly folded and organized, men's and women's clothing. Whoever stocked this place, they were thinking ahead.

She threw a change of clothes in Cole's direction and stepped behind a screen to swap her wet clothes with dry. He did the same.

After changing, he looked down at his new attire. Plain linen pants, loose and airy, with a button-up pale blue shirt, short sleeved and a little too big for him. Surprisingly, the room was warm and he didn't need extra layers of clothing. Emma said the submarine was sunken into the mud walls; that would explain the warmth. But he found it hard to believe everyone that had come here would swim down from the pier. There had to be another way in and out.

"My real name is Jennifer Jacobs. I expired eight years, 128 days and six hours ago, give or take a day." Cole turned to her voice. She had walked out from the screen and was wearing a light cotton dress, hugging her body in the few spots where the ocean water wasn't completely dry. Cole was mesmerized. He didn't realize how shapely she was. Her usual outfits were layers of shirts, pants with extra pockets, and jackets. She always wore a hooded jacket.

Emma walked towards him, talking as she advanced. Cole kept quiet and just took in her body.

"I am part of the Movement against LifeSpan, as I told you when the Collectors were coming for us. They were coming for me. I am one of the hunted. We have lived outside of the system, choosing to band together and combine our intelligence for an eventual trial against LifeSpan. They will answer for their crimes, and humanity will be the judge, not them."

"So you are a group of terrorists? What has LifeSpan ever done to you?"

"They have *oppressed us*, Cole. The entire world. They oppress people, they oppress weather, they oppress finances, nature, where you live, what you learn, who you marry, when you have children." Emma looked into his eyes. "They even oppress our ability to die."

Emma was standing in front of him now, a wild look in her eyes, as she was preaching her litany. He could see the passion; her disdain of LifeSpan exuded from her very pores. They had been walking towards each other as their conversation wore on. Once again, Cole found himself inches from her, but this time he didn't back away.

"They organized the entire world, Emma. They were there when nobody else would take the job. We owe our very existence as a civilization to LifeSpan. There are no more wars, there is no fighting."

"My people fight. We fight them on every front," Emma shot back.

"LifeSpan stopped us from killing ourselves," Cole said.

"They tell us when to die. How is that any different?"

"If you are gathering intelligence and waging a secret war against LifeSpan, what do I have to do with it? I don't want to fight LifeSpan. I work there, remember?"

"Well, I would guess you've just been fired." Emma smiled.

"I don't know Emma, I didn't want to be dragged into all of this. Why didn't you just run away, leave me there for the Collectors? I didn't do anything wrong." Cole reached out and grabbed her shoulders in frustration.

"They were using you Cole, promoting you. I was assigned to

you. I was using you for my reconnaissance. But something else happened. My judgment was clouded." Emma knew this wouldn't sit well.

"I was an assignment?" Cole backed away from her.

"You turned into much more than that, Cole, you turned into my friend. Something that was out of my control. I was sloppy. I let myself get too deep. I should have let you go, let LifeSpan control you. They control everything else, what's one more?"

"They can't control our feelings," he said, trying to see the silver lining here.

"*I* can't control my feelings," Emma whispered.

And suddenly they were embracing each other, kissing deeply. Cole ran his hands through her hair, pulling her close, afraid to lose her.

They continued kissing, ignoring the threat that loomed over their relationship. Inside this sub, buried in the earthen mud and hidden below the saltwater, they were happy. Once they reached the surface, there would be no rest; they were both outlaws.

Cole pushed her away from him, gently holding her at bay, his breathing heavy.

"I've always loved you, I just never thought you were interested in me, y'know, in that way," Cole admitted.

"Cole, it was complicated. It still is complicated. I was working on an assignment. I was living two lives." Her words were spoken softly, with the metal surroundings adding a tin echo behind him.

"We can return to the surface, turn ourselves in, tell them it was an accident. There were witnesses. They would know it was in self defense."

"There wasn't an outward threat, I reacted too soon. The witnesses would call me a madwoman. Cole, if we did turn ourselves in, what would you expect? They slap us on the wrists and let us go? We lead a normal life? That option is not available to us." Emma let go of him, shaking her head. "There is a reason I don't get involved with assignments. I told you I was one of the hunted. There's an explanation why I failed identification, why I can't buy anything, why I can't enter LifeSpan buildings."

She sat down on the edge of the bed, thinking about her next announcement. Cole sat down with her, taking her hands. The water was rippling against the metal railing, pulling back into the floor opening, and creating an erratic gurgling. The lighting was sparse, only illuminating half of their features. Emma lowered her head, unable to look Cole in the eyes. A shadow fell across her face.

She looked down as she spoke.

"Cole, I do not have any nanos in my body. When I died, they were taken out of me."

GUEST

The scrubbing bot was finishing its last round of the kitchen as Aunt Hester turned the corner, stepping in from the backyard. She shook off her shoes at the threshold, knowing the sweeper bot would be there soon. She had placed her glass down on the table and wanted to pour another helping of wine when the porch monitor chimed.

Finally, Cole was back from his day. If only he spent as much time at home as he did with that girl, we would get to know each other better. He's just like my sister, Hester thought as she poured the wine, the aroma wafting up to fill her nostrils.

The porch monitor chimed once again, an indication the visitor had not scanned the palm plate. Hester placed the glass on the counter quickly and rushed to the door. She had assumed it was Cole because she wasn't expecting any visitors, but if it were Cole, he would have scanned the plate and let himself in. Now there was someone here to visit and Hester had rudely made him or her wait. She was always thinking of someone other than herself.

She opened the door and greeted a sturdy-looking man in a long white trench coat. At first Hester thought he was a

Collector, possibly informing her of a neighborhood meeting. Her identification was half wrong, for this man wore a long trench coat much like the Collectors, except his was embroidered along the bottom edge with dark, rolling clouds.

"Hello, ma'am, I am the Praetor of Sector 655. I am looking for your nephew, Cole. Has he been in today?" the Praetor asked.

"Actually, I thought you were Cole. I haven't seen him in some time. He left this morning with a friend of his."

"Has he contacted you lately to check in? Or possibly told you when he would be back?"

"Well, to tell you the truth, it is really up to him whether he comes back tonight or not. He is smart enough to take care of himself." Aunt Hester thought he was rather pushy.

"Yes, he is quite smart, and very gifted. What is the name of his friend?"

"I have to go now. I'll tell him you were here when he comes back home." She moved back into the foyer and motioned to close the door, hoping he would take the hint and go on with his day.

"Well, that won't be necessary. How about I wait here for Cole, just a short while?"

"No, I don't think that would be necessary, thank you. Mr. . . . ?"

He stepped into the house. His brilliant white trench coat came swirling in behind him.

Aunt Hester couldn't argue with him; he was obviously a high-ranking official with LifeSpan, but she knew this was wrong. There was no reason for a Collector or any LifeSpan official to enter a home without a resident expiring. Still, she did not resist his entry and showed him to the kitchen, where he could sit at the round table.

"Would you care for some wine?"

"No, thank you. I will not intrude," the Praetor ironically replied.

"I'll just be upstairs, straightening up a few things. The wine is on the counter here. I'll leave an empty glass out in case you change your mind."

Aunt Hester went upstairs and glanced one final time to check that he was still sitting at the table. She had to get ahold of Cole and tell him to stay away tonight. This visitor wasn't sitting too easy with her.

When she reached her room, the door swished open and she ran to grab her digiscreen and call Cole. Hiding behind her bed, she scrolled through the address cards on her screen and tapped Cole's picture with her forefinger. The connection was initiated.

Thump thump. Pause. Thump thump. Pause.

Finally he picked up.

"Cole, this is Aunt Hester. Just stay out tonight. I hope you are having a good time. There's no rush to come home, nothing going on here. Emma is a nice girl. You two seem to be doing great together. That's all I had to call for. Just don't come home tonight. OK?"

She waited for his response after blurting out her frantic ramblings.

"Cole? Hello?" Aunt Hester looked down at her screen. The connection was still active, but there was no response. Then a familiar voice came across the transmission.

"I think you should come back down to the kitchen. We have a few things to discuss," the Praetor said.

THE FALLEN

Cole was speechless. He had never heard of anyone living without nanos. It was the core of their entire civilization. It was their identity. Here he was, standing across from the girl who had shown him how to be so free-willed, and yet, she was the one who was free. More free than anyone alive. Really living, except for one crucial point. Cole became frantic, his mind whirling.

"What if you are injured? Is that why you are hiding from LifeSpan? What now? Who did this to you?" Cole stepped toward her, reaching to cover her, needing to hide her from the world. He could be her protector now.

"It was my choice, Cole. The girl I was is dead. Jennifer Jackson expired for LifeSpan, and when she did, I took a new name. I am Emma Goldstein now. Everything you know about me, everything you love about me, is Emma. You wouldn't have liked me when I was Jennifer. I was blinded by LifeSpan, as is everyone else. I was lost."

"So we move away from anything to do with LifeSpan scans, we live and . . ."

"You don't get it. I can't just run off and abandon the Movement.

We've all worked too hard to quit now." Emma swept her hand
across the air, gesturing at the complex. She knew this would be his
reaction. To run. To hide. She would have to toughen him up if he
were going to finish the planned road before him. The Movement
had a destiny for Cole, and it was already in motion. She couldn't
let him run. How could she keep him here and . . .

"I'll join. Obviously, I don't have a future at LifeSpan, and even
though they haven't done anything to me personally, I'll stand by
you," Cole pledged.

"You don't know what you're asking. You may still have a
chance to live a normal life." Emma tried to hide her excitement.
He was hooked. The Movement would continue.

"I can't live a normal life without you. We can still move away,
and stay in contact with everyone else. I'll tell my aunt I have to leave,
to move out. Then we drop off of the grid, we . . . what's wrong?"

Emma's face had dropped; she was pale.

"Cole, your aunt's house is empty by now. They would know.
She has probably already been taken." Emma always knew this
wasn't a game. Real consequences were the result of her actions.
Emma had to be callous; she had to distance herself from the
"others," those who were still under the influence of LifeSpan,
including Cole's aunt, a casualty who would be sorely missed, but
a necessary casualty for the betterment of the whole. She looked at
Cole, and a wash of emotions fell over her again. She was trained
to distance her mind from any emotional contact with the "others."
However, she couldn't finish her mental disconnect, not when she
looked at Cole. She couldn't ignore his reaction to his aunt's house,
the only home he knew.

Cole had never thought of that. Like a fool, he was worried
about his employment at LifeSpan. If they were criminals, they
would surely trace him back to his family. The only family he had
was his aunt.

"We have to go get her. Maybe they haven't arrived yet. We could call her!"

"No, Cole, it's too risky. We have to wait here, let things calm down."

"Emma, I can't lose her." Cole stood, reaching a hand for her. "I sat by when LifeSpan stole my own mother. I even helped them!"

"This time is different. You are an enemy of LifeSpan. There is not a promotion at the end of this day." Emma tried to reason with him, but there was a new resolve in him. He found it, that elusive backbone of his.

"My aunt needs the two of us. With your sneaky hiding in the shadows, whatever spinning kick things you do," Cole teased. "And my amazing ability to point at people waiting to be kicked, we are unstoppable!"

"Great. Let's go find someone to chop," Emma agreed.

She had a real bad feeling about this.

Later that night, Cole was hiding behind the largest tree in Aunt Hester's backyard. Emma crouched along the blackberry bushes lining the property, about twenty yards from Cole. They had taken a non-linear route to her home, watching for any signs of Collectors. Emma moved along houses, through bushes and across garden beds without a sound or any sign of her passing.

His path looked like he was dragging an angry tiger by the tail.

Cole crouched, pivoting his body, and peeked around the trunk. The house was quiet. Dark. He ducked back again. It was possible Aunt Hester was not home. She could have broken her routine and gone for a walk, or was at a neighbor's house. He knew that was a stretch.

Emma was motioning to him. She pointed at the second floor.

Cole peeked again and clearly saw his aunt walk in front of the window, the lights dimming as she left the room.

She is home. I will go get her. You stay here, Cole mouthed the instructions slowly, patting the air and walking his two fingers on his palm.

Emma rolled her eyes. She could read lips. Ridiculous.

Cole reached the door, placed his hand on the plate and with a swish, he stepped inside. The lights turned on when he entered. He raced upstairs, trying to catch his aunt on her way down. She was sitting on the top step, arms folded across her knees. She looked like she had been crying for many hours.

"Cole. What have you done?" Aunt Hester whispered.

"I have come back for you." Cole grabbed her shoulders. "We can leave now. I brought friends. Come with me. It isn't safe here."

"Well," a husky voice broke in. "You have that much correct." The Praetor stepped out from Aunt Hester's room and into the hallway. Cole leaped back. "Now here, lets talk about these friends of yours."

Cole immediately retreated down the stairs. His exit was blocked by a Collector at the base, looking up at him. The Praetor at the top, Collector at the bottom.

Great, a Cole sandwich with a side of bad luck, he lamented.

"Cole." Hester's voice was calm. "Your mother warned me this might happen. You are so much like her."

"What would she do in this spot?" Cole asked.

"Don't waste this moment now. It's all I can give you. She would RUN!"

Hester pulled her digiscreen from the folds of her shirt, spun around, and smashed the screen into the side of the Praetor's face. He stumbled back, leaving a small opening for Cole to dive through. Cole did not waste a second. He ran down the hallway to the rear window facing the back yard.

"Window thirteen, open maximum!" Cole screamed as he plummeted through. The window popped open, and he rolled onto the first-floor rooftop.

Cole slid across the inclined surface, kicking and grabbing to slow his descent.

I can angle to the tree, grab a branch and lower myself to the ground, Cole thought.

He fell off the roof, smashing into the young tree. He twisted through the branches, still trying to desperately grab at anything. He missed every branch and hit the ground hard.

Emma was watching the windows for any sign of movement. She looked around the yard, surveyed the neighbors. She listened to the birds and commotion of animals around her. Emma knew signs of unrest. She also knew when it was too quiet, and right now, this was not right. Cole was not prepared for this. She knew if he was given the choice to fight or run, he would try to run.

Probably trip and fall in the process, she thought.

On cue, Cole smashed onto the roof, slid across the house, and dived face-first into a tree.

Just great! Emma broke from her cover and ran to the house. *Was he blind? Were his hands bound?* There really was no other explanation for his lack of control in that escape.

Emma reached him as he fell from the tree canopy, rolled him over and shook him violently. She knew they didn't have much time if he was already fleeing the home. They must be here. His eyes fluttered and he recognized Emma.

"Collectors. Here," Cole stammered, still too hurt to get up.

Emma reached into her bag and pulled forth a small silver ball.

She ran her fingers along the sides, found the impression, pushed hard and shook the ball. At first, a faint glow was visible between her fingers, and it grew more intense with each shake.

With her other arm, she pulled Cole up as the door broke open.

The Collector stepped out, billy club in hand.

"Close your eyes!" Emma yelled to Cole and threw the ball at the Collector's white coat.

Unfortunately, Cole never took direction well, and his reflexes were even worse. The ball burst into pure light, blinding the Collector and burning into Cole's vision. The world oversaturated. He stumbled back, blinking wildly.

"What was that?! I can't see anything," Cole yelled at Emma.

"I told you to close your eyes!" Emma pushed him through the yard.

"Well, I thought you were talking to the Collector!" Cole knew she was running. Her voice was trailing away and he could not keep up.

"Why would I warn him?!" Her voice was farther away. He continued running even as his nanos healed his eyes. His surroundings were clearer now, and he never slowed.

Cole ran as fast as he could through yards, across streets, and jumped over bushes and around pools. On he ran.

Emma knows where we are going, Cole thought as he ran. *Emma. My new life on the run with Emma, leaving a trail of destruction.*

His heart was beating so loudly, he was afraid it was a homing beacon for the Collectors to track him through the city. He jeopardized his entire future at LifeSpan. He was one of the most respected employees, easily climbing in his field. He had promise. He turned in his own mother for LifeSpan. He abandoned his Aunt Hester for the Movement. What a mess.

How did it all come down to this frantic run through the city, Collectors on him like a cat on the trail of a foolish mouse?

Yes, Cole thought, *that is what I am, a foolish mouse. Led to a trap by a chunk of cheese named Emma.*

Cole rounded the corner and slammed into a solid wall. For a moment, his surroundings blinked out, and he knew he was falling. Not knowing which way was up, his mouth smashed into the pavement, his teeth cutting into the back of his lips. His hands fumbled around for leverage as he tried to pull his knees under his body.

Cole heard screaming, but it seemed so distant. His mind told him it was a woman's voice, possibly his mother's. How could she be here? Filled with false hope, Cole opened his eyes, expecting to see her warm smile beaming down at him. Through blurry vision, with the salty taste of blood in his mouth, Cole looked up at the wall that impeded his escape. *Funny*, he thought, *I never saw a wall with white boots.*

From her hiding spot, Emma saw Cole fall and knew he wouldn't be getting back up anytime soon. Two Collectors were looking down at him, talking to each other. She hunched down lower, as the ugly one waved his white billy club in wide sweeping motions. *He's trying to find me, but that won't work on me.* Emma thought. *What can I possibly do now? There's no way I can drag Cole away with those watchdogs standing over him.*

She needed a distraction, which was her only recourse. Slowly, she inched backward down the sloping hill and ran in a large circumventing route to arrive behind Cole and his two towering captors. Looking around, she spied a ladder leading to the rooftop. A perfect place to throw something far.

She began the climb, quiet as a mouse, keeping Cole in her peripheral vision. *This is crazy. Why don't I just leave him? I can return to the Movement, safe. What do I need to risk my life for a compromised assignment?*

Emma reached the rooftop and scuttled over to the edge, looking down at her targets from three stories higher. *There has to be something up here that I can throw. Hopefully, they'll run after it like a dog chasing a toy. Then I'll . . . then what? Climb back down and drag Cole away before they return?*

Well, it'll have to be a far throw.

Emma quietly stalked around the roof and found a loose brick she could pry from its spot. Feeling the weight in her hand, testing its mass, she took a few steps and threw the brick as far as she could into the brush she was hiding in moments before.

Both of the Collectors immediately looked in that direction, but failed to give chase. They stood for what seemed like hours, staring in the direction of the decoy brick.

C'mon, take the bait. It's me out there. Go get me, Emma's thoughts were screaming in her head.

Silently willing the Collectors to take the bait, her elbows were aching with the stress of holding her head above the stout wall that lined the roof. Incredulously, the two Collectors turned their heads slowly, and looked right at her. Sucking in her breath, she ducked quickly.

Did they see me? Should I run? she thought.

"Hello, girly." A grating voice was unexpectedly behind her.

Emma felt a cold chill run along her spine. She rolled onto her stomach, and her eyes widened as a Collector stepped over her and grabbed her by the neck. Easily lifting her, she kicked and screamed to no avail. He made his way to the edge of the roof, and began the descent from the building's ladder, dragging her along as she choked and struggled. Emma grabbed at his wrist, clawed at his face, and pumped her legs like she was out-swimming a shark. The Collector did not alter his course, and he regrouped with his cohorts.

"Here is the little one giving us the run around. That must be her boyfriend," he said. "She was trying to help him. How cute," Ugly Collector was telling his companions.

I knew there were three. Emma's head was throbbing as he dropped her to the ground next to Cole. Desperately trying to fill her lungs with air, she had nearly passed out when the Collector was clamped down on her neck. She looked over and saw Cole open his eyes to meet her.

"Didn't leave me, huh?" he smiled weakly.

"I thought about it. But something held me back."

"Oh yeah, and what was that?" He started to cough.

"I love you too, Cole," she replied softly.

He stared back at her, dumbfounded.

"Did you just—"

"Yes, I said it, now shut your mouth."

That was an easy thing to do. He didn't know how to respond anyway. This wasn't exactly how this moment was supposed to play out.

He felt the end of a billy club press into his temple. Incredible pain overtook his body, unconsciously curling him into the fetal position. Emma screamed. His entire body was convulsing, jaws clenched, muscles tightened. The pain subsided when the club was pulled away.

"No bedtime stories for you kiddies," the tall one said with a wicked grin.

"You monsters! Leave us alone! We didn't do anything!" Emma began to stand. Cole reached his hand up weakly to stop her.

The Collector's club swung over to Emma, the end planted firmly on her neck. Nothing happened. With his other hand he reached out and grabbed her face. His large gloved hands were large enough to smash her eyelids down, clench her jaw shut and have her clawing at his forearms to breathe.

"Looks like we have a runaway. Are you part of the futile resistance? Playing out your dreams?"

"You are corrupt," Emma said through clenched teeth. "We will not stop until you are destroyed."

"Strong words for an insect." He looked over at his companion, who had his forefinger pressing gently on the side of his vocal cords, silently moving his mouth and talking, but no words could be heard. There was a small microphone implanted into his neck, adjusting and translating his movements into words for the listener. He then transferred his finger to the back of his ear to listen to the response from the other end. His head was nodding in approval before he removed his fingers.

"What are we doing with them?"

"This comes from the top," the ugly one began. "Keep the boy. Kill the girl."

"No problem." Without pause, the tall one twisted Emma's arm back and bent her down over his knee, face up. Emma tried to struggle, looking for some way to wiggle out of the iron grip. She kicked her legs and tossed her shoulders, to no use.

"NO! Let her go! Emma, fight him!" Cole cried out.

The Collector's right elbow rose up over his head, hand clenched, forearm muscles tensed, and came crashing down on Emma's torso. A sharp tree-cracking sound echoed around the alleyway as Emma's ribs shattered. Caught between his immovable leg and the thunderous crushing blow, her chest buckled inward and her spine snapped. Emma's arms raised from the force, and her struggling ceased.

Cole shouted in denial as he watched Emma's body slide off of the Collector's knee, her face a frozen mask of surprise and pain. She hit the ground limply, arms and legs falling in a cluttered bloody heap, all life fading from her eyes.

NEW EDUCATION

Cole jumped awake. He was leaned up against a smooth wall, sitting with his hands tied behind his back. As the rest of his body slowly regained strength, he realized his muscles ached horribly, and he was too exhausted to change his current position. Cole managed to turn his head slightly to take in the rest of his surroundings. He was in a small room.

If he were able to stretch out, Cole guessed his feet could touch the wall opposite him. There was very little light, bleeding in from a small opening high above. Cole stretched his head up but was unable to see the ceiling. It was impossibly tall. He tried to stand. His head was throbbing, and the room began to spin. He fell back to his knees and fought to keep himself from passing out. Where am I? Where was Emma?

Then he remembered, and Cole broke out in a sob, letting her memory fill his thoughts. However, he quickly turned his mourning to anger. Anger directed at LifeSpan.

Why would they want to keep me? It's my fault Emma is dead.

The door slid into the wall, and light poured into his small room. Blinding light, forcing Cole to close his eyes. He barely made out two figures standing in the doorway.

In walked a stout man with large, hairy arms and a slow, steady gait. Cole tried to see his face, but the backlight was too intense. The man peered around the room, then looked down at Cole.

"Hello, down there." His voice was cold. "Have you awakened already?"

The room suddenly seemed smaller, for there was no pity in this man's voice, no hope of reprieve. Cole knew this was not a place to recuperate.

"Where am I? What do you want from me? Why would you—" Cole began, and his intensity increased as he became more frantic.

"We are here to help you, of course. My name is Galen." The man bent low, close to Cole's face. "You have lost your way, child, and I can show you the path."

His breath smelled like old cheese, and his flabby cheeks wiggled when he talked. His brow seemed to be frozen in a continual furrow.

"Where is Emma? She . . ." Cole dropped his voice, and all strength left him. "She died." His eyes filled with tears.

"Oh, she is alive," Galen replied casually, watching Cole's expression light up, his eyes filling with hope. Galen reached down and untied Cole's hands. "You can see her when you are better. Now go to sleep. We will begin in the morning, after warm coffee and a cinnamon roll."

Galen turned his back and started towards the door.

"What will we begin in the morning? I want to see Emma *now*!" Cole began furiously.

Galen turned abruptly. His head snapped back to look at Cole so forcefully that his jowls had to swing across his neck to keep up. His eyes squinted in rage.

"I'm sorry, but I told you to go to sleep." Galen's hand flew out from under his robe, wearing a white glove. He spread his fingers wide, locked his arm open and extended the palm facing Cole. He could see a palm-sized white disc mounted in the center, with a series of wires running up the fingers, connecting to each fingertip with a smaller white disc. The wires' light grew in intensity and Cole felt a pulse run through his body. His head became heavy, his stomach knotted. The air became thick and his muscles sluggish, like being dragged under water. He put his arms out and felt that the plastique wall was close. He leaned against it for support.

Another pulse pounded him, and his eyes closed as his limp body hit the floor.

"Goodnight, *boy*," Galen hissed. He lowered his arm, and the glowing faded from his glove. With a sneer, he turned and exited the chamber, leaving Cole where he fell.

Cole awoke the next morning. At least he thought it was morning. Light was coming in through his window far above. He stood quickly in his cell. Too quickly. His head throbbed from sleeping in such an awkward position. He stumbled to the door.

I think my nanos are on vacation. Cole felt terrible.

"Hey! Can anybody hear me out there?" Cole croaked out from his dry throat, yelling at the solid door. "What do you want from me?"

He walked back to his bed and sat down, collecting his thoughts.

Let's look at this from a calmer point of view. At least I am not tied up anymore, Cole said to himself, taking small steady breaths. "Emma was not who she said she was. I ran with her, for some reason. I jeopardized my career, my entire life for her. And she goes and gets killed by a Collector. LifeSpan knows about the Movement." Cole couldn't even keep the story straight in his head, it was all so mixed up.

The door slowly slid into the doorframe, revealing Galen standing in the hall. He was smiling and holding a tray of steaming coffee and a dome-covered plate. As he stepped into Cole's small room, a guard was behind him, carrying a plush chair. He placed it immediately inside the entrance and stepped back into the hallway. Another guard brought in a tall stool and placed it on the opposite end, obviously intended for Cole. He left the room. The door swished closed with a muffled clank at the end.

"Good morning, Cole. I trust you slept well?"

Galen stepped farther into the room, placing the tray on the edge of Cole's bed. He looked up and smiled again as he lifted the cover on the plate, letting the aroma of fresh cinnamon rolls fill the dank, stale cell.

Despite himself, Cole leaned forward to take in the aroma. Looking up at Galen, he wondered if this was some sort of ruse. After his harsh treatment last night, how could Galen be so kind to him now?

"What's the matter, boy? Not hungry?" Galen pointed to the food. "It's a brand new day, time to start it off the right way. Let's discuss your daily agenda."

"You wouldn't let me talk yesterday. Why would I want to sit down and have breakfast with you?" Cole responded warily.

"What happened yesterday was a lesson for you. You will have many lessons in the upcoming days, when you —"

"I want to leave here, and see Emma," Cole interrupted.

"Well, your first lesson will be not to talk when I am talking. I could leave that as a warning, but unfortunately I will have to give you one demerit."

Galen sat his large bulk into the chair the guard had carried in. His body settled into the corners of the seat, his obese torso rolling over the arms. He seemed quite comfortable.

This left only the four-legged stool for Cole to sit on. The stool was a little too high for him to get comfortable. His feet only reached the ground if he slouched and pointed his toes, and then only barely scraping the floor.

"I don't care about being polite. I don't even know where I am, or why you've decided to keep me here, and until I find out or talk to my family, I won't be eating, reviewing agendas, or exchanging pleasantries with you." Cole thought himself clever.

"Well, then, I would guess our time is up for today." Galen rocked himself back up to a standing position and retrieved the serving tray with the rolls and steaming coffee.

The door opened and two guards came in, removing the chairs and the food. One guard took out a small white plate and placed it on Cole's bed. They left, leaving the door open.

"Before I take my leave, we still have to settle your one demerit." Galen fished in his vest pocket and took out a small red pill with two white stripes running vertically down its middle. He placed this on the plate.

He took a step back and stared at Cole.

Looking down at the striped pill, Cole was thoroughly confused. Obviously, he meant for him to swallow the pill, but to what gain?

"I'm not swallowing that. I don't even know what it is." Cole wrinkled his brow.

"You will eat this. It will cause you great pain," Galen replied.

Cole snickered out loud. It was a forced chuckle, meant to show defiance, but only affirmed to Cole's mentality that he was not in control here. Galen was so calm, his posture emanated total domination. Strained laughter seemed the only way to respond.

"Now that you told me, what the frag would I take it for at this point? If I'm being held captive, I sure wouldn't willingly allow you to hurt me."

"Because you need to learn something. You currently have your facts very misplaced. Number one, you have forgotten the greater good that LifeSpan causes in your life. I am here to help you remember the debt you owe to them. You are not my captive. You are here for reprogramming.

"Number two, you will do exactly as I say, when I say it, or you will only prolong this process, and further prolonging Emma's reprogramming."

Cole leapt to his feet. "You have Emma here too? Where is she? She wouldn't put up with this." Cole's mind was racing. From what he knew of Emma, she didn't mesh well with authority. That was an understatement. She would be fighting harder than anyone he knew. She probably already knocked out a few of the guards, maybe even Galen himself. But, that couldn't be. He saw her fall, he saw her body break under the Collector's massive blow. Even so, if there was a small chance she was still alive . . .

"You are a monster. LifeSpan is corrupt for sanctioning your actions. She's just a girl. Why would you hurt her?"

"Cole, my dear boy, I am not hurting her. You are."

"Oh? And how is that?"

"For every demerit you earn, she is given two. For every demerit you refuse to take, she is given four. So, let's relax and get this over with. Take the demerit, Cole, and I will see you at your next meal."

Galen left the room. The door swished shut behind him, leaving Cole staring down at his plate and the lone red pill.

Why would I take that? Because I think Emma is still alive? I saw her fall. I saw her eyes. I've never seen anyone dead before. I don't know anyone who has witnessed a real death. Everyone has his or her expiration, but apparently Emma was outside of that. She lived without an expiration. What did Mr. Stratus say? She had already expired? Her name was Jennifer. If she had already expired, how could she still be alive, unless there was a break in the system, unless LifeSpan was wrong. Of course something was wrong, or I wouldn't be in a place like this.

Hundreds of possibilities ran through Cole's mind.

Cole was pacing the room, looking back at the pill.

If there was a small chance that Emma was still alive, why would I want to cause her more harm? I do love her, and to save her any pain beyond what they have already done to her, I should take this pill.

Cole picked up the striped pill, rolling it between his fingers, and took a silent oath.

Whatever happens, Emma will be safe. When I get out of here, I'll tell the world. I'll stop LifeSpan, no matter the cost.

Cole tossed the red pill into his mouth.

He braced himself against the coming pain, and at first, nothing happened. He let his guard down ever so slightly, and then it arrived.

A wave of throbbing he didn't know could exist overwhelmed him. Worse than the Collector's baton, worse than anything his mind was anticipating. He fell to his knees, arms stiffened and hands clenched into fists. His skin burned, his head throbbed, and his stomach heaved. The small amount of food from the day before came up into his mouth, and he exhaled roughly to force the horrible tasting bile through his clenched teeth, drooling it onto the floor of his cell.

The pain lasted beyond his capacity to register time, and he slumped to the ground, his body stiff as a board. He felt himself pass out, then jolted awake, the nanos unwilling to let him give in so easily. So, as the time passed, Cole was cognizant of only varied levels of pain that ranged from stiffness, to shock, to convulsing and back to stiffness. Finally, mercifully, he passed out.

Cole stood along the pier, watching the water swirl around a floating stick, lapping along its side, trying to pull the stick under. They tugged back and forth, fighting each other continually, neither giving ground. Stick versus water. Cole took his eyes away for only a moment as a hand ran along his shoulders and down his arm. Emma wrapped her arms around him, looking for warmth. He could feel her breath on his neck. Cole moved up and pulled her closer. Turning, he looked into her eyes. The moonlight fell across her skin. Emma. Find me.

Cole jolted awake by the hissing swish of his cell door day after day. Galen and the two guards set the room. Cole fought back. Galen left a demerit for him.

Galen came in at night and gave Cole a thick blanket.

Galen took the blanket away before the next night.

Cole awoke, yelling Emma's name. Galen walked in, silver tray in hand, holding a brilliant white bowl, so white it was glowing in the poor lighting, blending into the smooth ivory walls. There was steam pouring out of the bowl, and Cole felt himself drawn to the contents. No matter what they were, his hunger was overwhelming. The only disarming feeling was the smell, or the lack of it. Cole wasn't sure he had full use of all his senses, so in the end, he dismissed the anomaly.

"Good morning, Cole. We have a long day ahead of us. Breakfast is here, nice and hot, just how I like it. Do you like your breakfast hot?" Galen was calm. His voice soothing and conversational. He glanced up the wall, towards the ceiling, completely oblivious to Cole. Or so he thought.

"I like my breakfast at home." Cole formed a fist, thinking to lash out, now when Galen was preoccupied. *Now. Do it.* Cole's mind screamed for action, and yet he continued to sit.

"Well, this is your home. You sleep here, you wake here, you are staying here. What else needs to be accomplished for you to call this your home?"

"Your home is where you choose it to be. I did not choose this place," Cole said defiantly. *Now. Jump at him! Jump!*

"Ah, yes. So, does a newborn child choose its home? Does the lost traveler choose his sanctuary?" Galen stared at Cole, waiting for an answer to his rhetorical question.

Cole shook his head, trying to dismiss where this conversation was going.

"You have chosen this place as your new dwelling, just the same as a baby would choose where to lay its head at night. More like the lost traveler, you have gone astray. It was brought upon him, as to you, by circumstance. You decided to act wrongly. We very kindly stepped in and brought you to a new safe haven. We are your new parents, giving you a roof over your head and food on your plate." Galen seemed quite proud of himself, but the mere mention of food sent Cole's stomach in a loop. He stood and walked over to the tray, reaching for the steaming rations.

"Not so fast, Cole. We have a few items for discussion first. Please, take a seat."

The guards brought back the stool every day. Cole sat.

This time his feet rested flat on the floor.

"Wasn't this stool a little taller?" Cole asked.

"Yes. You looked uncomfortable. I can give you comfort," Galen said.

Cole looked up at Galen. "Thank you."

"That's better, Cole." Galen leaned in. "See? We are making progress. Well done."

Galen handed him his breakfast.

OFFENSE

"We need to send a search group. We have to find out what happened. Something is wrong! Send anyone, send *me*!" Tym cried out to the ceiling, his head bobbing around in excitement.

"We cannot jump to conclusions," the Father exclaimed loudly enough for all in assembly to cease their separate conversations and whispers. How could he keep this group from running off in their own directions? He was experienced enough to see desperation sink into their tough exteriors.

The Movement was restless after a week of worry. Without fail, Emma had checked in with the underground group every night for years. She was meticulous in her reports and frequently sat to discuss her observations with the Father. Yet, she had not been seen for over ten days.

Gathered before him were the leaders of each division of the Movement.

He stood at the head of the table, nothing more than a large slab of weathered wood posts bolted together from the abandoned docks. To his left sat Wallace, chief scholar and orchestrator. He sat stoically in his chair, as always. His beard was meticulously trimmed to a neat point, riding away from his chin like a claw. He was a tall man. Some would call him lanky, but he preferred to think of himself as streamlined. Without Wallace, the Movement would be a disorganized mess.

"We have to believe she is in trouble!" Tym stood, waving his arms around.

The Father gently patted the air with his hands, gesturing for Tym to sit back down. Tym eventually composed himself enough to pull his sagging pants back up to his ribcage, and plopped down on his chair. He swung his magnifying glass back around his head, to just above his left eye.

"No," Gretchen calmly replied. Tall, imposing and the constant pessimist among the gathered council, it was no secret that she disliked Emma's forays into enemy territory. "We must carefully examine the facts. Emma was consistently involved with a subject who was deep in the LifeSpan network. This man, Cole, was an assignment that went too far. I think she has defected to LifeSpan."

"Impossible!" Tym jumped to his feet again, his eyes blinking rapidly. The action filled the room with clinking and ringing as various instruments, trinkets and chains settled themselves back into Tym's bulging pockets.

"Thank you for your input, Gretchen. The simple fact is we haven't heard from Emma. Of course, this is highly unusual for someone of her experience. Therefore, one assumption is Emma is in trouble. I highly doubt, after all her years and sacrifices for our organization, she has defected. While it is possible, please do not bring this investigation into the realm of hearsay. Let us only look at the facts."

The Father spoke in such a calm and reassuring tone, the room eventually settled down. Tym sank back into his chair, and Gretchen resumed her scowling.

"Very well. Perhaps Emma is simply slacking in her duties,

and failed to report. We should find out why, and decide whom to send out to find her," Gretchen stated to the group.

"I'll go!" Once again, Tym jumped, but failed to hold his balance, being pulled backwards by the sudden shift in weight from his backpack. He landed hard on his pack, rolling to the side, and spilling the contents onto the ground. Various springs, mechanized robot spiders and a cup of oil spilled out, among many other unidentified components. Gretchen glanced over her shoulder, hardly amused, as he crawled around to gather his scuttling gadgets. She made absolutely no move to help him.

"We also need to find Cole. If Emma is in trouble, he could be in a dangerous situation beyond his comprehension," the Father noted.

"Wallace, double-check Emma's secondary information check points." He held up a hand to stop Wallace from telling him how many times they had already checked the hot spots. "Just do it again. Do it for me."

Wallace bowed deeply, incapable of resisting his request.

The Father stopped and looked around this small group. So many relied on the decisions of these few minds. Wasn't that always the way it was throughout history? They would have to keep the wheel turning, and the Father was the one to do it. He paused briefly as he met each of their eyes.

"This may be the day we have feared," he said quietly. "Our collective intelligence points to us being exposed. However, we have received no sign from the outside world to verify this deduction. If we are not exposed, we are very lucky.

"Currently, we must act decisively, and with force. Each of you knows that it is never my first choice, but I feel we have run out of options. We will send Gretchen's soldiers, undoubtedly the greatest offensive force at our command."

"No!" Gretchen objected. The failed assignment is not worth —"

"Gretchen, remember his lineage. You owe him that much, at least," the Father interrupted.

"They are not ready for full deployment. I need a little more time."

"Time is what we don't have to spare! Don't you get it?" Tym threw in quickly.

"Gretchen, how much would you need?" the Father asked.

"One week. Give me at least that and we'll have a slightly better chance at success," Gretchen implored.

"It's already been over a week! You think we can sit around for *another* week while your boys shine their shoes and do push-ups?" Tym was turning red, motioning the push-up part.

"Very well then." The Father stood. "Gretchen, you have four days, and your army goes with our blessings. Tym, we need your skills to help the team when they go into the field. Gather as much reconnaissance and communication tech gadgets as you can. They'll need it to keep in touch with us."

Sci Tym jumped back, slowly pulling his Master Sci glove from his pack while singing a dramatic fanfare for effect.

"Make no mistake, there's no turning back. As we reveal Captain Ian and his soldiers, we are also revealing our weakness. If they are captured, or worse, if they do not return, we have no other recourse. This mission must not fail. Emma is too valuable to the future of our opposition, and Cole is bound to our destiny. Remember, we have four days. Then we toss everything into the fire. Let's hope we live through the flames."

THE CAPTAIN

Captain Ian walked down the line of soldiers, his boots clicking loudly on the hard tiled floor. They were standing at attention, hands clasped behind their backs, feet positioned slightly apart.

The soldiers stared forward, chins held high, and did not flinch as Ian stepped in front of each one, opening and closing their vest pockets.

They were equipped with a tactical vest of Sci Tym's design. Shoulder straps ran up and over, securely fastened to the torso. The vest was adorned with numerous pockets of various shapes and sizes, each bulging with supplies and offensive combat components. Sci Tym had even loaded the vests with a few surprises of his own.

Under the arms and along the side of each vest were webbing and buckles, connecting the front and back panels securely against the torso, form-fitted to each soldier. The suits and all of the items attached were non-magnetic. Sci Tym was adamant about every single piece formed from a high-density plasteel of his own recipe.

Their pants were loose and tucked into the tall buckled boots that ran up to mid-calf. Long, narrow sheaths were sewn into the sides of the boots, fastening thin daggers for emergency use. That's what these soldiers were trained for, emergency use.

I guess that's what this is, Ian thought.

Captain Ian knew they were walking into an unfamiliar situation and cursed Cole for forcing them to play their hand at this early stage. He had trained Emma. She was too slick to get caught. This *boy* was the real reason he was leading his army into battle. There was a high probability of engaging a Collector. He also knew they were not ready for that, not yet.

The soldiers stretched and moved, testing their absorption panels sewn into their suits. These panels were shaped around each muscle and separated at the joints to move with the men. They lessened injury from falls, punches and even pressurized energy blasts.

Captain Ian looked back down the line of soldiers. The first assembled army in over 250 years stood before him.

This army of ten soldiers, including me. Captain Ian knew it wasn't the size of the dog in the fight that mattered.

Not exactly the masses he read about in histories of famous war campaigns, but it would have to do. He had also read numerous historical speeches given by great leaders before sending their troops into treacherous situations.

Let's see what I can do, Captain Ian thought.

"Soldiers, fall in!" he yelled from deep within his chest. Every soldier snapped to attention and walked over to their captain.

"We have received news from Wallace. Emma has been found." The soldiers let out a cheer. Captain Ian raised a fist. The room fell silent immediately. "Listen up! We are focusing only the mission facts. Wallace does not have a confirmed sighting of Emma. However, he has located her assignment, Cole. We all know Emma. Every one of you has worked with her. Some in the field, most in the fighting ring. She always has a plan. *Always.* If Cole is important to Emma, he is now part of our mission.

"What we are about to attempt transcends any logical thought. *Tonight* we are openly opposing LifeSpan. We shall endure! *Tonight* we put our training to the test."

Captain Ian paused.

"Wallace has confirmed Collectors are guarding the site."

Only one man shuffled.

"Make no mistake, we are entering enemy territory. Our mission is not diplomacy! We are taking back what belongs to us, and woe to any that stands in our path. We will engage!"

Their response surprised Captain Ian. He expected a hearty "Yessir! Instead he received the cheer, "For Emma!"

"Let's show them what we are made of!"

"For Emma!" came their reply.

"We shall endure!" Captain Ian yelled.

He waited, looking each man in the eyes.

"For the Movement!" Captain Ian cheered, and the soldiers echoed.

Many of them will die tonight. A man wants to know what he's dying for. Captain Ian knew. *For Emma.*

The gray transport lumbered down the street, covered with dust and dirt. Nobody gave the sad looking truck another glance. That was the point, for if they could see through the solid, armor-plated exterior, they would be surprised at the cargo. There was no driver. The coordinates were already programmed into the guidance system.

Captain Ian was seated in the back with his soldiers. He looked again at their faces, some preparing internally, eyes closed, breathing controlled. Others were reviewing their buckles, checking the fit and stretch of their armor. Ian was thinking about their destination: the esteemed Montgomery Hospital, naturally long-since converted into a museum.

After the introduction and acceptance of Nanomedicine, hospitals were one of the first institutions finding their services no longer needed.

According to Wallace's spy network, the reprogramming facility was buried underneath the museum. A perfect cover. The museum rarely received visitors.

Each soldier was studying a computer drawing on their digiscreens: a small map rotating on a central axis, pulsing in and out. The emerald-green framework and translucent walls were a digital representation of the underground passages in the museum. Their information was extracted from echo transmissions measuring the surrounding pavement and lower sewer readings.

The readings were taken at a safe distance, stressing the range of their machines, while surrendering high-definition renderings. Because of this rather patchy process, there were large sections of the underground map that were missing, leaving many variables, and as a byproduct, many potential traps.

Captain Ian did not enjoy variables. Nor did he like faulty information that could lead to his team being stuck below ground, without a map for extracting themselves, the enemy surrounding them.

After the soldiers committed the map to memory, they switched over to a digital recording of Cole and Emma, running from the Collectors. They could not find any records on Cole, registered with LifeSpan, but that was to be accepted. Most likely, they were trying to erase him from the system. Luckily, Wallace had secured the security footage before it was purged.

Captain Ian focused on Cole's image, freezing the footage.

If any harm has come to Emma, you will answer to me, the Captain promised.

REPROGRAMMING

Cole was strapped tightly to the table. Looking around the room, he saw two Doctors clothed in long, flowing, silken white robes. They waited patiently, arms hanging beneath the many folds of fabric cascading down their bodies. They were looking across the room to a black window. Cole did not struggle. Galen had said they could no longer be friends. Cole was a failure.

After weeks of education, he had let Galen down. If only he had listened better, Emma wouldn't have had to die. Galen said Cole had too many demerits, and she paid the price for his insolence. He deserved to be reprogrammed. Emma died for him, and he could not change.

Cole had fallen in a deep depression, void of any desire to change.

The Doctors continued to wait.

Galen promised that after reprogramming, they could meet again. Galen would be there for him. He was always there for Cole. Cole's mind drifted through the last few weeks . . .

An electric voice broadcasted through the room. "You may commence with the reprogramming. He is of no use to us."

The Doctors followed the Voice and began. The process was painful, as nano groups were taken out of his system and run through a central reprogramming machine. Cole's remaining nanos raced to repair the extraction wound as the newly reprogrammed bots were forced back into his body. This was repeated as another nano group was extracted, and the repair bots picked up the pace.

During the process, Cole was humiliated by the Voice, forced to repent and constantly repeat the glory of LifeSpan. "We are lost. LifeSpan is the compass." Cole begged for them to destroy him. He didn't deserve another chance. *Where is Galen now?* he wondered.

"Because you have information we need, Cole. You are the resistance leader. Galen no longer cares for you. Your family despises you. You have failed your mother," the Voice continued.

"No. She was leaving to get better." Cole couldn't remember anymore.

"You controlled Emma. You are too important for us to lose you. You must be punished for starting the Movement. You betrayed Emma. You are hurting everyone you loved. You saved Emma. Saved the Movement. Destroyed your family."

Insult. Praise. Insult.

The reprogramming continued as Cole gave up.

The Voice did not relent.

Ian's men stormed the hospital, clearing room by room. Their training paid off, as they neutralized every threat. They stomped guards, overwhelmed unsuspecting museum workers and eventually burst into a room of Doctors and Scientists standing over a thrashing man. Captain Ian recognized Cole. He gave the signal for his men to take out everyone else.

It was a one-sided battle, as trained soldiers quickly took control of the room.

Soon, Captain Ian stood over Cole.

"Cole! We are sent by the Father to bring you both back. Where is Emma?" the Captain asked.

"She's gone. Far from us." Cole was trying to get his bearings.

"Where can I find her? We have to leave."

"Galen said I could have saved her. It wasn't my fault. We tried to run. She's broken. They broke her, but I wouldn't break, and she was punished. We are all LifeSpan in the end . . . ," Cole mumbled, and drifted away.

Agent McHenry approached the two of them.

"Captain, I request we leave him. Continue looking for Emma," McHenry suggested.

"Hold. We came for Cole too."

"What were they doing? What is all of this?" McHenry asked as he looked around.

"I . . . don't know. . . . They were reprogramming me." Cole stood, leaning heavily on Captain Ian for support. "There is a machine where the nanos were fed. They changed, reprogrammed, and threw them back into me. Emma would have loved that power."

Captain Ian looked around, realizing this machine would be invaluable in Sci Tym's hands. Cole could still be a liability if his nanos were reprogrammed to be pro-LifeSpan.

That's all right. We have a solution for nanos in the body, Captain Ian thought.

"Duggan, McHenry, gather up Cole and pull this machine. It's all coming back with us."

Cole and the two soldiers busied themselves with tracing wires and pulling apart the processing array. As it turned out, the reprogramming pod was a cylinder, no larger than an oversized backpack, but heavy enough for two men to barely lift.

As Cole's senses were clearing, he remembered the Voice.

The Doctors were always looking to the tinted window. That's the heart of this place. The brains. Cole knew it must be destroyed.

He ran from the room, leaving McHenry and Duggan to drag the pod away.

Cole approached the booth with caution. He noticed the door was open, unable to slide shut from a fallen Doctor casualty from the soldiers' raid. He heard movement inside the room, and decided to take them by surprise.

I hope there's only one, Cole thought. *Why can't I stay out of trouble?*

He jumped over the body and charged into the room. A heavy-set figure fell back as Cole grabbed him by the collar. They tumbled back, each fighting for the upper hand. Cole knew after his reprogramming, he had very little true strength left, and his adrenaline was slowing down. In one last push, Cole pulled the man around and threw him with newfound energy. He hit the main control dock hard and slid off.

Cole stepped back to see if this Doctor would rise.

However, this was no Doctor. Galen looked up from where he fell, blood pouring from his face.

"Cole, my savior, you've returned to me," Galen said with a weak smile.

Cole wanted to run over and help him. Galen was his friend, after all. Cole was the one who was tainted.

I turned in my mother. I was the one who hurt . . . Cole's mind raced.

However, with the door blocked open, Cole could hear Galen's voice over the speakers, echoing through the room. It was the Voice.

"It was *you*." Cole didn't know what was real anymore. "*The*

Voice! How could you! You were my teacher. You said LifeSpan sent me here for reprogramming." Cole tried to sort through the lies.

"Never! I came back to save you," Galen reasoned.

"From whom?" Cole asked.

"The Movement, of course. We knew you were the leader. Once your mother was taken away, the mantle passed to you. We knew they would try to rescue you. So, we were prepared." Galen smiled. "Your friends are trapped. See for yourself."

Cole looked down into the room, as Captain Ian threw a Doctor across the room.

"Oh, what have I done?" Cole asked quietly when the Doctor landed.

Cole turned back to Galen, but he was gone.

I can still use the information here. The screens surrounding him were logged in from Galen, and Cole's name was still flashing through the procedure. His files were here, his life was here. Cole could end this now, try to erase his entire existence according to LifeSpan.

However, connected to Cole's file were others. Loved ones' files. The whole Jenkins line was here, following his mother's last name, which Jon took as his own.

He opened the digifiles: Jon Jenkins, Mary Jenkins, Hester Jenkins.

He saw his father's memories playing above him. Cole saw his harsh treatment at the hands of the Doctors. Cole wept as he watched his father thrashing in his seat. He witnessed his draining.

Cole watched the recording of Galen torturing his mother and his aunt. He saw them fall under his glove, drained of life.

Cole's innocence was drained with them, and he vowed to stop LifeSpan at all costs.

"Time's up! Move out!" Captain Ian ordered. "Where is Cole?"

"No, you cannot take him," a Doctor said, holding the side of his bloody head. "He still doesn't understand the glory of LifeSpan."

Captain Ian turned, grabbed the Doctor by his coat, and leaned in. "Do I look like someone who cares about the *glory* of LifeSpan?" Ian smiled.

He pulled the Doctor up as he stood, still holding the Doctor's coat, and threw him across the room. The Doctor slid across the floor toward the door. His body was abruptly stopped by an outstretched white boot, and a large, cloaked figure stepped into the room. He was not smiling.

Agent Rufus saw three Collectors walk into the room. "Party's over, boys," Rufus said to the soldiers, under his breath.

The Collectors spread out.

"Duggan, McHenry, find Cole and get him out! Tell the Father we are sorry for his loss. Emma was a true soldier." Ian never took his eyes off of the Collectors as he spoke. Walking sideways, his hands were moving around his armor, checking his pockets, loosening straps. His men did the same. Some were even digging their heels in, like cats ready to pounce.

The lead Collector reached into his robe and produced the standard billy club. They realized anyone who would openly challenge a Collector was a fool, and anyone who was wearing armor was an instant threat. Hopefully they were a challenge.

Captain Ian was nervous, but careful not to let it show. He couldn't let his soldiers down, not now, not while facing the one threat they had trained so hard to beat. But their training had been cut short, and Ian doubted they were ready.

The Collectors were an incredible force, true, but they also had weaknesses, and his men were charged with finding those and exploiting them. They had run this scenario too many times to count in the virtual simulator.

One thing Ian did know was their strengths, enough to give them all the respect as fellow soldiers.

Inexperienced and outnumbered. Yes, eight to three is not in our favor, Captain Ian thought. *We will take casualties today. Emma was the first to fall.*

"For Emma!" Captain Ian yelled.

His soldiers echoed and charged forward.

The Collectors stood against them like stone pillars parting rushing waters.

A red-bearded Collector faced off against two soldiers and Captain Ian. He was the unfortunate one to have three on him, but he didn't seem worried. The Collector spun and dived, flaring his heavy cloak all around him, keeping the soldiers at bay.

The soldiers watched for an opening, finding none. The soldier on Captain Ian's left ran out of patience and decided to charge into the Collector, baton raised.

The Collector grabbed the edge of his cloak and pulled quickly, dragging the hem across the soldier's chest as he reached his target. The soldier felt a burst of pain and looked down to see that his armor was cut across his abdomen, exactly where the plates separated under his rib cage. Blood was pouring out of the opening, and he dropped to his knees, arms pulled in tightly to stem the flow. The Collector stepped back, letting his cloak fall, blood dripping from the razor-edged hem.

Captain Ian looked down at his fallen man, saw another fall in the corner of his eye, and cursed. He took a step back and reached into a pouch tied to the back of his belt. *Let's try this*, he thought.

The middle Collector was actually on the defensive. His two attackers were fearless, to the point of being reckless. He had a small bruise on his cheek from a lucky blow and was able to retaliate with a few kicks and punches of his own. Their armor had proven to be very resilient against bludgeoning; it resisted his force, dissipating it through the panel he struck.

He calculated the most productive use of his offense, tucked his billy club back into the jacket clip and retreated a few steps to prepare a strike. The Collectors were trained in the old way of fighting, the Bellicose Method, by Nimbus himself. They knew a time would come when they would exert their true force, not just escorting the recently expired to the Grand Hall of Collection.

He saw the fear in these two soldiers. He could probably wait for them to be sloppy. Their eventual exhaustion would lead to mistakes, but he was never the patient one. He curled his fingers to resemble a claw and dashed forward, angling his arm down.

The lead soldier pulled his foot back, thinking he was trying to pull him down, just as the Collector planned. Instead, he leaped at his chest. The soldier was off balance and unable to defend against the full weight of the Collector pouncing onto his chest, crouched like a feral cat. Both men fell, with the Collector landing on top.

The soldier was pinned and trying to tuck his knees between them to kick the surprisingly heavy Collector off of him. He could see his comrade beating on the back of the Collector with his own baton, to no avail. The Collector barely noticed his strikes as he reached forward and grabbed the soldier's neck covering. He pulled down with both hands, tearing the armor from his neck.

Suddenly the Collector had his billy club in his hands and pressed it to the soldier's neck, smiling triumphantly as he released the sonic wave against their nanos. Nothing happened.

"That only works on your puppets. I tore those nanos out from my body long ago. You cannot affect me," the soldier spat in his face.

"We've had some recent upgrades, thanks to that rogue girl." The Collector tilted the billy club, angling it so the soldier could see two wires running out of the bottom and back up his sleeve. The Collector depressed an alternate button on the club and an incredible surge of electricity discharged through the weapon and into the soldier's neck. The soldier's scream brought a quick glance from those battling in the room, pausing the fighting momentarily.

The current of power continued to course through his body as the Collector held his baton there. Even after the soldier was dead, the Collector continued driving it more deeply into the soldier's neck as the flesh burned away, smiling all the while.

Agent Rufus knew he had to switch tactics. His partner fell to this electric Collector, and beating him did little to stop the berserker. Rufus dropped his baton and dug in one of his pockets. *Posterior Pouch L15*, as Sci Tym called it.

I don't care where I get it, as long as it works, Agent Rufus thought as he slid a slender tube out of its plastique sleeve. He threw it at the Collector's shoulder, where it shattered.

The Collector stood, staring at the soldier, and reached over to touch the sticky goo making its way down his shoulder.

"Well, now." He was brushing the gel with the back of his hand, only spreading the sinuous jelly further around with his glove. "Is the child finished with his tantrum? Now you throw your juice at me? Is this supposed to stop me from frying you like your friend?"

Agent Rufus fished another tube from an adjacent pocket strapped to his arm.

"No. But this should slow you down." He popped the top off with his thumb and splashed a pale green liquid at the Collector.

His reaction was quicker than the soldier had anticipated, diving to the side. The Collector almost avoided the solution entirely. Unfortunately for him, only a small amount of Tym's combustion fluid needed to combine with the jelly.

Dense blue flames leaped up the Collector's arm, spreading across the sticky jelly, feeding off of the chemical reaction's energy. The Collector flew into a rage, trying to remove his jacket before the flames spread. It was too late. The chemicals bonded into a liquid magma, soaking through the fabric and devouring flesh and bone. His arm became useless as the muscle was dissolved from the bones. Still, the magma spread, eating away his abdomen and dripping wherever he flailed. His legs were soon destroyed, removing his ability to stand. The Collector slumped to the ground, attempting to rise, to no avail.

"One down and two to go. No problem," Agent Rufus said.

He turned to survey the room, assessing where he would be most useful. He saw his comrades sorely pressed to fend off the other Collectors. Five men were down; only Captain Ian, one other soldier, and he were standing. Suddenly, the odds were no longer in their favor, if they ever were to begin with.

Captain Ian met his eyes and flashed two fingers then three in a circular motion.

The sign for retreat.

He fully agreed with that decision, and ran to his Captain's side. They joined their last soldier and the three of them went running down the hall. Behind them, they could hear the low electronic whine as the Collectors charged up their energy suits to follow.

Ian saw the bright silver line running down the hall, embedded in the upper part of the wall. Just like outside, and all across the city, these metallic tracks would allow the Collectors to move at incredible speeds. Most of the population thought this speed was a powerful technology given to the Collectors to aid in their expiration retrievals. It was, but it was mostly to spell doom for anyone attempting to flee a Collector's wrath. The track was a highly charged magnetized connection from the strip to the Collector's chest plate. The whole system ran on a specialized frequency. Fortunately, the soldiers had another surprise in store.

Glancing over his shoulder, Ian saw the first Collector swing around the exit and smoothly enter the hallway, his feet settling back to the ground after being pulled the short distance by his magnets. The other Collector joined him in the hall, getting his bearings. They floated off of the ground a few inches and accelerated towards Ian and company.

"Attention, soldiers, we are running Scenario Three Six Two. Wait for my signal." Captain Ian said over his radio. As they ran, each soldier pulled a drawstring from around his wrist. A long pocket ran up the lengths of their arms. The pocket's contents were single flat stilettos. These custom blades, shining silver from edge to edge, were hinged on the widened end and held tiny springs loaded into their hilt.

As the soldiers ran, every downward swing of their arm dispensed a stiletto, tossing them behind the men. As each of the blades flew out from the pockets, they were no longer under tension, and their springs popped open in mid-flight. Folding out from itself, each stiletto became a five-pronged star, dropping onto the ground below.

Another folded blade dropped into the arm holster to take the vacant space and was just as quickly thrown behind.

Soon the hallway was littered with blossoms of silver, each side laser-sharpened. The magnetically charged Collectors glided over them with no way to maneuver around the soldiers' trap.

Captain Ian knew this was a fatal mistake, for the stilettos were made of the same compound as the gleaming tracks on the wall. The two Collectors each attracted a dozen of the blades. Tuned into the exact frequency as the track and the stiletto stars, their magnetic chest plates could not distinguish between the two. The clusters rose in the air and flew into the Collectors. The sharpened points had little trouble piercing the suits, and blood splashed out of their backs. Overwhelmed, their suits powered down, no longer supporting the Collectors' levitation. As their feet touched the ground, both Collectors slumped to their knees, spitting blood, and collapsed to the floor.

Thanks again, Tym. I don't know how you did it, but you found the right tuning, Ian thought, and the soldiers ran out into the night.

ESCORT

Cole walked the halls to his new home, hidden deep underground.

We are heading to safety, lying low for a while. Captain Ian was very clear the night of their escape; nobody would know what had happened. Emma was gone. His aunt and mother were taken from him. His own father was handed over. His old life seemed like a series of terrible conclusions, each outdoing the previous.

The Movement's headquarters were actually in an elaborate underground city, long forgotten in the LifeSpan expansions. On the surface, LifeSpan thrived. Citizens had no idea their current town was built on top of history.

Literally built over everything, Cole joked. *New houses placed on top of the old, leaving this town as a shadow. The basement of humanity. Come on down for some fun and leave the sunlight behind.*

It had taken Cole the better part of four days to learn his way through his section, let alone the extra floors of the building around him. The Father stressed that Cole was never allowed to be without a guard.

Today, he was guarded by Sci Tym. He was the only one in the complex Cole considered a friend. Their immediate connection so long ago in Emma's house was a turning point in Tym's life too. He knew the Father was a friend to him, but he was always so serious, burdened with responsibility.

Tym didn't have that weight on his shoulders when Cole was around. Looking over at his friend, Tym felt guilty for deceiving him while Cole was alone here. The Father had been watching him secretly with tiny video drones, another great invention of Tym's. The Father and Tym had reviewed the footage, and had concluded that Cole was not a threat.

They had noticed a hardening of character, but nothing they were worried about. They needed to evaluate the long-term effects of his time in the LifeSpan reprogramming facility. So far, he was the same Cole they remembered, but with an edge.

That was why the Father agreed to meet with Cole today. This was a momentous time for Cole. It was his first meeting since he was liberated by Captain Ian and his soldiers.

Any mention of the soldiers around Sci Tym was a topic to be avoided. Tym was overcome with sadness for the fallen soldiers. They had risked so much for Emma, and they didn't even know she was never in the facility. Instead, they were left with rescuing Cole.

Upon their return, the soldiers were especially vocal about their disappointing mission. To make matters worse, when Tym was unavailable to guard Cole, Captain Ian took his place. He keenly felt Ian's hatred. Cole reminded Ian of his soldiers' sacrifices and their fruitless rescue mission.

The two men stopped walking, and Tym nodded toward a door. It was pale gray, totally smooth from top to bottom with no other markings or switches on the door facing. It didn't seem out of place from any other door, except this one did not automatically swish open when they stopped.

"This is the Father's room, isn't it?" Cole asked.

"Yes. He has wanted to see you ever since he heard you were free," Tym admitted.

"Then why did he wait until now? I've been out for days." Cole couldn't help blurting out his frustrations.

"Already that long? Time flies. . . . Well, that's a good question." Tym was stammering, wringing his hands as he bobbed back and forth. "He is a very busy man and he, uhmm, had other appointments to attend to, and he—"

"Tym, you are a very bad liar," Cole cut him off. "You could just tell me he didn't trust me and wanted a few days to watch me."

Tym smiled at the blatant truth in his statement.

"You really are a trouble maker, aren't you?" he joked with Cole.

Then he stepped forward and placed his arms straight along his body at both sides and bowed to the door, tucking his chin in as much as possible, moving his head only a fraction. Cole thought this was an absurd way to greet a locked door. Usually, the visitor would place his palm on the surface, and if the resident were expecting you, the door would swish open. Obviously, the Father would be expecting them.

Without touching the door in any way, it swished open to reveal the room beyond.

Tym ushered Cole inside, and immediately his eyes were drawn to the sheer scale of such a place. The walls, reaching up over fifty feet before they met the ceiling, were completely covered with makeshift shelving. Each shelf bowed under the weight of many books. Thousands and thousands of books were littered throughout the room! The floor beside him, the desk to his right, and even the elongated conference table were stacked with books of every shape and size. Some looked very old. They would have to be. Cole couldn't remember the last time a book was published outside of a digiscreen novella. A book was very rare to have, not because of any illegality of the product, but more so because of the ancient process. It took so long to actually bind and complete a crafted novel. Most books written were published as they were typed, immediately available as a digiscreen download. Books were even released chapter by chapter if need be.

"I see you are impressed." The soft-spoken voice brought Cole out of his wonderment and he realized it was the Father's, coming from the center of the room. Cole stepped forward and peered around a stack of novels over twice his height. Indeed, the Father was sitting at a large, wooden, carved desk, incredibly old-fashioned. He appeared at ease, grinning, and his eyes twinkled.

Unfortunately, the Father was not alone at his desk.

Captain Ian was standing at his right. Arms crossed behind his back, his face was a scowl of disgust as he looked Cole over.

His hatred for Cole was very apparent. Cole understood the gravity of losing men in the field; "fallen" was how they were referred to around the Movement's membership. With even that being considered, there was still one question that remained, and Cole almost voiced it aloud. Why was Ian so angry with him? At this point, it must be personal.

The Father nodded to him and Captain Ian stood straighter.

How was that possible? Cole mocked.

The captain tugged his many-pocketed vest and nodded to the Father.

Ian turned and walked straight for Cole, staring him dead in the eyes as he crossed the room. Cole tensed, feeling a confrontation on the way. At the last moment, Ian turned slightly and only clipped Cole's shoulder with his own. Still, it felt like he was slammed by a boulder, and Cole stumbled back half a step.

With a sarcastic huff, Captain Ian left through the sliding door. Cole watched him walk down the hallway as the door swished

shut. Surprisingly, he could still see the captain even after the door
was closed. It occurred to him the door was made of a one-way
vision-blocking material, and further revealed that the Father and
Captain Ian were watching Cole and Tym standing before the door
as Tym had given the signal, a respectful bow. Possibly, they could
hear them too.

Cole realized he would have to watch his step in this new
underground. It clearly was not his home.

"Hello, Professor Lander," Cole joked, using his alternate
name. "I *am* impressed. I never knew there were so many books
in one place outside of a museum." Cole was brought back to his
gawking. He didn't doubt you could have all of these books on
a digiscreen, but the actual original manuscripts were definitely
exciting to have access to. Who had read these before him? How
many places, homes, and cultures had these books been passed
through?

"Please, call me Father if you are comfortable. Everyone else
does." The Father stood, looking around the room, following
Cole's gaze across the bookshelves. "Truthfully, these were from
a museum. It was a long time ago, when LifeSpan was vigorously
expanding their corporate borders. Many historical institutions
were no longer needed. Hospitals, libraries, treasuries, to name just
a few.

"Cole, sit down." The Father waited until he found a seat. "I am
sorry for your losses. I knew your mother and your Aunt Hester."

Cole wept. Finally, after all this time, he found a connection to
his family. He thought back to the meetings with Emma, and this
Professor Lander—the Father. Given the circumstances, he was
now the only family Cole had anymore.

They talked for many hours. Cole relived his tragedies, and the
Father listened.

Again, Cole stood at the entrance to the Father's room. Of course, this time he knew that whoever was sitting in the room could see him. Cole bowed lightly, holding up the two glasses and a bottle of the Father's favorite drink for his new-found mentor. At their last meeting, the Father mentioned his love for apple juice, of all things. The door swished open.

"Hello, my friend." As always, the Father's voice was instantly soothing, draining Cole of all tension, inviting and welcoming him as a kindred spirit. Cole stepped inside and worked his way around a few containers full of newly acquired supplies. Canisters of what appeared to be liquid cooling tanks, heat registers and a jet-black coat, so immensely dark that it absorbed the light that would have reflected on the fabric.

What is the point of that? Cole resolved to ask later.

"I see you brought a most delectable drink. Let's share. Please sit."

Cole grabbed a plasteel cube close to where he was standing and sat quietly, waiting for the Father to start their session.

"Today, you will choose our topic." The Father poured himself a glass, and leaned back in his chair.

Cole was taken aback. They had many of these sessions over the last few weeks, and he was always questioned and guided, and their conversation usually ended in deep thought. They had discussed his interrogations at the hands of LifeSpan, his days with his aunt, and his broken future with LifeSpan. They had shared a deep sadness at the loss of Emma, her time here with the Movement, and her incredible courage. Cole knew his life was forever changed and he had nowhere to go from here that would not involve the Movement. That's what he should be asking about.

Cole looked the Father in the eye.

"Let's talk about you."

"Well done, my boy! I was waiting for this request." The Father hopped in his chair with excitement. "I was actually just like you. I used to work at LifeSpan, back before you were born. In fact, you could say I started Division 3. More or less."

"What happened? Did you meet a rebellious young woman who introduced you to a secret society of freedom fighters?" Cole thought himself pretty slick.

"Hardly. That would have been more glamorous than what actually happened. The gradual downslide happened over many, many years." The Father took on a nostalgic pose, looking back through the years, peering across their room.

"I was noticing during my time overseeing the incredible developments in our global company, a few benefits to society were grossly overstated. Lifespan became greedy and unprincipled."

Cole learned a great deal that day and his respect for the Father strengthened. Years ago, the Father discovered LifeSpan was corrupt, and nobody realized it. They tried to silence him with demotions and threats, but he escaped and was hunted by the Collectors.

"I was eventually caught by them, y'know," the Father revealed. "They beat me, severely. Tortured me with their billy clubs for many hours before they bound me. They were going to take me back to him. To Nimbus."

"You escaped them again?" Cole was mesmerized. "How?"

"Luck, my boy. Pure luck. I leapt out of the transport, rolling and squirming like a worm. I happened to be next to a venting pipe when I hit the ground. I dived down an active gas-exhaust line, into the sewers. The pipe was full of flames and smoke so thick I couldn't breathe."

"What?! How did you survive? What happened?" Cole was on the edge of his seat.

"I burned. My clothing melted along with my skin. I felt my bindings burn away, and I fell free, hands flailing before landing in a pit. I was on fire, all of me. I could feel my hair and skin falling from me. The nanos did their job and kept me conscious. Instinctively I rolled, attempting to smother the flames from my clothing. However, I was choking on the rising gases. Unable to breathe, wracked with pain, and still on fire, I fell to my knees and died."

"Wait, repeat that last part again. You died?" Cole asked.

"It's true. The Collectors looked down at their scanners and knew my life had ceased. Called off their search and— Are you alright, Cole?"

"Yeah, yeah. Please continue, so I know this is real and I haven't been meeting with a ghost for the last few weeks."

"Ah, that. Unbeknownst to LifeSpan, I had a group of nanobots dedicated to one purpose. They would jumpstart my heart if ever the need arose. I awoke some time later, gasping for air as the smoke machines turned off. There I was, back from the brink, lying in a pool of silver iridescent syrup. My nanos. They must have been disrupted when I died. I gathered up as many as I could in a discarded metal jar. For this second life, I took the title of the Father, and continued my fight against LifeSpan."

"Where do I come in to all of this? Why do you trust me inside the Movement?" Cole asked.

"Oh, my boy, you are full of many talents. For starters, Sci Tym and I have tried for years to reprogram groups of nanos. Suddenly, you return with Captain Ian's men and LifeSpan's closely guarded reprogramming pod. You know their systems; you have an incredible knowledge of computer technology. You are a lot like me, Cole. Except, for right now, your body can still heal."

"I know I have the nanos in my system. They are in everyone, and they help you." Cole turned away, hanging his head. "They are supposed to help, but Galen was able to hurt me, and he said it was from the nanos in my body. Somehow, he set them against me."

"Yes, Cole, you have survived where others would have perished. You learned first hand that the nanos can hurt. They control your body's every function; every cell is tuned in to their frequency," the Father explained. "The nanos can only control your body from the inside. Galen was able to turn that against you. He was able to disrupt their original programming, albeit only briefly, but effectively. The very instruments of your health turned on their host and started to damage you on a cellular level. Then they repaired you, on a cellular level. It was a vicious cycle of rending and mending."

Cole sat down and digested what the Father was telling him.

"Father, how do I stop them from hurting me? I don't want anyone to be able to control me like that. Not ever again."

The Father turned away from Cole, and let his robe fall beyond his shoulders to expose his back. Cole caught his breath. Looking at the Father's back, he was aghast at the amount of damage evident. His skin was rippled and stretched.

The results looked like he was wrapped in a spider's web of loose flesh. As the Father moved his arms to shuffle his robe back up, the skin twisted and shifted, like it was meant for a man twice his size. The color was a pale yellow with vibrant swirls of pink just under the surface.

"The nanos can be removed. Unfortunately, there is a side effect to eradicating them from your body."

"You can't heal. Is this what happens when fire touches your skin?" Cole asked, sympathetically reaching out.

"Yes, Cole, skin is not very durable when exposed to high heat. It melts like wax. Hurts, too. But without the nanos, I could do very little against the flames," the Father replied, tying off his robe belts and pulling the collar more closely to his neck.

"Well, at least you are free. I still have men like Galen searching for me," Cole lamented. "So I hide. We all hide, unable to act!"

"Who says we are not proactive?"

"Why else would you all be down here, hidden from the surface?" Cole reasoned, believing he was just stating the obvious. "You have hundreds of defenseless residents, just waiting for Galen's glove to visit and break you all."

"Is that so? Why do you believe his glove would have any power here?"

"His glove controls nanos . . . ." Cole was connecting the pieces now.

"Cole, the only one here with nanos by choice is Tym. Everyone you see, including me, is free." The Father walked over to Cole now, laying his hand on his shoulder. "Easy part is getting them out of your body. You just have to die."

"Then why don't the nanos pour out during the expirations?"

The Father paused and smiled.

"Ah, my boy, you are finally starting to think for yourself," the Father congratulated.

The Father walked across the room and exited, the door swishing shut behind him.

Cole jumped from his seat and ran to keep up.

"Well, if I wanted to die, I may as well return to the surface and have the Collectors do the job!" Cole yelled.

"That would be too easy. Besides, we actually enjoy you being alive. Don't you?" the Father responded with a wink, continuing down the corridor, leading him further underground.

"The hard part is destroying them, so I trap them. They are confused, but very much alive. Those little machines are always ready to bond with another host." After walking in silence, the Father turned into a small room and unlocked a heavy iron door located in the far rear. He stepped inside and a series of motion-activated lights illuminated a wall of shelves. Each shelf was filled with plastique jars. Hundreds of them.

"The only way to get rid of the nanos in the body is to fool them. When they sense that a host has died, they have nothing to control. Their biological programming ceases. This makes the nanos retreat from the body. They pour out as an oily liquid, out from every orifice, every pore, moving on their own accord," the Father said.

"Where do they go?" Cole was shocked.

"They try to find another host. They are always searching for a host. It is their sole purpose when they are not fused with a body. When they bond with another group of nanos, they share their information and assimilate."

"So, when they leave the body, that's when you trap them? In these jars?" Cole stepped into the room, walking up to the nearest shelf and peered inside the tinted jars. There was indeed an oily liquid inside, no more than a cup full at the most. A casual glance could mistake this for syrup, but it . . . moved. Slowly the liquid climbed up the side of the jar, and swirled inside, shifting with each small successive wave.

Cole remembered the pain and humiliation Galen was able to inflict on him. He was beaten down just to heal again. Never in control of his body. He hated LifeSpan for having that power. Now he had the reprogramming pod to make sure nobody had to go through that again. He just wanted the nanos out. He wanted to be in control of his own body.

"Father, kill me. As soon as you can. I need to die," Cole begged.

THE REMOVAL

Later that night, Cole was led to a provisional room built in the far corners of the Movement's headquarters. It was roughly square, only six feet across, made of clear plastique and reinforced with bands of plasteel. There was a single, clear door leading into the room, with a locking bar on the outside. The floor was a floating metal grate built over a funnel.

"I know you have been trying to reprogram the nanos and leave them in the body, but for now, this is the only way." Cole placed his hand on the old man's shoulder. "I don't want to wait. I don't want anyone to have this power over me."

"Cole, if you would please remove your clothing so the nanos have nowhere to go except down, through the grating." The Father was gentle, his eyes sad.

They looked into each other's eyes and knew there was no other way.

Cole looked at Tym, who was checking the controls and trying to avoid Cole's stare. The room began to hiss, and Cole glanced up at the large tanks of gas mounted to the ceiling. Tubes from these tanks fed into small holes at the bottom of the room. Cole knew what they would bring: death.

"Remember, you don't have to do this if you are not ready," the Father chimed in.

"I'm ready." Cole removed his clothing and stepped into the room.

The grating was cold on his bare feet. The room had a rusted odor, like metal stored in a wet warehouse. Cole turned around and noticed a crowd was forming outside of his enclosed cube. For many of them, this was his test to prove loyalty to the Movement. Some still believed Cole was an agent of LifeSpan. Suddenly conscious of his nakedness, he crossed his hands in front of himself, shying back from the edge. Cole never would have thought he would die in front of so many people.

"Anytime, Sci Tym," Cole announced loudly. *Time to die.*

Tym threw a lever, turned a series of dials, and there was a loud series of clanks. A slow humming began, gaining intensity as the tanks above Cole were primed. He remembered the Father telling him the nanos would do their best to heal him almost as fast as the gas would kill him. The balance was a strange effect, being cured and dying at the same time. Your own body turning against you, in an effort to save you.

Cole locked eyes with the Father, threw him a small wink, and the gas tanks emptied with an extraordinary exhalation of pressure from above him. In one instant, Cole was blasted to the ground, his hands flying forward to stop him on all fours. He immediately began to choke. His eyes watered. Cole looked out of the plexi chamber to find solace in the Father's eyes, but could not see past the fogged reflection. All around him was white gas, enveloping him. He felt like he was falling through a cloud.

His choking continued, and he felt his body strengthening, but he remained on the ground, back arched like a feral cat. He glanced down at his arms and saw his skin buckling. Just under the surface, it moved and flowed. His eyes stopped watering. Still, the gas filled the chamber, squeezing the air out of the cube, forcing its volume into the space provided, greedy in its use of the remaining oxygen. Cole was inhaling gas and exhaling gas. He became lightheaded, but again the feeling went away as quickly as it arrived. He was falling down a mountain, with nothing to do but grit his teeth and close his eyes, waiting for the end to come.

"What is happening? This is taking far too long." The Father was standing over the seated Tym, staring at the same electronic readouts, trying to sort out the various physical readings including heartbeats, pressure, oxygen levels and stress readings. Cole was fighting. Well, the nanos were fighting for him, and they were doing an amazing job.

"I'm sorry, Father, I do not know." Tym was bobbing in his chair, alternately wiping the sweat off his brow and randomly swiping screens away with his gloved hand. "The tanks are nearly empty, and Cole is in fine shape. He hasn't even passed out yet! The nanos appear to be winning. They are marvelous creations, adapting faster than I had predicted. I don't see how that is possible, but I've been proven wrong once before. I was very young, and had just returned home, or was I just leaving to go? I happened to be very young—"

"Tym! I believe Cole would like to hear your story at another time. Let's make sure he can do that, yes?" The Father was acting nonchalant, but Sci Tym was snapped back to reality.

"Yes, yes, of course. Those nanos are able to balance his entire body systems, including the mind, and not even miss a beat . . . Remarkable. Must be a recent improvement . . . I'll have to trick them."

"I don't care *how* they are doing; Cole is suffering, and we need to get them out of him before the gas runs out. And we need it done two minutes ago!" The Father spun to the crowd and raised his hands in an empty-palmed plea.

It was Captain Ian who stepped forward, hand crossed over his chest, head bowed slightly in salute.

"Sir, if I may suggest the Compound 2-XR we were preparing for our next mission," Ian proposed.

Tym was the first to object, talking loudly and quickly enough before the Father gave the go ahead. "I don't know if that would be right for this situation. We haven't fully tested the effects on the subject's epidermis. The cellular layers were heavily compromised at the last run."

The hissing of the gas tanks and Cole's low moaning were the only sounds. All eyes fell to the Father, for his decision was not merely for Cole, but a confirmation that he really would do anything necessary to accomplish his goals. He trusted Captain Ian explicitly in the field, but couldn't help wondering at his current motives against Cole. He knew Tym shared his distrust.

The Father looked deep into Ian's eyes, trying to gauge his intent. He might just want Cole out of the picture, still considering him the main reason for Emma's demise. But would he do so in the open, with everyone watching? No, Captain Ian would wait for a more opportune time when no one was watching.

With a mental note to watch Ian more closely in the following months, the Father made his decision.

"Ian, my friend," he began, dropping his title on purpose to establish this as a humanitarian request and not an order. "Fetch the compound. And hurry! We have to end this."

THE BEACON

When Ian returned, he was holding a canister no thicker than a club and shorter than his hand. It was indented so fingers could grip it securely and adorned with two yellow stripes running widthwise. The shape made it easy to be thrown, and the stripes were a universal sign for "stay away." Ian took one last look over at the Father, and after receiving a nod, twisted the top of the container until he heard a loud snap. Captain Ian took two long steps, jumped at the containing booth and pulled himself up the ledge. With his free hand he wrenched the secondary exhaust cap off, holding his face back from the gas backlash.

Captain Ian glanced into the containing booth and saw Cole thrashing on the ground. His hands were holding the side of his head as he was kicking and wriggling from an unseen web. Ian dropped the canister into the cell, replaced the cap and effectively sealed the Compound 2-XR gas inside. Even though he still resented Cole, he hated to inflict this kind of pain on him, but there was no turning back now. Cole's nanos would never give up.

Ian jumped the distance off of the booth and landed with a thump, one knee bent down to absorb the impact. When he stood facing the crowd, they were solemn. Then each expression changed into wide-eyed disbelief, some pointing behind Ian at Cole's containment. Ian turned to comprehend.

That's when the screaming began.

Cole was throwing himself at the tank wall, clawing at the plexi surface to no avail. The air in the tank began to change as the old gas began mingling with Ian's new chemical weapon. The air was thick, and turned a dark green. Cole's screaming was louder than the machinery, a tortured howl, echoing down the corridors and raising the hair on the back of Ian's neck.

"Galen!" Cole shrieked, "*never again!*"

"*Tym,*" the Father yelled. "You need to figure out what is happening, and find a way around it!"

Tym wasn't listening. He brandished his Master Sci glove, and suddenly every digital screen jumped free of their devices and was layered in the air before Tym. The information obeyed Sci Tym; he was the orchestrator now. He leapt into a furious dance, swiping and pulling information screens, overlapping the previous screens of information with the next at such a speed, the Father lost track of what was happening. He had only seen Sci Tym this furious with his Sci glove once before, when they first decided to build an intricate hub of information and establish the Movement. Back then, Sci Tym worked day and night, erasing histories, breaking into security systems as, piece by piece, he liberated the members of the Movement.

Now it looked like he was reading the entire history of nanos, every version and every schematic written about those infuriating little bugs. Tym was furiously sweating without the ability to wipe, so he resorted to blowing through his lower lip, angling his breath upwards. The screens layered more and more quickly. He was breaking down the new models, searching for matches, sending signals to Cole, and hoping for a return blip, verifying the newest model. Tym knew when Cole was born and he knew when the nanos would have been injected. How could these be so advanced?

Unable to focus through the pain, Cole was calling for Emma, calling for his mother, calling for his father, to no avail. *Where were they? Why can't they hear me?* He saw the faces of Tym, Galen, Gretchen; his feelings cycled from hatred to friendship, torture to relief. His throat hurt. Pain coursed through his veins. He was hot, then cold, and hot again. Cole was drifting. His mouth was open to his jaws' breaking point, but there was no sound. Numb from the cold, too much, so bitter. Cole held his arms out for an embrace.

Is anyone here? Mother, take me away. Mother, where are you now?

Cole slumped to the ground, all of the air removed from his lungs. His body gave an instinctive spasm, his eyes flickered and he gasped his last breath. The Father and Captain Ian rushed to the holding cage under Cole, and saw the small pool of storm-cloud gray ooze. The nanos. They collected into the funnel-shaped bottom of the small room, through the grate. The nano pool was no bigger than a cup of spilled water, but the Father and everyone else assembled knew there were millions of nanos, eagerly searching for a new host. They were unable to climb the slick walls of the funnel catch, but that didn't mean they would stop trying. They would never stop trying, for that was the nature of the nanos.

Cole was dragged to the floor space between the cell and Tym's control booth. He was not breathing, his body the color of a hard-boiled yolk.

"He's dead," a hushed voice said from the crowd.

Many of those assembled had their nanos removed by choice. However, none had witnessed an extraction like Cole had just suffered. His nanos fought back. After this mess, there probably wouldn't be a volunteer in a very, very long time.

"Well, of course he's dead. That was the point," the Father snapped as he threw a blanket over Cole. "Tym, get over here!"

Tym was already running with a face mask draped over his shoulder, the clear tubing snaking down around his legs, threatening to entangle his short, wobbling struts every step. This forced him into an awkward stumble, on the edge of disaster with his hurried pace.

His arms were raised high over his head, each hand holding a long stick. One red, and the other black. The air was crackling around the sticks, and he was very careful to keep them as far apart from each other as he could. The butts of the sticks were attached to thick, black cording that appeared to be plugged into Tym's backpack. The true path was hard to distinguish with the amount of buckles, straps, wires and pockets in Tym's overburdened wardrobe.

The Father was kneeling over Cole, applying a clear gel to his chest, as the crowd tightened around the scene. Tym stumbled past the Father, with the poles in hand and his legs predictably entangled, sending him skidding across the distance. He fell ungracefully on his face, unable to put his hands in front to cushion the fall lest the poles get any closer to each other. They were already throwing enough sparks to force the crowd into a small retreat.

Tym fell a few feet shy of the nano cage collection. He was flopping side to side like a fish out of water, incapable of using his hands and completely unable to lift himself off the ground. Finally, Captain Ian leaned over and grabbed two handfuls of Tym's jacket.

Suddenly, Ian froze. He was looking at the nano cage.

"Tym, since you seem to have all the answers," he said as he raised his hand and pointed at the bottom rim sunken into the ground, "what is that?"

A few of the audience members that were next to the team also looked over to the rim. The trapped nanos were many feet below the edge, safely contained in the smooth funnel. However, there was one small speck moving along the top as an insect would walk around the edge of a saucer, searching for a spot to jump down safely. This speck was about the size of a small, black ant. It was moving slowly, searching and pulsing a deep red.

The speck stopped, crested the ridge and moved off of the rim, progressing across the floor at an increased speed.

Tym suddenly found the energy and angle to boost his bulk onto his heels. He focused all his attention on the small crimson anomaly as if facing a tiger head on.

"Captain, please hold these." He handed the poles to Ian, slid off his backpack and walked carefully to the nano cage edge. He reached in his vest and removed a small plastique jar with a suctioned lid.

Within a foot of the pulsing gnat, jar outstretched, he fell upon it.

Captain Ian wasted no time running to the Father and Cole, electric rods pulsing, the cords dragging Tym's backpack. The Father finished applying the gel on Cole's chest and laid a metal disc over his sternum. Captain Ian crossed the poles over the disc, and Cole's body jumped.

After a few tense moments, Cole gasped for breath.

He turned to face the crowd and smirked as best he could. The Father looked down at him, also smiling, and helped him to a seated position. The crowd parted the distance from Tym to the Father, and Cole was able to see what was in the jar Tym now held aloft. A small red pill, with two white stripes running vertically down its middle. It was the demerit Galen had given him on his first visit. He had unwittingly swallowed a trap.

"Tym! Put it down, and get away . . ." Cole warned.

The captured specimen pulsed more powerfully than it had before, and the jar became superheated, forcing Tym to drop it, shattering the container and releasing the item once again. It pulsed brightly one last time and let out an ear-piercing whine. The screech filled the corridor, making all in assembly cover their ears. The shrillness was unbearable, echoing endlessly through the corridors. The ruby beacon became so bright, it drowned out all of the other lighting and cast a deep red glare on everything and everyone.

Tym pulled another container clipped to his shoulder and wrenched the cork loose, pouring a putrid yellow fluid onto the pill. The sticky goo surrounded the pill, muffling the light and noise. However, as it was pushing against the muck, the glow brightened, and the siren's volume increased, if that was possible.

It all ended as the Father grabbed the sticks and shocked the red beacon with a glorious blast of electricity. The red light faded away and the screeching died, leaving everyone's ears ringing with the aftereffect.

RETRIBUTION

The relief from the silenced beacon was short lived. The assembled citizens rubbed their heads and ears as their hearing returned. However, a deep quiet passed through the crowd, edged with a palpable fear. The beacon was obviously from LifeSpan. This could not bode well for their hideaway. As usual, they all turned toward the Father for guidance. He looked fatigued.

"Maybe they didn't hear the signal, eh?" Sci Tym tried to joke.

High above the city, the airspace was usually very quiet. The breezes and soft winds could continue without obstruction.

Today, the calm was broken by hundreds of hovercopters, each carrying five Collectors as its crew. The LifeSpan logo was emblazoned on the copters' sides.

They were waiting. Strategically placed across the countryside and tuned into one station, they waited and listened for the signal. Collectors were a funny breed; they each hoped to outdo each other, gaining reputation among their elite brotherhood. However, when approached, they would swear undying loyalty to LifeSpan and insist there was no desire for personal gain. Thus, when Choppers Six and Eight received the blaring signal from subject Cole's homing beacon, the two crews were silently overjoyed, and ready to enact judgment against those responsible for their fallen brothers.

Before the Father could respond to the assembled questioning citizens of the Movement, a call broke through the air.

"Collectors! They are here! Inside the compound!" The call was repeated hundreds of times as the alarm was sent from soldier to mother to child. Soon the Movement was abuzz with activity, shelving was knocked over, possessions were grabbed and families began frantically trying to find their missing loved ones.

Throughout the numerous underground tunnels, screams were coming from every direction. The Father recognized them as death screams. Unfortunately, they were not a cry you ever forget. The Father knew the Collectors were taking no prisoners this time, and the complex was lost.

"Captain Ian," the Father said, "I fear we may have our very own Battle of Borodino upon us."

"Let us hope we have better results than Napoleon," the Captain replied, and gave a solemn nod.

Allie ran as fast as her stout legs would carry her, trying to make it back to her room. Her son would be waiting for her there. She had told him if there was ever trouble, to return immediately to their quarters and hide in the cupboard, and she would return for him.

The only thought racing through her head was his safety; he was everything to her. They were one of the newest recruits to the Movement, rescued by Tym after her husband mysteriously disappeared. Tym had told them about secret projects her husband was working on, and that he would not be returning, but the Collectors would.

On that fateful day, Allie had retreated as the Collectors' transport arrived, with three of the robed enforcers entering her home. As she watched in horror with her son and Tym, hidden a safe distance across the street, she witnessed the end of her normal life as the three Collectors destroyed her home, erasing all that she had built. She returned with Tym, carrying only her son and the clothes on their backs.

Today, the Collectors were back. The location has changed, but her terms had not.

Allie repeated her oath: *My son is not the property of LifeSpan.*

She rounded the last corner, descended a small set of stairs and arrived at her door. The lock was thrown—a good sign. Once Allie entered, she called immediately for her boy. The cupboard door flew open wide and he ran to her waiting arms.

"We have to get out of here, now. Everyone is at the far east exit. We have to be fast; they are closing the door shortly and we can't miss the exodus. We rehearsed this. Do not be afraid. I have you now."

As she finished her explanation, half of the lights blinked out, flickered and resurged. The Collectors must have been taking out the electric grid. Of course, Tym had backup solar pumps trying to keep the facility lit. Unfortunately, the energy pump didn't have enough juice remaining after Cole's recent death chamber had pulled most of the reserves out of commission.

Instead, the entire facility was basked in a pale glow with half the normal illumination, throwing shadows across every corner, enshrouding the maze of metal and plasteel in a soupy haze.

Allie pulled her boy close to her and ran into the hallway. Their vision was blurred, with the sparse lighting only revealing a few steps ahead of her. Luckily, she knew her way around. Allie took the same route daily.

She kept one hand in front of her and the other clutched in a grip only a mother could sustain on her son's clothing. They could hear discharges of electricity, pulsing through the air, crackling in the dark. People were screaming; children were crying. It was a nightmare to run through the dark maze and not try to help her fellow residents. Nevertheless, they pressed on, for the far east exit was close, and Allie was not leaving all she had fought for.

Five Collectors rounded a corner, shoulder to shoulder, each holding a crackling billy club in each hand. Before them were women from the washing room staff, who were frightened, and rightly so. The Collectors were not the typical image of LifeSpan political correctness. They were white demons with eyes of fire and teeth gritted so hard, their jaw muscles clenched shut.

"Why are you doing this?" the brunette woman managed to ask between sobs.

The Collectors advanced.

"Because," a strong male voice carried from across the room, "they have no care for human life." The Collectors turned to see who intruded on their scrap.

A lone soldier stood in the doorway, wearing his chest plate. He held a long metallic pole in both hands, about four feet in length and capped with a solid metal ball. He hefted it like a small flagpole, with the weighted end held taunting the Collectors, pointing them out, challenging their might against his own.

The Collectors barely gave the women another thought as they advanced towards the soldier.

"Ladies, run! Do not look back!" He was hopping from foot to foot, fully aware he stood no chance against five Collectors. His only hope was to last at least two minutes so the women could get beyond the reach of these Collectors-turned-killers.

They looked at each other, confused.

"Where do we go?" the same brunette woman yelled toward the soldier.

He was caught off guard, hoping the women would just run. He didn't take the time to think about this information. If he said it aloud, the Collectors would know where the secret rendezvous was. On the other hand, if he didn't tell them, they could run into another pocket of Collectors. If he revealed this information, then he would have no choice but to hold the Collectors at bay.

"Go to the far east exit. Tell them Agent Duggan will be a little late."

"Who is Agent Duggan?"

"I am! Now get out of here!" He charged forward as the women ran down the hallway, taking the first sharp left and never looking back.

His pole swung towards the lead Collector with all his weight behind it. The Collector raised his arm and caught the pole in his side ribs.

The pole stopped dead. The momentum instantly stilled.

Agent Duggan tried to pull the rod back, but it would not budge. He couldn't figure how the Collector was still standing. That blow should have broken his ribs, or at least staggered him slightly. He pulled again, frantic to retract his only weapon.

It was too late. The other four Collectors surrounded him.

He felt their hands reach out, and each squeezed different parts of his body more tightly than a mechanized vise. The one he felt the most was the large hand gripping his neck. Agent Duggan began to scream but was silenced when the Collector ripped his throat out, muscle and blood coating his gauntlet. Agent Duggan's body fell and was kicked to the side. The Collectors advanced to the east.

EXIT

A small group had already gathered in the far east exit room. It was a huge gallery room, about forty feet across and twice that in length. The room echoed every sound, including the shuffling feet of the many refugees and their varying levels of conversations. Most were in a hushed whisper, trying to make sense of the commotion throughout their underground home. The lights were dim, slowly powering down, losing their glare at each passing moment. The secret to this room was the reinforced wall at the far end. It was covered floor to ceiling with cabinetry of all sizes and was the main supply room for the dining areas. Cole gathered the group of frightened family members together. Children were crying while the adults looked to the Father. He had always been the one to give them solace in their times of need, and he silently stood with his hand on Cole's shoulder. Cole's head was spinning. He could hear screams echoing down the halls, through the vents, only emphasized by the soft sobbing of those in the room with him.

"The time has come. We are being forced from our home by those who do not understand us," the Father began.

"Is it true the Collectors have . . ." A frightened girl was having trouble finishing the sentence. "Is it true the Collectors have killed people here?"

The Father looked to Cole with compassion, and as he opened his mouth to answer the concerned mother, a shrill scream echoed down the hallway and into the dark room they were huddled in. There was no doubt in anyone's mind that the Collectors were killing. The scream shook them to their core.

Fear settled in.

The Father burst into motion. He began spinning paintings on the wall in a complete circle, with small gears shifting and clicking in the walls. He opened various cabinets and threw small levers hidden under the floor panels. Cole couldn't figure out what was happening until he saw the far wall began to shift upwards. It was only then he realized the cabinets didn't run all the way to the ceiling, which left room for the wall of cabinets to move upwards, only about two feet, but it was enough. Cole felt the air pressurized through the new opening under the cabinets. There was clearly another space beyond.

"This escape was devised expressly for this purpose. The opening should be large enough for any of you to slide under and through. It is not large enough for the Collectors to pursue.

"You will be following Cole. Treat him as if you were talking to me. He is your Father now." It was a resigning sentence. The Father turned his back on those in assembly.

Cole couldn't believe what he was hearing. These people had been with the Father for an untold number of years. Cole still had so much he wanted to talk to him about. He wanted to yell his own denial, but couldn't find the breath. He locked eyes with the Father, and knew it was over. The dedication to these people, the families, everything. They tried to live a life away from LifeSpan, but the Movement just could not survive. Cole nodded. His shoulders slumped with responsibility, and he walked away from the Father.

They began sliding residents of the failed Movement under the escape door to live another day. When Cole slid through after the last resident, he turned to help the Father through.

Instead, the wall slammed shut with the Father remaining behind.

"When can we stop running?" The question was called out for the fourth time.

Cole knew he needed to answer those who were gathered with him. He tried to ignore their pleas, but they looked to him for guidance. They wanted him to save them all, but what could he do?

Everyone dear to me is dead because of me. I am the plague, reborn.

"I don't know," Cole answered quickly.

"Where does this tunnel lead?"

"Where is Sci Tym?"

The questions kept coming.

"I don't know."

"How many of the group survived? I thought the Father was right behind us!" They increased in desperation.

"*I don't know.*" Cole stopped and faced the group.

"When will the Collectors give up? When can they leave us alone?" they pleaded.

"Never!" Cole screamed. "They will never stop. We are all going to be crushed. We don't belong in this society, none of us. Things have changed. This world has changed to force us out." Cole raised his hands in frustration and ran his fingers through his hair. "For all we know, this tunnel was never finished. We could all be trapped down here. Hopefully this opens to a miraculous freedom field, far away from here, out of LifeSpan's reach. We can all pick berries and dance among the flowers! Is that what you want? Is that what you think? What do any of you really know anyway? You have been hiding from the real world for so long you forgot how to think straight. You look to me for answers. I'm afraid I have none for you."

Tym felt the rumble long before he heard footsteps. Something big was heading his way, and fast. Based on those attributes, he really didn't want to be in its way. He was still about forty feet away from the Father's room. The entrance was hidden. If he could only get inside . . . Should he risk it? Tym had a better idea. He was a Sci, after all.

He jumped over to the nearest doorway. An old plasteel frame was barely holding the metal door in place. The room inside would be large enough, if Tym could fit through the opening.

Note to self: you could lose a few pounds, Tym thought.

He stood back from the frame, reached into his backpack and pulled out four metallic discs. Tym threw two discs onto the ceiling above him, where they adhered to the surface immediately. He tossed the other two discs onto the ground, about a foot from him. The discs glowed and connected wirelessly to each other. They projected light across to each other, flickering briefly and eventually settling on an exact image of the empty doorway he was facing.

The rumbling grew louder, and Sci Tym jumped behind the projection as a group of Collectors rounded the corner. Tym could see through the screen, for his side was still translucent. However, when the Collectors stopped to peer down this new hall, the illusion held, reflecting back a digital copy of the dark surroundings.

They stood there for many minutes, deciding which course to take. Tym nervously peered back, counting the men. Eight of them. Two teams, it would seem, as four had a faint red stripe running around their collars. Luckily, they turned back to the intercrossing hall and continued their original course. Only then did Tym notice they were dragging hardware pieces from a large cube, complete with tubing and hardwires.

The last use for the cube was to help Cole die. The Collectors must have known its purpose, but how?

Before he could think too deeply on the issue, they were almost out of his sight. Sci Tym knew they couldn't see through the projection and began a crude dance, wiggling his fingers and mocking the retreating Collectors. It felt good to heckle their looting party. Luckily for Tym, he had developed this disc projector just last month to hide members of the Movement, like the Father.

Unluckily for Tym, the Father was a lot thinner than he was.

The trailing Collector gave a fleeting glance down the hallway, and noticed a khaki colored pocket, bobbing in the air.

EPSILON

As the gate closed behind the Father, twelve Collectors filed into the far east exit room. They scanned the area, expecting an ambush or at least a larger group of refugees. Instead, they faced a lone old man.

The Father paced around the room, keeping distance from his deadly foes, while forcing himself not to look at the secret exit in the back of the room. If the Collectors noticed he was looking at the false wall, the escape would be for naught.

Now that the whole of his fellow Movement members were safely out of earshot, the Father decided to reveal information long kept secret.

"You, with the red around the eyes. I see you squinting as you stay behind, away from the lights. Their illumination bothers you. Epsilon, that is your name. What, may I ask, is your number?" The Father spoke in a soothing, matter-of-fact voice.

The Collector was confused. He looked to his brothers for advice on how to answer this inquisitive man.

"Epsilon Fourteen," he finally admitted.

Sci Tym jumped back as the Collectors returned to his hallway, in full sprint.

Maybe they dropped something, Tym thought.

Immediately he pushed the thought out of his head and began calculating. Eight Collectors against one man. But this was Sci Tym, and the calculations flowed through the air, trajectories of targets, differences in their gait, the differing height of three that were taller than the others, the loose boots of one. There were approximately 12.3 seconds before they reached him. Plenty of time for a Sci of his talent.

Tym unfastened the latch at his belt and ripped the whole of it from his person. He had built a safety mechanism into the back of each pocket, exclusively activated by his unique signature. Usually, Tym grabbed one or two pouches from his belt after some thought about their application, releasing the contents with a simply swipe of his finger along the belts inside. In this situation, with eight Collectors rushing him, Tym dragged his hand down the entire back of his belt, releasing the locks. He threw the belt over the screen.

The Collectors could see movement from the edges of the screen. There was definitely someone behind this false wall. An enemy. He would be easily crushed under a sea of raging Collectors. Suddenly, flying in the air from behind the security screen came an assortment of trinkets. Jars, containers, pouches and beads rained down, spilling their contents onto the group.

"Ah. Fourteen. Rather late in the batch. Did you know there were only twenty-one in your group? The problem with the eyes was eventually fixed, only for another issue to arise. You were a good batch. I was especially proud of my Epsilon line," the Father explained.

This made the Collectors pause. How could he know these details about their origin? How could anyone know those details?

"You think we are impressed by your knowledge? We know your speech to be only a ruse. You lie to us so your friends may have a chance to escape," a Collector, circling to the Father's left side, called out.

"While it is true my friends are running from you, the real truth is found within yourselves. You know me from the past. You know me in your heart, your programming," the Father quietly replied.

Indeed, the Collectors gave pause. He *was* familiar, from a dream. A dream they could not remember on their own, without the gentle coaxing of their parental architect.

"We . . . killed you!" Epsilon Fourteen lowered his arms. "You burned."

"Yes, your suspicions are revealing my face to you. I am your Father. All of you are my children, my creations."

Tym pushed through the doorway and fell into the Father's office, moments before the hallway erupted in a circus of effects from Tym's belt.

Electro-magnetic pulses deactivated the Collector's billy clubs, as another bubble of techno goo bonded two Collectors together, before they were dissolved from a bouncing plastique ball of acid. The Collectors tried to kick the containers away, hoping to send the jars anywhere but at their feet. Some of the jars rolled. Others shattered when a boot hit them, releasing a chemical gas or a powerful bonding glue. Explosions splashed body parts down the corridor. Bright sunbursts stole their vision. Metal discs spun in lazy magnetic circles, emitting super-heated plasma blades, severing the feet from three more Collectors.

A few Collectors were brave enough to reach for the pouches

and attempt to toss them aside. Four Collectors suffocated when one of those late-blooming traps exploded, enveloping their bodies in a dense foam.

Tym knew they would have their hands full in the hallway. He closed the door, and started looking through the room. From what he could tell, he was the only member of the Movement to visit this room since the Collector invasion. That was not very good news.

Here he was, inside the Father's most private of spaces, while everything around him crumbled. Was he really the only one left alive?

Father, be safe, Sci Tym thought. *We need you now more than ever.*

Tym could handle himself. It was everyone else he worried about.

Focus. Just grab what you came for and get out of here, Tym reminded himself. *And if I ever get out alive, I'm starting a new life with half the amount of food I eat now. Nothing but trouble, this bulky figure.*

Tym shuffled through the collected digiscreens on their planning table. There wouldn't be any helpful information on the screens, and he was afraid to turn anything on right now. However, they were still too valuable to leave behind.

He filled his bag with the Father's journals, which contained locations of safe houses, meeting spots and a few decoding books for the Movement's messages. At least he could keep this information from the wrong hands.

Perhaps it was possible to rebuild at another site, with a new team.

Sci Tym was brought out of his planning as a new light source grew from behind the plasteel desk. It pulsed and repeated, in succession. A pattern of light, signaling to the Father. Where was the signal's origin?

More importantly, from whom?

Sci Tym knew the Father's passcode. Luckily, he hadn't changed the sequence, and the digiscreen opened. The screen shifted, pulling a stock image forth, and from the other side, Trina was emerging into view.

"Trina?!" He knew it was her. He could never forget her.

Before his image reflected onto her side, Tym angled the digiscreen to the floor, hiding her view of him.

She started talking as soon as the sync was complete. She was speaking in a hushed tone. "Alexander. Your location has been compromised. *They* know. *He* knows. Please. If you are there, you have to leave."

Sci Tym wanted to look into the screen and tell Trina everything was all right. Which was only partially true. He did not know his fellow members' fates. There was also a huge risk in revealing himself to her. This could be a trap.

Could Trina be a double agent?

"Father, please. I need to know you are safe. Why are you not responding?" Trina was crying; that much was obvious as her voice cracked. "I need to know Sci Tym is safe."

He snapped the screen up, looking deeply into his Trina.

"I am here," Sci Tym said.

Trina was shocked and relieved in a mixed emotional display. She could barely speak, so Tym decided to jump right into the most burning question.

"How did you learn about the Movement?" he asked.

"I am sorry we never told you. I have been secretly working with the Father for many years now, Tym. It was the best way to keep my secret. We all know you are . . . passionate about your studies, and you would have worried for me."

"I worry for your safety even now as we are speaking to each other. Where are you?" Tym asked her.

"I am safe from prying eyes, if that is your question. I wish I could tell you more, but LifeSpan knows where you are. You have to find the Father and get him to safety. You don't have much—"

"It's already too late," Tym interrupted. "I am afraid the Movement has scattered. Many have died from an invasion of Collectors to our home."

"Oh, Tym, we feared it would come to this."

"The Father was separated from me. I know which exit he was heading for—"

"Tym, listen to me. LifeSpan has entered forbidden territory. Nimbus must be stopped." Trina looked around, and leaned closer to the screen. "He has been absorbing the muscle memories and basic instincts of expirations for years. He wanted to become faster, stronger. That is why the Father tried to leave LifeSpan."

Tym knew this story. That's why the Movement was formed, to have Nimbus answer for his crimes on a global trial.

"Recently," Trina began, "Nimbus went too far. He absorbed an *entire personality*. The very being of a human. And he wants to do it again. He is using the expiration technology for his own gain."

Now this was something Sci Tym did not know about.

"Are you saying people are expiring and being absorbed?" Tym was raising his voice with every word, fighting to keep control. This was a grave crime against all of humanity. This went against every ethic of what the Scientific Community stood for.

Humanity was not a pawn for one man to command at his leisure.

"I will take him down. He will answer for his injustice," Tym vowed.

"I know just when you can. Listen carefully, Tym. Nimbus has been on his airship for almost a year. It's time to land and resupply. I believe this is your moment. Get to the port if you want to make a difference."

"So, we take out Nimbus . . . Then what? He still has control over every living person on the planet!" Tym knew there would be a large void to fill if Nimbus was no longer sitting at the head of LifeSpan.

"Luckily, I have a plan." Trina smiled. He loved when she did that.

The Collectors stopped surrounding him. The twelve of them were confused. They were searching their inner demons. Their memories flashed with intense training sessions and painful surgeries.

Through it all, the Father was there, in their memories. He stood in the rooms, watched over them. He trained them on morals, following orders, the greater good for all of LifeSpan. He was there, in their minds. Deeply instrumental in their creation.

"Epsilon . . . *Bono malum superate,*" the Father quietly stated. Those were the trigger words he placed in their programming long ago.

Overcome evil with good.

The four Epsilon Collectors turned to their brothers, awakened by their Father's call to arms. They were not in control of their actions. Reaching out, they began an intense struggle within, and as their minds screamed out against this action, they grappled with the other, newer models in the room, fighting, choking, striking with their billy clubs. The Collector civil war raged instantly, as they defended themselves from brothers, teammates, and newfound enemies.

The Father walked towards the wall to escape, ready to join Cole. However, before he reached the exit, incredibly strong hands grabbed his jacket and wrapped around his neck. The Father clawed at the forearm and twisted his head for air, to no avail.

"Theta . . . Theta Twenty-One, and you are not my Father," was whispered in his ear.

Cole and his group walked in silence for almost two hours before the exit was in view. They gathered together and looked out at an open field. It was nighttime. The city was on the horizon, with only a faint hovercopter hum in the distance.

"You saved us." A child was pulling on Cole's pants.

"You saved yourself. I was just there to push you through the exit." Cole dodged the praise. *These people need to go. There is nothing I can do for them now.*

"Alright. Everyone. It's time to go now. I'm sorry this unraveled like it did, but at least you can be happy to live your life out as it was intended. I suppose we will be dying of old age. Free of expirations."

"What about the Movement?" a voice called from the back.

Cole couldn't believe they were still interested in resisting.

"It's done. That's all we had. I will still fight on, I don't know how, but I will find a way. The Movement has died, but LifeSpan lives. I cannot have that." Cole looked around at the thirty or so refugees standing before him. He never was good at speeches. "If you want to stay with me, I can't stop you. I should probably mention, everyone that has ever stood with me has died."

Yes, terrible at speeches.

"Cole, you need to believe in yourself before others will believe in you." The statement rang through the tunnel from a newcomer, walking towards the group.

Cole couldn't see his face, but he recognized the silhouette.

"Tym! You are alive!" Cole rushed over to his old friend. He noticed he was alone. "How did you get here?"

"I took the far east exit," Tym replied, and instantly followed up with, "The Father was not there. Plenty of dead Collectors, but he was missing."

"We will find him, Tym. We will not stop until we do," Cole stated.

"Yes. The Movement continues?" Tym was hopeful.

Cole turned to his group one last time.

"This is no Movement. This is a Revolution!" Cole threw his fist in the air. "The offer still stands. You can leave now, and live your life out as you want. You can find a spot in the world and hide. If you are lucky, no harm will come to you. If any of you would like to take that path, the exit is there. Anyone who will stay and fight, the choice is before you."

The revolutionaries all stood their ground.

"Excellent," Cole said. "Tym, tell me you have a plan."

"Why, yes, I definitely have a plan." Tym was tugging at his pants to keep them from sliding down.

Where was his belt? Cole wondered.

DUO SCI

Cole jumped awake when the window opened, the cold breeze blowing across the room. He reached behind his back for the plasteel blade strapped at his waist, ready to throw. However, standing before him was Sci Tym.

Within the last few months, Cole had not slept in the same safe house longer than two continuous nights. Their plight against LifeSpan was in full swing, with pockets of resistance swelling throughout the world. Cole was their reluctant leader. With Tym at his side, they were the driving force behind the rebellious mindset.

Now it was time to set in motion their most daring plan and, hopefully, put an end to this part of his life. There really was no turning back now. Maybe there never was. Nimbus had been aboard his airship consistently for almost eighteen months now. Cole knew from reliable intelligence that the cloud city had to come down to the surface and reload. There simply was not enough power to keep the massive headquarters afloat, so they were told.

Here they were, after their escape from the Movement's headquarters, watching and waiting for this cloud to touchdown.

They needed to get to him, to stop Nimbus and relinquish his control of the globe. Cole needed it done now.

Oh, sure, that's easy. Just kindly ask Nimbus, controller of all things, "Could you give up now?" Cole thought. There were only two problems with this pathetic plan.

"Tym, I think we have been approaching this all wrong." Cole jumped out of bed as Tym was setting down breakfast and digging in another random pocket for seasonings.

"I knew you didn't want the multivita shakes anymore. This should be better for today." Tym was actually unwrapping individual sweets, pastries and what appeared to finally be some meat. "This should be right today."

"No, Tym, not the food!" Cole knew it was hard to get Tym focused, but he wasn't any better for the crew. "I'm talking about our plan. I'm tired of waiting and I'm tired of watching that city float above us, with Nimbus still ruling everything."

"Well, Nimbus owns the skies, literally. He is the only ship allowed at that altitude. It is his space." Tym glanced upward, peering through the ceiling, into the clouds themselves. "I actually think the clouds ask him for permission."

"Alright. I'm past that thinking. He is just a person. We just have to find a way to get to him. If he won't come down, I'm going up."

"That's ridiculous. You can't just fly up to his floating city, knock on his door and ask him to open up and have a chat with him." Tym's voice was rising, and Cole knew where this was heading. "Hello, I'm Cole. The once-favored child of LifeSpan, friends with Sci Tym." He looked at Cole. "Y'know, he doesn't like me very much?"

"Yes, I know that Tym."

"So, personal friendships aside, and past missions aside, and killing all the Collectors and destroying nanos and all. But could you just land this city and go gas yourself?"

"We haven't tried that yet." Cole played along.

"Yeah, that's perfect. Then we can inherit the *whole fragging world!*" Tym screamed, arms outstretched.

Cole and Tym sat solemnly, staring at each other.

That was problem number two.

What would they do with the world? Why would they want it? There was a chime at the door.

Cole reached in his pocket and pulled out an imaginary watch, pressed the non-existent button and pretended to read the dials.

"Ah, yes, right on time," Cole quipped.

Tym laughed at the absurd notion of following a timepiece. Cole was enjoying the freedom since his death.

The door chimed again.

"Open for guest," Tym announced.

The door swished. A short, unassuming Sci walked into the room, looked around immediately, following corners, memorizing the room, seeing patterns and recording anomalies.

There's only one thing Cole hated more than working with one Sci, and that's being in a room with two Scis. He looked over at Tym, who watched the newcomer with an equally intensive evaluation. Their eyes met.

"Hello, Sci Tym," the newcomer greeted.

"Hello, Walter Nigel. How's the Doctor blending Sci business coming along?" Tym always picked on him for being cross professions.

"It helps me get into the Control Room."

He immediately had the attention of them both. Finally, time to infiltrate. Cole leaped across the room and grabbed a seat, pulling close to listen.

As Sci Nigel laid out the logistics of breaking through the safety mechanisms, Sci Tym was taking all the credit for such an adventurous approach.

"I can be very convincing, y'know," Tym said, looking at Nigel.

"I would have said no to you. Generally, I don't want to get involved with these things. But there is one person I cannot say no to."

There was another chime at the door.

"I knew it! You turned us in! LifeSpan is here!" Cole jumped into a defensive pose.

The figure walked in.

"You are half right," Trina said. "But I hear there is a resistance, and it's gaining momentum."

Trina always arrived at the right time.

SHUTDOWN

Dr. Nigel led the charge himself, ducking around corners and using his security codes to pass through the laboratory with ease. He knew his orders, and Trina was close by. They could not fail. Cole needed him. The world as they knew it needed him. This was his time.

"Control Room secured." Nigel was surrounded by screens. They projected on the walls, were built into the consoles, and grew from every available surface. Plasteel panels lowered from the ceiling grid, also filling with maps, flow charts and percentage readouts.

Trina secured the door and joined Nigel, ducking around the information screens. She knew he was opening too much information. He was a talented Sci, but this was outside of his experience.

"What we need to access is every sector for LifeSpan, and therefore, the world," Nigel explained. "According to Sci Tym, we need them all open to begin the shutdown of each sector."

"You make it sound so easy, but I'm telling you, it's not," Trina interjected. "There are safeguards in place, with processing times, and I know LifeSpan doesn't have an auto reset—"

"Ah, Trina, you speak the truth." Nigel dropped his pack off his shoulder, reached in, and pulled out a tangled mess of wires and power discs attached to a white gauntlet, each fingertip covered in a series of small white discs.

"Where did you acquire a Master Sci glove? *Doctor*." Trina was suddenly suspicious.

"It appears Sci Galen is not around to utilize his glove. Don't worry. Sci Tym spent some time and updated this one for me."

"That's what I'm worried about."

They looked at each other for a moment, realizing there was no turning back from what they would be starting. Trina nodded, and Nigel returned the silent acceptance. They settled in and began sorting through the screens in front of them. Trina was pulling the regional data, organizing the populations by nanoblocks, age groups and upcoming expirations.

Dr. Nigel began his calculations, digging deep into the mainframe of nano maintenance. He thought back to his early days at LifeSpan, full of wonder, as most new Doctors were before the Receiving, a great cerebral download of collected knowledge.

"Trina," Dr. Nigel began, "do you remember your first unlock?"

"Yes, of course. It was one of the greatest days of my life. I always knew I wanted to become a scientist. My Receiving was scheduled the same day as my mother's expiration. She was always so supportive. Her unlock was architecture. She loved buildings, always working on the cityscapes, while I was so interested in the human body. The day I Received and all the knowledge of past Scis was unlocked, I thought my head would explode. My mind was exhausted. I felt . . . powerful. I felt like I was part of something grander than myself, bigger than all of my mother's buildings." Trina looked over at Dr. Nigel. "What about you? When did you Receive?"

Dr. Nigel began to reply when his screens let out a beep and doubled in size, completely filling every space around him in holographic displays. Galen's glove lit up like a beacon, and Dr. Nigel smiled.

"We are in," he announced.

Trina could see it now: every sector around the globe was sorted into even further providences. She always knew LifeSpan controlled the nanos; she just never really knew the sorting. The entire planet was connected into an assimilated hive, while staying segregated by region. *Why the division?* Trina wondered.

"Remember what Sci Tym told us. Do nothing else. We are only here to shut down the nanos. This will give him time to reprogram . . ."

Sci Nigel began moving screens with the gloved hand and pulling files with the other. He knew the key was deep in the archives of LifeSpan. With luck, they could find the override and shutdown the system. Almost there. He flung the projected files to Galen's glove, which he had palm facing up. The digifiles stacked into the glove's force field. After many moments, Sci Nigel paused.

"This is it: the entirety of the local system. Ready to test the glove's modifications?"

"Don't fail us now, Tym. Go," Trina replied.

He charged up the glove and slowly closed his open hand. Held in the force field, the files crumpled. Dr. Nigel crushed away the system, and when his hand closed, the light faded from the glove. It was done.

Trina watched her screens, as every sector faded. The lights of nano control blinked out, one by one. The nanos of everyone in the world went offline.

We did it, Tym, we did it. Trina breathed a sigh of relief.

THE GARDENS

Nighttime encompassed the exclusive gated community of Northern Orchards. Many of its residents were slumbering peacefully and waiting for what tomorrow would bring. Aside from the outdoor lighting used to boast the exteriors of these well-kept mansions, there were hardly any auto illuminators still active.

This made the fourth house on Cedar Lane more noticeable, for every light was on. A glance in the window would show only two residents, older in their years, sitting in the main study while a slow-burning artificial log blazed in the fireplace.

"Honey, the time is almost here." A sweetly melodic voice floated in the air. "11:11pm. What a perfectly appropriate number for a mathematician, don't you think?"

Henry smiled at his wife. She had spent a lifetime in vocal studies and instruction, which kept her voice sounding as sweet as the voice of a woman half her age. Her statement rang true as he glanced once again to the front door. Two minutes, fifteen seconds remained.

When he was a young boy, going on eight years old, he had figured his expiration time based on his remaining LifeSpan pocket watch countdown. Many in the world population never sat down and figured the exact expiration time until it was closer, like, say, within ten years or so. Henry figured his expiration to the minute, over eighty-four years in advance. He saw it as an engaging mathematical challenge. Oh, how he loved mathematics and calculations. They were so perfectly stable.

"You look good today. As handsome as the day I met you. I noticed you left your wedding ring on the table," Adel replied, removing the blanket draped across her knees and carefully folding it over the arm of her chair.

"I wanted you to keep it. I don't know why, I just figured there should be something here to remember me, remember our marriage," Henry admitted.

"I have a whole house full of memories, beautiful gardens you planted with fountains and pools, beautiful drawings and paintings of your favorite plants. I see you all around, I feel you in the air. I doubt that will leave this place. It's permeated into the walls. As far as our marriage, you really did great for the last sixty-two years. Not many are granted a LifeSpan so long together. It's a shame we were never allowed children."

"It's funny how the small things work themselves into something great." Henry's worries were put to rest with Adel's comforting words. "At least you have eight years, three months, two days and three-quarters of an hour left. Not like me. Today I fig—" He glanced at the clock on the far wall and his words froze.

"What's the matter, Henry? What is it?" Adel asked, rising to her feet so quickly the folded blanket was disturbed and crumpled to the floor.

His mouth was dry. Barely able to breathe, he whispered, "The time. Something's wrong with the time."

She turned and looked at the clock. 11:12 pm. One minute past his expiration.

That was impossible.

Henry bolted to his desk, digging furiously for his LifeSpan digiscreen organizer. His wife ran to the dining room table and picked up her LifeSpan pocket watch. It glowed, recognizing her nano signature. She opened it and saw her active dials ticking down, as usual. She picked up her husband's timepiece, which, of course, did not glow in recognition of her, and returned to the front room, searching for her Henry.

He was crouched on the floor, scrolling through his digiscreen, trying to access the LifeSpan official documents virtual table.

Adel briskly walked to him. Holding his pocket watch between her thumb and forefinger, she touched the backing onto his exposed neck.

The watch glowed, accepting Henry's unique nano signature, and the front popped open. Adel could clearly see the dials had all stopped moving.

Expired.

"Henry, the dials . . ." Adel began.

"Have all stopped. I figured as much," Henry finished for her.

He continued scrolling through, ultimately zooming into a document on his reader. "I've found it! The LifeSpan report, dated when I received my expiration and was given to my parents." He skipped through the document cover, and read aloud:

Henry G. Reingold
Subject #6621-7782-11
Expiration 33582.23.11.0

"Something is wrong. I shouldn't be here. I shouldn't be —" He nervously looked back and forth, like a caged animal.

"Henry, relax. We just need to contact the LifeSpan offices," Adel tried to reason.

"No!" Henry cried. "I shouldn't be here, I . . . I can't! This has never happened! *The world is balanced. LifeSpan is the scale.* Nature has a balance, a structure, just like mathematics. What have I done?" His voice was growing shrill as he stood.

"Henry, please. There has to be an explanation! Something is wrong. Let's work to fix it, like a mathematician . . ." She placed a hand on Henry's shoulder, only to have it immediately shaken off.

"There is nothing wrong. This is an infallible institution, and there are no mistakes. I should be expired; the Collectors should have come for my body. Where are they?" Henry's voice grew very quiet. "I can't live any longer. I shouldn't shame you that way."

Henry dropped his digiscreen, put his arms in front of him in a feeble show of distance, and backed away from Adel. She was crying now, tears running in long streaks down her cheeks. Henry was staring at her, too absorbed in the overwhelming wrongness of the situation, unaffected by her misery. He could only shake his head and wave his hands, fending off an unseen swarm of bugs. Henry began to back away, his eyes darting around the room, expecting to be struck down as an abomination of nature. His back struck the glass door that led into his prized garden. Adel began to falter for him, her shrieking emphasized by her uncontrolled sobbing.

Henry was trapped. His mind whirled, finally settling on a desperate plan. He threw the door open and loped into his backyard. It was the stumbling, frantic run of a man fleeing a great danger, except this danger was in his mind. He knocked over a potted plant, the dirt and leaves spraying across his meticulously swept patio. Henry darted the length of his property, which sat high atop a mountain outcropping. Adel jogged out the back door, across his lovely gardens, and as she screamed, he lunged off the mountain's edge. His last thoughts were of trampling his wonderful garden.

DUEL

Cole was worried for Tym. Their hideout had been stormed by Collectors shortly after Trina left. Cole was bloodied in more than one spot, his pants were torn and now his jaw was throbbing with pain. He was bleeding all over the vest Tym gave him.

Sci Tym had forced this vest on Cole as he fought the raiders, yelling for Cole to flee.

I think Tym escaped. I ran the best I could, but they were everywhere, Cole remembered. *Then they were all over me, capturing me and throwing me into the lion's den. This was Nimbus's sanctuary.*

Nimbus was not happy when the Collectors dropped him off. He still wasn't happy. He had just thrown Cole across the room, again, more violently than minutes ago.

Maybe one of these pockets has a napkin? No time for jokes, Cole. He knew Nimbus was toying with him. If Cole was within a few paces, Nimbus lashed out. He moved faster than anyone Cole had ever seen. Faster than he thought possible. Nimbus struck with a viper's snap, and Cole was easily flung away each time.

"You dare oppose me? I have created and destroyed entire civilizations! You cannot reverse what I have set in motion."

Nimbus spoke softly and so matter-of-factly, most people believed every word. He was lecturing Cole, playing with him, keeping pace across the room and around the furnishings. "Finally after millennia of war and senseless slaughter, we have halted our own self destruction. We have evolved. We have strengthened ourselves to erase the fear of death itself!"

"Nothing was erased! You veiled peace while you cut our lives short. Your self-imposed expirations mean nothing." Cole was gaining momentum now. Although they had been debating these same issues ever since the Collectors dragged Cole aboard, he knew the only chance Sci Tym had was for Cole to stall Nimbus.

Sure, this is going so well, Tym. Take your time. Thanks again for the vest. I'm probably going to die wearing it, Cole thought as he jumped to his feet and took his time connecting each clasp on the front. Acting smug, he replied, "You have no power over me."

Cole barely saw the fist this time. He tried to dodge it by snapping his head back. The move saved him from a direct hit; however, his shoulder caught and he tumbled across a desk. Digiscreens and building models landed with him as he slid over and down.

Nimbus stared down at Cole. "Are you implying the expirations have anything to do with fear? They are in place to eliminate fear."

Cole reached over his head and grabbed the desk edge, pulling himself to his feet.

"It's really quite sad, Cole. If you give someone an expiration date and have them truly believe the allotted time is all they have left, the human body will rebel upon itself." Nimbus turned his back on Cole, walking away. "You see, the body and mind work together, and when the mind gives up, the body follows. Then the natural expiration process has begun."

"I suppose you never had that problem?" Cole asked. "Are you beyond human? Some kind of immortal?"

Nimbus did not turn back to face Cole as he stopped. Nimbus glanced at the ceiling, deep in thought, and he closed his eyes. Cole had asked the correct question. Finally, he was on the right path.

Nimbus was actually keeping his mind clear. Holding the other voice at bay was a constant struggle, but Nimbus always found a way. He was in control.

"Oh, I assure you, I am very much human. Just like you. Although, you are nothing but a boy when compared to my age," said Nimbus. "I opened my mind to immortality. I have learned of the limitless possibilities within our souls.

"You see, we do have the technology to enter immortality," he explained. "In fact, when LifeSpan was but a fledgling child itself, we willingly gave the secrets of immortality to the entire populace."

Nimbus looked back at Cole. "Oh, it was perfection, continual life, free from our single biggest fear at that time, our oldest foe: *death*. But then something happened. The population grew reckless and bored. Accidents were rapidly increasing as the populace lost respect of their bodies. They relied on the nanos to repair almost any amount of damage. There was no care for person or property. We sped along at a rapid pace of almost constant upgrades to the Nanomedicine technology. But that wasn't our worst problem."

"I think I can guess." Cole started walking a wide circle around Nimbus. This topic kept Nimbus thinking, which meant distance between them, and Cole hoped that meant less kicking to his head. "The people wanted to live their own lives, free from your oppression."

"Not oppression, Cole. They wanted order restored. Written on the very fiber of our being is the availability of death. Humans treat it as a finish line, with your entire life as the race to be judged. Will you have a gold medal at the end of it all? Will there be an end? If there is nothing to lose from death, we cared for nothing

during life. We stopped trying, my boy. We stopped improving."
Nimbus paused, and turned to face Cole.

"They just needed someone to tell them when to end their life,"
Nimbus stated matter-of-factly.

REBOOT

Dr. Nigel slid the glove off, dropping it to the floor. His body felt heavy, and so very tired. The nanos were not feeding adrenaline or energy into his tired muscles. He closed the distance to Trina, with the sensation of trudging through water.

"So this is what it feels like? Without help from my friendly nanos?" Dr. Nigel quipped. "I believe running is out of the question. It's a good thing we just have to sit and wait for Tym now."

That much was true. Sticking to the plan, Trina sent Tym the signal. He was reprogramming the nanos. Breaking their connection to LifeSpan was one-half of the reboot. The other was their healing ability. Trina devoted her life to improving Nanomedicine. If this reprogramming was successful, it would enable the populations to still have the healthy, repairing benefits of the nanos without the LifeSpan-controlled expiration.

Tym's message blipped back to Trina's digiscreen. *System reboot in 7 minutes.*

"Nigel, we have a brief moment before systems are back up with Tym's personal touches. Before we were rudely interrupted by this whole saving-the-world nano-style, you mentioned your date of Receiving. I would very much like to hear about that."

"Ah, yes. I was only a boy at that time. Young, perhaps eight or nine. I showed great promise, and when I excelled beyond my peers, the LifeSpan Praetor of my sector noticed," Nigel reminisced. "I was entrusted with a vast amount of knowledge at this very sensitive age. My cerebral Receiving was not taken well, and I spent nearly a week in my room. Mumbling, typing excessively. However, I learned to control the information. I studied and grew. I researched and built my reputation with determination. I haven't updated my nanos since that original Receiving."

The wall screens began their slow glow, booting back to their original brightness, as the nano population came back online. Nigel knew millions of people would be feeling better in just a short while. It was an odd feeling to have your nanos turned off. Many would not realize what had just transpired.

Nigel turned to Trina. "In fact, I would deduce, your nano tech is more updated that I am."

Trina stared at him with newfound respect. He was a true Doctor — pledged to help and driven through his research. That's what also made him a good Sci. Perhaps the future would lead to merging of more professions.

"You should be proud of what you have accomplished," Trina said.

The room filled with light. Every screen was back to full capacity, and across the globe, nanos were back online. The spider-webbed grid of interconnected LifeSpan control was gone. Dr. Nigel felt his breathing come more easily, his hearing grow clearer, and he stood straighter, puffing out his chest.

"Welcome back, little guys," he said into his arm, petting his skin.

"Now, that is weird," Trina laughed, and pulled out her digiscreen.

Systems back. LifeSpan's out. Great job Tym, she typed.

No sooner had Trina sent the message than the room began to shake. Trina grabbed for the desk, thinking the whole building was coming down, only to realize the room wasn't moving; instead it was every screen pulsing and wobbling, creating a vertigo in their control room. Trina could barely hold herself up.

"What is happening?" she cried out.

Dr. Nigel was also attempting to stand while looking at his data, trying to find an explanation. The screens split off again, like before, with each separate Holowall showing the many sectors across the world. The data began re-sorting on its own, categorizing the populace. Listing their nanos. The models. The types. The origins.

Nine screens shifted to the center of the room, their edges turning a pale red. Dr. Nigel noticed that these were the earliest models of nanos still active in the world. Most likely their hosts were simple folk, filling basic duties to help their particular sector. The spider web reconnected to them, back to the LifeSpan database, becoming one hive mind.

FORCE EXPIRATION. 'blip'

The screens emptied. Every name. Gone.

"NO!" Trina and Dr. Nigel screamed together.

Thousands were on those screens. Parents. Friends. Children. Expired.

Trina grabbed her digiscreen and called Tym. She was aware their connection could be traced, but no longer cared. "Tym! The system is shutting down. It's reconnecting everyone and forcing expirations." She stared at her screen. Where was he? "Tym, we need you. Something went wrong. Please Tym, people are dying. The system started with the oldest nanos; maybe that can help you. It's picking them off in order of . . ."

Trina looked up at Dr. Nigel. "Oh, Doctor, *when* was your last Receiving?"

Cole could hardly believe this conversation.

"Are you playing with their lives *and* their souls?"

"Oh don't be so melodramatic, Cole. Humans are vegetation, slowly withering away. We are nature's greatest fertilizer! They just need someone to tell them when it's time to enrich the soil. We are in charge of writing our own history now," Nimbus continued calmly, watching Cole walk the perimeter of his council room.

"That's you? You are the creator and destroyer? The Father told me about your *history* together. He was your prodigy! Did you think you could just erase him too?"

"The Father," Nimbus spit the name out. He pointed at Cole. "Do you even know his real name?"

"Yes, he told me it was Alexander." Cole retreated around the desk, keeping distance between them.

"Correct, *boy*," Nimbus mocked. "I knew him as Alexander *Jenkins*. The children learn of him early in their education as Dr. Montgomery. They sing his name. We love Montgomery, for he has created a great many things. We even named hospitals after him. Do you remember?"

Cole felt the air leave his lungs. His mother's diary suddenly came flooding through his memory. Alexander was the name of *her* father. Could this be true? Was the Father of the Movement his grandfather?

Nimbus continued to smile as he took a seat in his high-backed white chair. "I find it ironic that somehow I have become your enemy when your trusted leader keeps his own sordid past from you. The Father, indeed."

"He was a Father to me! He was a great man who knew evil when he saw it, and he was the only one who would stand up to your kind! Just like Emma!"

Enraged by Nimbus's dismissive tone and hoping to take advantage of a now-seated and defenseless Nimbus, Cole ran at Nimbus, closing the gap with pure hatred fueling his rage.

"Our kind? Why dear boy, the only thing he was a Father to was his greatest creation. We were partners, that is true, but he was the one who created the Collectors."

Cole stopped his charge, still twenty feet away. Again, he was caught totally off guard by Nimbus and his revelations.

"That's impossible," Cole refused. "The Collectors have been around since the beginning of LifeSpan. You said so yourself. That was hundreds of years ago."

"So was our partnership. You still haven't opened your mind! How could the mortality rate change so drastically overnight?"

Cole was trying to follow.

"If the nanos repair our deficiencies automatically while keeping the body in excellent physical condition forever, what is the *obvious* side effect?" Nimbus led Cole to the answer, waiting for his response with a smile.

"Immortality," Cole replied.

"Exactly." Nimbus was still sitting. "Cole Jenkins, your grandfather left LifeSpan and decided to start a family. He was 270 years old when your mother was born. I am three years older than him. He should have respected his elder. I was always wiser."

For the second time tonight, Cole felt his legs go numb. Why couldn't he gain the upper hand with Nimbus? It seemed he was being led along all this time. He felt his head spin, and had no choice but to sit down across from Nimbus, place his hands on the tabletop for support, and watch the room spin around him.

The two sat staring at each other for some time. Cole was losing this debate.

"If you are so old, and you say it is directly linked to the nanos in your body, in all of our bodies, why wouldn't you set the expirations of the entire world population to live hundreds of years?" Cole was grasping for a mental handhold.

"Let me ask you this: would you readily accept the sudden change in a lifespan?"

Cole thought about the question. In one aspect, it would obviously allow civilizations the benefit of time, eliminating the need to rush through projects, family time, work, love. On the other hand, Cole could see the attraction for procrastination that would last a lifetime.

Nimbus assumed the lecturer role once again. "The human mind is comfortable within the arms of repetition. Psychologically, we can handle change, as long as it comes in measured bursts. We saw the signs in our early test subjects, some of the first humans with nanos fully integrated into their systems. There were discoveries everyday. We were fueled with a powerful inner energy, tuned motor skills, sharp minds; everything was amazing and new. The testing continued with incredible success, until we revealed to our test subjects that they would live for hundreds of years or longer."

"How did they take that?" Cole asked.

"Unexpectedly, not very well at all. I thought they would be overjoyed. We were handing them practical immortality!"

"Is that when you took it all back? The great introduction of forced expirations?" Cole pushed his chair back and stood once more.

"You are half-right on that one. Alexander and I worked together for many years, generations to be exact. We slowly worked expirations into the system. The fools, they were happy to die. I could not let the combined evolution of mankind go to waste. There was an incredible amount of potential stored inside each nano. I only needed a moment before their death to absorb the advances."

"Unfortunately, our next step drove your grandfather to . . .

extreme measures. Which, in turn, left me to take extreme prejudice against him. He fled LifeSpan with information I would be—"

"I heard the story. He told me you hunted him. Like an animal! I won't let that happen again, not to anyone!"

"So driven, yet so naive. Cole, you are out of your element. What do you propose? Returning civilization as we know it to the chaos of its previous incarnation? Are you their savior now? Come to kill me? Do you even think that is possible?"

"Let's find out. You have to be stopped. This is wrong. Civilization doesn't need you to tell them when to die."

"No, Cole. It would seem your friends are doing that for me," Nimbus teased.

"What are you talking about?"

"Trina? Dr. Nigel? They have failed. Blood is on their hands, and the toll is rising."

Dr. Nigel could only stare, his entire body numb.

"What have we done?" he whispered. The screens shook and lined up, side by side to one another. FORCE EXPIRATION. Twelve screens. Eighteen screens. Twenty-nine screens. He could hear Trina yelling. Distantly. He failed. They all failed. And humanity was paying the price. He was Dr. Death. He was the Sci of Pestilence. He fell to his knees as another group of screens shifted, lined up and turned red.

Trina was there, grabbing at his coat, forcing him to his feet. She was screaming at him now. He could see that, but heard nothing. Cared for nothing. It was over.

Trina threw the worthless Dr. Nigel onto his workspace. She knew their only hope was Galen's glove, and as she slipped on the gauntlet, the screens responded. She threw her palm forward, pushing the screens apart, throwing them across the room, to the ceiling, and shuffling them in the air. They sorted themselves, gathering again, and she threw her hand out, scattering the screens once more.

She could not control the glove. She was never trained in that, but she could scatter the screens with just the force of her will.

"Nigel! You have a duty to uphold. You took an oath to heal humanity no matter the circumstances! Get up! They need you. The entire world needs you now." She threw her hand out again, and the screens came back faster. They regrouped, and flew past her. Trina swung around. FORCE EXPIRATION. Too late. That was a huge group, over fifty-six screens. Trina was sobbing between her pleas to Nigel and her frantic screen sliding. "Doctor!! Your mother knew you were the healer! There are more mothers and sons, hopeful of their futures. They need you now. They need a Doctor." Trina's voice cracked as she wept for the dead, and the Doctor stood.

"Give me the glove," Dr. Nigel said. His voice calm. "It's time for a Receiving."

With Galen's tool, he tore the screens back, creating force fields around them, shuffling the rest with such ferocity, the holograms buckled. Trina ran back to her station and pulled updates on population counts, searching for the last nano model forced into expiration. She checked her digiscreen with her message still searching for Tym, unanswered.

"Trina, I know how to stop this!" Dr. Nigel yelled. "The system will not stop expiring until it believes the last model is gone."

"Right, and everyone is dead." Trina thought that much was obvious.

"So, we just have to skip a model."

"How do you think we can do that? Now we are into millions of people for each forced expiration."

"Unfortunately, some more will have to die. I have calculated that a massive Receiving will take the amount of time to hold back the screens for two more expiration blocks."

"Then, when the system hits a batch of screens and they are empty, it will believe the expirations are finished!" Trina understood.

"There's only one catch," Nigel explained. "The next expiration block is mine."

"No! There has to be another plan!"

"It's alright. I can save them."

Trina saw the screens break out of the glove's force field. They collected, and Nigel fought them off. She also saw the far left bank of screens listing the nano model 525-9. They were all flagged for a Receiving, and a small blue graph grew next to each name, upgrading them to the next level. Nigel's plan seemed to be working, as each name was taken off the list and added to the next tier. There were still millions of names to go, but they were filtering off at an incredible pace. She looked over to Nigel. He was sweating now, flipping data, building force-field walls from old information, confusing the database. The technology fought back. It realized there was an obstruction to its orders, and the screens were collecting in the room again. Nigel could not hold them back as the pile grew larger than even he could handle. Swelling to over 320 screens, the edges grew red.

"Nigel! Break them up!" Trina's heart sank as the screens flashed. She knew the expirations were happening in her city now. Soon it would happen in this room.

"I believe Dr. Nigel has unwittingly stumbled into my fail-safe. If he were a true Sci, he would have seen that coming."

"What would that be?"

"Millions are expiring as we speak. Nanos across the world are shutting down, and taking their hosts with them."

"Well, then I can wait for your nanos to die. I have none," Cole answered.

"That may be so. Unfortunately, I tire of this conversation, as riveting as it was. Today will be your last day on my Earth." Nimbus's posture became very limber and he stalked forward, his body perfectly balanced. He swayed with a deadly grace, raising his hand in front of him as he crouched down, fingers stiffened, formed into wedges. Nimbus gathered his internal power, breathing deeply.

This time was different than the last. Cole knew he would not be tossing him around and chatting. The time for talk was over.

Cole had no escape. Looking around the room, he knew he was doomed. Nimbus crept closer. Cole ran to the doorway, clawing at the panel for exit. He looked for cover around the existing furniture, anything he might be able to use as a weapon. Meanwhile, Nimbus continued forward.

Cole knew he had lost. There was no escape. What was he thinking? How could he have hoped to unseat the immortal Nimbus?

Nimbus paused, back leg tense, rising on the balls of his feet. Cole stood less than ten feet away, ready to dodge, if he could. Their eyes locked. With a growl, Nimbus leaped, right arm extended, his hand formed into a wedge, fingers clenched.

It happened so fast, Cole would have had better luck dodging a lightning bolt.

He heard his chest crack as Nimbus struck.

Emma, I'm sorry. Wait for me. I'll be there soon.

Nigel was exhausted. His head throbbed with concentration. He only had to hold on for a few more minutes. He could see the new group of screens gathering and checked on the progress of his massive Receiving upgrade. It was a race to see which one would finish first.

Either way, I'm gone, Nigel thought. *What good have we done today? What freedom is this, with so many dead? Dr. Nigel, the first Doctor in millennia responsible for global genocide.*

He threw his hand up. The glove pulsed with energy. Sci Nigel used all of his willpower to move a stack of files 200 thick across the room and scattered them to the floor. *Well, that should buy some time.* He gasped at the effort.

"The Receiving is almost finished! Nigel, add yourself to that list. You can skip ahead!"

"No, not until everyone is finished. The Receiving is rightfully theirs." He threw another batch of force fields.

"That's just it, Nigel. Look at the upgrades! They are almost finished!" Trina was pulling her own statistics up, looking across the globe, sobered by the lack of data. She knew entire countries were wiped out.

She was right; the list had a few hundred left. They were going to make it. Dr. Nigel searched and pulled up his digifile. He knew the next step would be tricky. In order to get his file flipped into the Receiving list, he would have to let go of the massive pile collecting once more. Only for a second. It could spell disaster. What right did he have to save himself, after he destroyed so many?

I can still do good, Nigel reminded himself. *I am still a Doctor.*

Nigel let go of the barrier. The files rushed out. He grabbed his digifile and flipped it to the Receiving list. When he returned to the forced expiration group, they had combined with three other piles in the middle of the room. Nigel pushed and pulled at the digital mass. He threw force fields. He screamed, and swiped, and waged a digital battle with Galen's glove, to no avail. The pile grew, file upon file, with the stack five times larger than any before.

Trina saw the desperation in Nigel's eyes. She looked to the Receiving screen, and the last names jumped over the list. Dr. Walter Nigel was the only name left. Any joy Trina could muster was immediately stolen away as the files dominating the center chamber began glowing red. Dr. Nigel panicked.

"Hold it back, Doctor! You are almost finished with your Receiving!" Trina held her breath with hope.

"Don't you see, Trina! I am still on this list, with the forced expirations. If the upgrade finishes first, I'm safe, and the Receiving list is empty. If the files force their expiration first, I'm done. Either way, my name empties the list, and the system stops."

"Your progress bar is almost complete. You are coming with me today. Back to Sci Tym and the Revolution! We need you!" Trina yelled back across the room.

"No, Trina. It looks like you will be traveling alone," Dr. Nigel stated. The last digifile flipped past him and joined the crimson-edged group. The red intensified. He looked to the Receiving screen. Eighty-two percent complete.

FORCE EXPIRATION.

"Doctor! NO!!" Trina left her station and ran to him.

"I was a good man." He doubled over. His gut was on fire, his heart screamed. "I was a good man, I was a good . . ." Trina was there, holding his head in her lap. The nanos turned on him, and shut him down. She wept.

The Doctor's digital nano signature burned off in his model purge. His name was erased from the Receiving board as it reached ninety-six percent completion. The red files emptied as the Doctor withered away. 2,608 screens blinked out with him.

The system jumped to the next model, 525-9, searching for files. With Dr. Nigel's quick thinking, this entire batch was missing in line. The chronology was broken, and the system paused.

EXPIRATIONS COMPLETE.

Trina cried for the Doctor. She cried with anger and pity. She cried for the insanity of the system. She cried for the dead. So many dead. Her station was still calculating the lost files, reaching over two billion forced expirations. She was still crying as light returned to the room and the door swished open.

Sci Tym rushed in, beaten, his clothing torn, dried blood covering half his face.

"Trina, bless the stars, I've found you." Tym stumbled to her. "We have to get out. We were ambushed. They have Cole. I know where he is."

Nimbus told the truth: Cole was no match.

His force was so powerful, it would have blasted through Cole, which was why Nimbus was so shocked to see Cole bounce away from his punch and slump down against the wall. It was only then that Nimbus recognized the vest Cole wore as a power-absorbing protectant, much like the Collectors' robes.

Well done, Sci Tym. You bought the boy another minute of life, Nimbus thought. However, where Nimbus had struck was now a small dripping tear in the fabric. A broken container, about the width of a hand, was still strapped into the pouch. Its contents had splattered on Nimbus.

He stood and tried wiping off the black shimmer. *What foolery is this?* Nimbus stepped back and furiously tried to wipe off the goo. Then he noticed it was moving. The black liquid raced up his arm, faster than water. It climbed Nimbus's neck, swarming into his eyes, mouth, ears. The nanos in the goo were prepared for one purpose: Destroy Nimbus. They were reprogrammed by Sci Tym and they were very efficient.

Cole was shocked awake by howling. The pitch was unlike anything he had ever heard before. Shrieking with pain, Nimbus pulled at his face and his skin churned. Cole had no sense of reason to the scene in front of him. He felt his chest where Nimbus had struck and saw the broken container. What else was in this vest from Tym? Cole turned each pouch inside out. They were empty, except one, which held a folded piece of paper, torn from a book.

He recognized the writing as Sci Tym's.

> This vest can absorb punches,
> so don't get hit in the face.

Thanks, Tym, Cole thought. He continued reading.

> Throw the container at Nimbus.
> The bugs are angry at him,
> but they won't hurt you.

Always there for me. Cole rolled his eyes.

Nimbus had stopped screaming and lay still.

Cole crawled over to Nimbus, intent on confirming his death. His skin was tightly stretched across his face. His prominent cheekbones were breaking through, creating gleaming white islands. Nimbus no longer had muscle tone of any kind. His neck and eyes were shriveled away, leaving an empty shell of the once-imposing man. Sci Tym's ruthless nanos must have eaten him from the inside, at the molecular level. Cole felt his own stomach flip, bile rising in his own throat.

This was a terrible way to go, for anyone.

He laid down on his back, exhausted. He threw his arm over his eyes and tried to think.

"You'll have to wait a little longer, Emma, wherever you are. Apparently I'm harder to kill than you thought. If only you could see me now."

What Cole did not see was a slow-moving puddle, iridescent blue, searching for a new union now that Nimbus was gone. The nanos could *feel* Cole. They knew a life form was close. They were looking for union. They moved together, rolling over one another, working their way towards their unsuspecting host. The swarm leaped up the side of Cole's face, and poured into him.

"No! Not again, no!" he screamed. He choked on the invading horde. The advancing nanos assimilated organs, muscles and tissues. They bonded with his every cell, flowing through his bloodstream, repairing damaged bones and torn membranes.

When the body was repaired, the nanos entered Cole's mind.

He tried to fight the takeover, but alas, these were Nimbus's nanos, which were on a scale far beyond any left on the planet. These nanos were evolved and held the information of ages.

Cole was filled with vast knowledge. A massive Receiving smashed through his mind. Over 300 years of developments, civilizations, inventions, skills, martial arts, technology. Cole was swept away in a torrent of information. He tried to stand, and was knocked back down. He tried to at least get his feet under him, kneel, but he fell down. Cole rolled and kicked. He grabbed at his head and screamed. He yelled to ground himself in the massive hurricane that was Nimbus and his stolen knowledge from forced expirations.

Cole was lost in the storm, and drowning fast.

Cole . . . His name was called, from a distant place.
Cole . . . *I'm here.* The sound gained momentum.
Come to me. I've been here a long while, and can show you the way.

The voice echoed through his very being. It was familiar somehow.

The storm still raged.

Jon *pushed* his thoughts, took control, and calmed his son.

I'm here now, my son.
We are together again.
Daddy's here.

Cole was absorbed in his embrace.

EPILOGUE

Under the close watch of Sci Tym and Trina, Cole's recovery was a series of successes and setbacks. His physical body endured, of course, as Nimbus's nano strain perfected Cole's core.

However, his mind continued to battle, unable to cope with near omnipotence.

Weak as he was for the following months, the Revolution carried on.

LifeSpan was thrown into a chaotic company-wide purge, as humanity lost faith in their beloved saviors, and overthrew the Praetors in every sector. Sci Tym had cleansed the nano technology, assuring that humanity was stronger in keeping the nanobots active.

Expirations were abolished, but the nanos remained more efficient than ever.

Yet, through it all, Cole carried the true hope for all of mankind, locked away in his mind. He charged Sci Tym with finding the key.

"Great news! Amazing, really." Sci Tym was hopping at the end of Cole's recovery bed. "We have finally finished with the isolation of your cerebellum. Well, the categorizing of data from the thalamus to the right hemisphere . . ."

Cole looked over to Trina.

"We can separate your mind," she clarified.

"Umm, yes. That's the simplest way to explain, I suppose." Sci Tym was still smiling.

Cole sat up in bed. His vision was cloudy, flashing through history, scenes, thoughts, memories, calculations. He paused, closed his eyes, and tried to calm the mental storm. Jon was there to help him form a complete thought.

"If you can categorize the advancements, I want you to arrange for a worldwide Receiving," Cole said slowly, with a strained voice.

Sci Tym was confused.

"Father, that's not what we had discussed," Tym started. "We can remove the information, and once they are sorted, we can decide the best course —"

"I told you not to call me that." Cole frowned at the title. "Also, *we* are not deciding anything. The advancements Nimbus hoarded are for the people. Everyone. They are the building blocks of civilization. They are from our greatest innovators, and Nimbus hid them for far too long."

Trina stepped forth. "I believe there is a way. Nigel talked of a tiered approach to Receivings. Before we were aware of the true nature of LifeSpan, he mentioned a digital file storage, a mini checkpoint accessible inside your mind, unlocked only when you had a desire to access the information."

"Of course! We could still arrange a massive Receiving of the locked mental files only." Sci Tym was catching on.

"Then if you wanted to learn about biological sciences, for example . . . ," Trina started.

"You could access only those files, and digiload to your mind!" Cole finished.

"Genius. We could make it work. I just need to borrow your soul," Sci Tym joked with Cole. The three of them sat for some time, happy to be in each other's company. Even though they lamented their losses, they prepared for the great Receiving.

So it was, as it always should have been.

Cole filled the world with knowledge. Pure, organized intellect was absorbed. With Trina's organization, there was an accessible library within the mind of every nano-carrying human.

It was known as Nigel's Gift, and few could envision a more fitting tribute.

www.ingramcontent.com/pod-product-compliance
Lightning Source LLC
Chambersburg PA
CBHW020310200626
46814CB00006BA/2179